Murmurations

By

Teri Hall

ISBN: 978-0-578-28433-0 (paperback)

Acknowledgements

Good friends read the drafts of this manuscript, and each had an important role in shaping the final book. Christy, Deb, Scott, Donna, Jen, Kelly, Monica, Kamarie, Caragh, Carolyn, and Richard—many, many thanks. It takes a special person to put up with "Will you read this semi-finished novel" sorts of requests. Each of you is very special to me. I count myself lucky to have so many people I trust and love.

Meat

IT WAS MY fault it happened. I hadn't seen any other people in so long I felt almost safe, and because I felt almost safe, I got careless. I was in a hurry to get the last of the potato harvest into the house before dark. It had been a long day of hauling them, trip after trip, from the garden in a neighboring yard to my own back yard. The wheelbarrow made it faster, but even so the light faded rapidly toward the end of the day. I'd left Tyrone locked in the house just to avoid having to keep him on leash while I was making trips back and forth, and when I got the last load home he was eager to get outside. It seemed quicker to leave the French doors off the kitchen open while I brought the potatoes, bucket by bucket, into the house, and let Tyrone wander in the yard. I was dumping the last bucketful in the sink, feeling pretty proud of my bounty, when a sound made me turn, and I saw him.

The boy stood in the doorway, a knife in one hand and Tyrone's collar in the other. Tyrone was struggling—the collar was twisted tight against his neck and he made a coughing noise, trying desperately to fill his lungs with air. I could see his legs shaking and then they relaxed as he lost consciousness, his body hanging limp from the collar. The boy—maybe seventeen at most—was wild-eyed and skinny, wearing a dirt-stained jacket. He stared at me, obviously surprised to find a living human inside the house. Without thinking I lunged at him, trying to loosen his grip on Tyrone.

"Let him go!" I managed to knock the boy's hand away and Tyrone slumped to the floor, taking deep, gagging breaths as he regained consciousness. The boy yelled something and lunged back at me and then I felt his knife in my side, an oddly dull sensation. I stumbled backward, some part of my brain sending alarms about the stab wound, while another part clicked through my options. Tyrone struggled to stand and scrabbled to me, jumping frantically, still not in full control of his body, knocking me off my feet. Behind the boy, a man appeared, gaunt and grimy, and from my vantage point on the floor I saw him take the boy by the shoulders and shake him. He was saying something but I concentrated on reaching my holster; I needed to get the gun. Once I had it, I pushed myself off the ground, leaning hard on Tyrone to leverage myself upright. I pressed one hand against my side where blood was seeping, warm and frightening, through my shirt. Gripping the gun with my free hand I pointed it at the two of them, the man and the boy.

"It's meat, damn it, and we're taking it!" The boy screamed the words at the man, shrugging out of his grip. He started toward Tyrone.

"It's her *dog*, boy." The man grabbed the collar of the boy's filthy jacket and pulled him back, eyes on my gun. "And you're about to get killed over it."

"I *will* shoot you." I stiffened my arm and aimed toward the boy, waiting, hoping he didn't notice the shakiness of my voice.

He stared at me, something like hatred in his gaze. "It's a damn dog." Tears sprang from his eyes and that made him even angrier. "We're *starving*." He tried again to squirm out of the man's grip on his collar.

A wave of nausea passed over me and I tightened my grip on the gun. Blood dripped onto the floor in front of me—my blood. I steadied my arm as best I could, and put my finger on the gun's trigger, ready to kill them both.

"Wait!" The man shoved the boy back, stood in front of him. "We'll go. Don't shoot."

"Go *now*!" It was my turn to scream. I advanced on them, still pointing the gun, and they started backing out of the kitchen, through the French doors. Standing in the doorway, I watched as they stumbled down the steps of the deck. The man turned toward me halfway down the sidewalk that led to the back gate, a horrified expression on his face.

"I'm sorry, Ma'am." He looked at his boy and then back at me, shaking his head, and then they both ran for the alley.

I stood leaning against the door frame for a minute or so, watching, hoping they were really leaving. Tyrone pushed against my legs, whining and growling. I had to get the door shut, get the bars in place, but my legs turned to rubber and then I was sliding down the door frame to the floor. Everything slipped out of focus except the sound of Tyrone snuffling in my ear, and soon enough even that faded away.

— —

I don't think I was out more than a few minutes. When I woke there was a man standing over me. All I could see was his silhouette in the open doorway, darker than the fading light behind him. Scrabbling, I raised the gun, which was still in my hand, and pointed it up at him. Immediately he raised his hands above his head and took a step back.

"I'm not them," he said, his voice low and quiet. "And you need help, lady, or you're going to bleed to death."

"They were going to eat Tyrone. I'll shoot you, too, if you try to eat—"

"This Tyrone?" The man held his hand out toward Tyrone, who sniffed at his fingers. "If so we're all good, because I don't eat dog." He knelt next to me. "I need to move you over so I can get the door shut, and then we need to see to your wound, okay?"

I remember trying to say something, but I couldn't string the words together. I remember when he moved me out of the doorway, he was gentle. I remember watching him put the bars over the French doors, moving quickly, checking that they were firmly seated in the brackets. After that, everything went fuzzy again. Then it went black.

New Beginnings

ALL OF IT all started long before that boy tried to kill my dog. Years before, really. There were plenty of clues along the way, but it's easy to be oblivious and people will always err on the side of easy. All the pieces of the machine were there, some hidden, some not so hidden, but they seemed disparate, intertwined as they were in the constant barrage of every-day mundanity. Nothing added up to the inexorable engine of ruin that we could all, finally, see so clearly, until it was too late. Lots of people were surprised, including me. But when I look back now and really think about it, the only surprising thing was that it took so long for everything to shatter.

When it all hit the fan, so to speak, it was spring. The days were getting longer, the air was warmer and everyone was enjoying the respite from winter's endless months of daylight-savings-darkness. Nobody seemed to care that spring was starting a full month early, or that high temperatures were setting records. We all just looked at it as a gift after an especially harsh winter—shut off the heat, fold the sweaters away in the back of the closet and break out the shorts. Global warming? Climate change? There *were* articles online and the evening news anchors droned on about melting glaciers. People talked about it in line at the grocery store, but then they shrugged and went about their business. What was there to do about it? What was there to do about *any* of the headlines?

I was at work in the middle of month's end, reconciling all the accounts-receivable payments that inevitably landed on my desk at the last minute. My boss kept walking by, surreptitiously eying the pile of checks.

I knew he was worried that the Jackson account hadn't paid off their bill. They owed us for a huge project and I had a feeling my own paycheck might be hanging in the balance if they didn't ante up.

I didn't hate my job, but I sure didn't love it. It was what I could get, newly divorced and relocated to Billington, a small, coastal city nestled between the sea and the foot of a range of mountains that had looked, to my weary eyes, like a place I might start again. It was as good a place as any. I'd never lived anywhere longer than a couple of years since I left home at seventeen; my longest stay in any city had been the last one, where I'd met Roger and, stupid hope still fluttering in my heart, married him. That didn't work out so well, so I'd driven a U-Haul filled with my meager belongings as far as the gas money took me. Which was Billington.

My boss, Pete Hill, owned the biggest construction company in town, but he was usually running in the red, due to his penchant for extravagant vacations. I'd only worked there six months and it seemed like he was always on his way to the Bahamas or just back from Acapulco. He liked the sun, and Billington was rainy and gray most of the year.

My desk was tucked into a little alcove in the back room, facing a cinderblock wall painted the ugliest pale yellow I'd ever seen. When I started the job, I'd asked if I could swing the desk around to face the room, but Pete said having employees' computer screens viewable at all times was the only way to keep them from spending all day surfing the Internet. I spent a lot of time observing how the dust settled on the yellow-coated mortar lines of the cinderblock wall, making everything look even dingier.

"Anything from Jackhole?" That was Pete's nickname for Jackson Development.

I didn't bother to turn around. I had just reviewed the online statements and I knew nothing had been transferred. "Not yet." Pete hovered for a moment more, but finally went back to his office to watch more of the news channel he always had blaring on his wall-mounted flat screen. It was his favorite way to spend a day, tilted back in his tufted, leather office chair, making sarcastic comments to no one about the latest atrocities the reporters were covering.

There were plenty of them. A modified strain of Ebola in Africa that none of the vaccines could touch, school shootings in three different states in the past week, some weird flu that had hit the East Coast and then spread like wild fire, and of course, more climate change fears. It had gotten to the point where I just didn't turn on the old television in my house. By the end of a day of forced listening at work, I didn't want any more bad news.

"Holy shit."

Pete's voice intruded on my concentration. I backspaced the entry I'd just made, reentered it, referencing the amount twice to be certain I got it right. He'd give me one of his long-winded lectures if the books were off by a penny.

"Holy *shit*."

Louder this time. I heard his chair creak as he leaned forward like he always did when some reporter really pissed him off. I realized I was frozen, my hands over the keyboard, my head turned halfway toward his office door, waiting for the storm to pass. Becoming still, like a rabbit who scents a wolf, was something I did without thinking; it had been my only defense for so many years when I was growing up. Taking a deep breath, I reminded myself—as I had for all my adult life—that I wasn't a child, that I didn't need to be afraid of every blustery man who crossed my path. I opened the next envelope.

"Julie!"

I groaned, quietly, so he couldn't hear. He never called me in his office unless he was going to give me a lecture, or work to take home. I had plans for the weekend; plans I was actually looking forward to for once. I'd just adopted a puppy—Tyrone, an ungainly, seven-month-old mutt—and our first formal obedience training session was on Saturday. Adopting him had been an impulse move, not something I had thought out very well, but I'd been feeling purposeless in some deeper way than usual. I'd been feeling alone, of course. I was used to that; before my marriage I was alone, and actually, during it. But the divorce had seemed like the finalization of some fact of my life—some unalterable fate. I was twenty-eight years old. I was damaged in ways that I couldn't heal. I was beginning to realize I would probably *always* be alone. The realization felt almost like relief, but

it left me weightless, unmoored to anything at all, to the point that sometimes I felt as though I might just float off the planet. I knew myself well
enough to know I'd need to find a reason to keep breathing.

Some part of me has always known that I'm irreparable, and that it couldn't
be different, given my history. Our history forms us. We can move on from
it, walking or running, but it marks us, and it shapes our perceptions, for better or worse. Mine had left me wary, to say the least, of trusting my fellow
humans. But I could trust a dog. Dogs never did anything to be mean. Dogs
never spent time planning how they might hurt you most with the fewest tell-
tale bruises. And I needed something, some sort of meaning of my own, if I
meant to keep going. So far, Tyrone was working as a distraction, and in any
case, he was my responsibility now. The obedience training seemed like a way,
a safe way, to fill at least a part of the empty, weekend hours.

"Julie, get in here now!"

Pete sounded close to hysterical. I jumped up from my chair and poked
my head into his office. He was leaning on the edge of his desk, staring at
the flat screen. His face was pale and when he saw me, he just pointed at
the television.

I followed his finger to the screen. There was a reporter holding a mi-
crophone, standing in front of a familiar, institutional-looking building. In
a blue banner at the bottom of the picture, the words *Breaking News, Mercy
Hospital, Bioterror, Hacker's Flu Fatal*, and *Quarantine* were scrolling past.

The reporter looked scared. Someone—I couldn't tell if it was a man
or a woman—lurched into camera range holding a sign, but before I could
make out what it said the station switched to the studio where a woman
with too much makeup on sat behind a newsroom desk. She had one finger pressed against her earpiece, listening to someone in the control room.

"Mercy?" I frowned. "Do they mean *our* Mercy, in Bond?" Billington's
too small to have a hospital all its own; the closest one is in Bond and it's
called Mercy Hospital. The building that flashed on screen before they
switched to the newsroom looked like it.

"Be quiet!" Pete held a hand up at me as if it would stop the flow of
words from my mouth. Which, of course, it did. "Listen." He didn't take
his eyes off the screen.

The screen split into a picture of the woman in the newsroom and one of the on-scene reporters. The woman looked up at the camera.

"Right, we've had a temporary streaming problem but we're live again at Bond's Mercy Hospital with KNG's Derek Wilson. Derek, can you tell us if the reports of a fatality are true?"

Derek's half of the screen enlarged. He had that blank look reporters get when they're listening to a time-lagged question from the newsroom, but then he nodded and addressed the camera. "Carol," he said, "it does appear that there has been at least one fatality here in Bond, and scores more nationwide. Reports are that Hacker's Flu, as they're calling it, is spreading like wildfire. There may be more cases inside here at Mercy, but we cannot confirm that." Derek turned toward the hospital and the camera zoomed to the entrance. "The hospital doors are locked and calls to the switchboard have gone unanswered since earlier today when, as we reported in a KNG exclusive, a hospital spokesperson told us they intended to implement lockdown procedures until they could ascertain the extent of the outbreak."

"I thought they were just being dramatic when they said that earlier," Pete mumbled.

Onscreen, the camera angle widened; there was a smallish crowd of people milling around outside the hospital entrance. Some were holding signs, but I couldn't make out what was on them. "As you can see," Derek said, "there are demonstrators here at the hospital, who started congregating about twenty minutes ago. We're not sure if they are representing a particular group or if they're just citizens with loved ones inside. A few of them have tried to gain entry to the hospital." Derek's voice took on a heightened tone. "The police are just arriving now."

The camera tracked a couple of police cars as they pulled up to the front of the hospital. A uniformed officer got out of the first one and once his partner joined him, they approached the crowd. For a moment the camera focused on them talking to one of the sign-holders, but then the picture jerked and swerved, blurring. Someone shouted something and the camera steadied; one of the policemen was on the ground. The camera remained focused on the officer on the ground, but Derek's voice came over the airwaves, cracking, almost a shout.

"One of the officers has just been assaulted, Carol. It looked to me like two of the—protesters, I guess we'd have to call them—ran toward him and then he was down. I can't tell whether there was a weapon involved or not, but his partner has his gun drawn—"

The camera panned the scene, showing more and more people streaming toward the hospital doors. Some of them seem to run right over the policeman on the ground, and I could see his partner trying to get to him. Two men stopped a few feet from the camera and looked toward it. It didn't seem like they said anything to each other but suddenly they were both running straight at the camera as though they planned it.

"Derek." Carol's voice cut in, sounding almost conversational. "Is there any indication—"

The video feed went black.

I just stared at the television, waiting. The picture came back up— but it was Carol sitting behind the desk in the studio, looking horrified. She nodded at someone off-screen and looked into the camera, eyes wide. "We've lost the signal from our KNG news team. As soon as we can we'll bring you more breaking news from the scene at Mercy Hospital, but for now, let's go to our local weather. John Stanton is here with the latest."

They switched to the studio weather set where the meteorologist stood in front of a map looking stunned. He quickly recovered himself once he realized he was on camera and started pointing at sections of the map, stuttering about precipitation and wind speed. When the picture went black again I thought for a moment something had happened to the whole television station, but then I realized that Pete had the remote in his hand—he'd turned the television off.

—　—

"That's it." Pete pushed himself off the edge of his desk and went to the safe—a big, oily-looking black antique that he was always bragging would withstand a direct dynamite hit. He crouched in front of it, fiddled with the dial and swung open the door. "Hand me that bag over there." He pointed back toward his desk without looking at me.

"What?" I'd never seen that safe open before.

"That bag, right there," he snapped. He set bundles of cash on the floor in front of the safe.

I didn't see a bag on his desk, but there was a reusable canvas grocery bag deflated at the foot of the coatrack. I held it out toward him and he grabbed it and started stuffing bundles into it. When the bag was full, he set it aside and reached further back into the safe. Carefully, he slid out a hard-plastic case. It looked like a case for some sort of power tool to me, maybe a drill. Pete grabbed the bag of cash and the case and set them both on his desk. It felt like he didn't know I was in the room anymore. He popped the latch on the case and opened the top. Inside, nestled in specially fitted, foam compartments, were two hand guns.

"Yep." Pete nodded. He closed the case and picked up the bag. That's when my presence registered again. "Um." He frowned at me as though I were a pimple on date night. Then he opened the bag and took out two bundles of bills. He handed them to me. "It's the best I can do, Julie." He waited for me to say something, but I just stood there holding the cash.

"Seriously, I need the guns for me and Barbara." He sounded defensive.

"What are you doing?" The blocks of money felt heavier in my hands than I would have expected. I had no idea what was going on.

Pete sighed. "Look, I'd offer to take you, but there's no room at . . . there's no room where I'm going. With Barbara and me and her damn sister, we'll have all we can do to last six months on the supplies I put back." He shook his head. "I never planned on her sister, but I know Barbara won't take no for an answer." He tied the cloth handles of the grocery bag together and picked up the gun case. "Better use some of that," he nodded at the cash in my hands, "to buy a gun for yourself now, if you don't have one. Arnie's Sports will still have some if you get there fast." He watched me, waiting for something, some reaction I was clearly not having.

"All right, time to go." Pete shifted the bag of cash and the gun case and dug into a pocket, fishing out the building keys. "Now. I'm locking the place up just in case I'm wrong and this is all a false alarm. But I don't think I'm wrong."

"We're leaving?" It was the middle of the day. Pete never closed up early. Well, he never let *me* off early, anyway.

"Did you not see the news just now, Julie? Bioterrorism. *Fatal flu*. People going fucking crazy. Yeah, we're leaving." Pete waited, foot tapping impatiently, for me to get my jacket and my purse. He held the front door open, watching the street like he expected a mob to show up, until I was outside on the sidewalk. Then he locked both of the locks and started toward his truck. Halfway there, he stopped and turned.

"Might want to put those in your purse," he said, pointing at the bundles of cash I was still holding. "Good luck."

I watched him get in his truck, start it up, and drive away. He didn't look back.

—— ——

I stood there on the sidewalk for a long time. I kept waiting for something to happen: for Pete to drive around the block and pull up laughing about his elaborate joke and how easily I fell for it, or for a wild gang to burst round the corner, screaming about plagues and attacking anyone in sight. But the street looked like it always did—quiet—a block off the main shopping district, filled with shabby storefronts in one stage or another of disrepair. A couple of cars passed by at the intersection up the block. A woman came out of the computer repair shop a few doors down, holding a rag and some window cleaner. She spritzed the display window and started wiping. After a minute she noticed me standing there, just staring. She shielded her eyes with one hand, smiled uncertainly.

"You all right?" Her voice was friendly, calm.

I draped my jacket over the bundles of cash and nodded. "Yep, just forgot what I was doing for a second." I laughed, but it sounded strained to my ears.

The woman didn't seem to notice. She looked up at the sky, eyeing the dark gray clouds high above. "Looks like it's going to come down."

I followed her gaze. "It does." I waved a little wave at her and started toward my car.

Murmurations

I PULLED OUT of my parking spot and turned the Kia's radio on. Usually I left it off, more interested in the possibility of the murmurations the noise from the car engine might engender. They seem to come through more often when there's some ambient noise. The wind, the water from a stream or the tub faucet, the sound of a fan. In the car engine, sometimes.

I've heard murmurations—that's my name for them—all my life. As a child, I thought everyone heard them. It wasn't until I went to school that I realized the other children didn't, at least not that I could tell. Neither did the teachers. I never asked my mother if she heard them; the murmurations seemed like a sort of magic to me when I was young, and something about my mother's alternating fragility and numbness, her worn-out pragmatism, made me certain she didn't hear anything close to magic. There was nothing fanciful about her. Nothing that made me think she would *listen* if there was something to hear. And of course, I didn't ask my father, because I didn't ask him anything.

At school, I didn't share my murmurations with any of my friends, just like I didn't share what was happening to me at home. There was an unspoken rule there: be *normal*. Be like everyone else. And even though some of my teachers acted like they cared, I knew that their caring went only so far.

I knew this from experience. Once, Ms. Janburg, my fifth-grade teacher, asked us to keep journals. She said we should write the truth in them, the truth about anything we wanted to say. She said she would read them every week and grade us on our writing, but that anything we shared was confidential. I wrote a lot of things in my journal, but they were cautious truths, the kind that can't come back to bite you. I described walking to school in the soft, early morning, and what the stars looked like through my bedroom window at night. I always got an **A** for my entries, and after some time passed and Ms. Janburg seemed to have kept her promise about confidentiality, I decided to take a chance.

I wrote about a different kind of truth. I wrote about my father hurting me. All that week I watched Ms. Janburg to see if she behaved any differently to me, a tiny ember of hope kindling in my chest. I thought maybe, just maybe, there was a way out. When she passed our journals back on Friday, I flipped to the last page of my entries with a pounding heart, my hands sweaty. I was hoping for a message from her, a *See me after class* or a *Meet me in the school parking lot and I will take you home with me.* But all there was on the page was the regular **A**, with a *Great job!* in red ink. Great job. Those two crimson words broke something inside of me.

It didn't occur to me until many years later that Ms. Janburg probably hadn't even read my entries that week. Perhaps she was unusually rushed and didn't have time to read all her students' work. I didn't realize that if she *had* read my journal, she might have done something. At the time, it just confirmed my idea that nobody cared, that there was nowhere to turn for help. I didn't know back then that sometimes, often, in fact, what happens to you in life can be ascribed to plain old crappy luck. That, and crappy humans.

And so I kept both my secrets and tried to be *normal.* My murmurations became one of the few things that were just mine, one of the few things that I could take comfort from. There *was* some comfort there, because even though I couldn't understand them, they made me feel like there was more in the world than just the ugly bits I knew about.

At least they used to make me feel that way, when I was a child. As I grew though, I stopped wondering so much about what they might be. I stopped being open to that feeling of comfort they used to give me—stopped thinking they might mean something important. Life was painful, and just getting through it however I could left little time or energy to investigate meaningless mysteries.

As an adult, I wondered if the murmurations could be a medical issue. I had a physical, had my hearing checked. The doctor answered my purposely vague questions with pronouncements about tinnitus and various other audiological conditions, but none fit what I experienced. To me, the murmurations were like a voice, speaking some strange language, and I couldn't believe they were due to some anomaly in my ear drum.

Over the years, I tried to determine whether they were connected to my own life. I analyzed whether their tones matched my circumstances: Were they sad when I was sad? Were they neutral when I was bored? I couldn't seem to find correlations. I ended up deciding they must be something like synesthesia—the condition some people have where they see numbers as a certain color, or taste lemon when they feel the sun on their skin. The murmurations were just a part of me. A part I would probably never understand. And if *I* couldn't, certainly nobody else would. So I continued to keep them to myself.

The only person I ever told about the murmurations was my ex-husband, Roger. It was early in our marriage, when we were still happy, or at least when we were still pretending to be. We were lying in bed together after sex, almost asleep, when the furnace in the old house we rented kicked on. I half-listened, sleepy and warm in his arms. And the murmurations began. I followed them with my mind for a little while, the ebbs and the flows, letting them speak to me, and then I opened my eyes.

Roger was looking at me with such tenderness. He was the only man who had ever made me feel valued, like he wanted *me*, not just my body or my laundry skills. I'd told him on our fourth date that I couldn't have children, and he'd just shrugged. He seemed to accept me despite my deficits. At first, I felt safe around him in a way I don't think I ever had with a man. I can still picture his hands, how beautiful I always thought they were, before they left bruises on me.

I smiled at him, reached over and touched his lips, whispered to him. "Do you hear it?"

He smiled back at me. "Hear what, honey?"

"The . . ." I didn't know how to tell him, at first. "The murmuring." I sat up in bed. "The sounds, coming from the furnace."

He stretched and sat up next to me. "Of *course* I hear the furnace. It's got to be twenty years old." He grinned.

"No." I stopped smiling. It was important to me that he understand. "It's not the furnace; it's not coming *from* the furnace. I explained it wrong. It's . . . it's that things *like* the furnace—it could be the wind, or a fan, or the water from the faucet—those things help it come through. At least, I think they might."

His face changed, grew serious. "What are you talking about?"

I didn't like the look on his face, which had gone from serious to worried. "The murmuring." I hugged my knees. "It's like voices. Not voices, I mean, but like, *language*. Something is saying something." I could tell I wasn't explaining it in a way he could understand. "It's like those flocks of starlings."

"Starlings?" He looked totally confused.

"Yes." I remember thinking, at that moment, *stop now, stop before you ruin it.* But I didn't stop. I wanted to be close to him. I wanted to be understood. "Those huge flocks of starlings, when they make those shapes in the sky. I showed you a video, remember?"

I had been so struck when I first saw one of those videos, way back when I was a kid. The moving flocks of birds were called murmurations. *They are just like my sounds*, I'd thought, watching how they moved, this way and then that, all as one, making strange, beautiful shapes in the sky, shapes that seemed to be communicating something. They *looked* just like what I sometimes *heard*, and I called my sounds murmurations from then on. I'd watched every video I could find of them, over and over, but whatever they were saying, it was a mystery. I couldn't tell if it was sinister or serene.

It reminded me of a toy— already retro when I was a child—called *Wooly Willy*. It was a simple piece of cardboard with a face printed on it, covered by a plastic bubble. The plastic held in metal shavings and there was a magnetic wand that you could use to move them around from behind, so you could draw eyebrows and beards and moustaches on the face.

From the front of the board it looked like the metal filings were moving magically, all by themselves. I used to make swirls and swoops with them instead of facial hair, just to watch them move. The starlings' murmurations looked to me like something was controlling them all from behind the sky, with some huge magnetic wand. Like something was speaking through them. They were writing something on the sky, but I couldn't read it.

It was the same with *my* murmurations. They felt like a communication. Sometimes they were mournful sounds, sometimes neutral, as though they were just humming about a mundane day. It always felt as though I was just on the verge of understanding them, but I never could. When I was younger, I thought that they emanated only from machinery. We lived in the city, and the predominant noises were all from machines. So I'd only ever heard them around cars, or heaters, or fans. It was easier, then, once I outgrew thinking of them as magic, to ascribe them to some manmade phenomenon. But I went to summer camp one year—a rare attempt on my mother's part to spare me from my father's attention for two weeks—and there, all the noise came from nature. I heard the murmurations in a stream, and in the flames of the campfire, and in the wind. Stronger, as though the lack of busy, city noise let them come through better. That's when I decided they came from something bigger than humans or their machines. I thought they came from the *world* somehow—maybe something even bigger than the world.

⁓ ⁓

Roger stared at me. "Honey, are you serious?" He moved away from me on the bed, his lip curled as though I was a spider on the sheet.

"Never mind," I smiled as I said the words. "Let's just go to sleep."

"You were joking?" He wasn't convinced.

"I think it's just some subsonic thing." I mumbled the words, words I had said many times to myself, to try to explain my murmurations away.

"Huh?"

"Like with the birds." I turned toward the nightstand so he couldn't see my face. "The shapes they make, it's got to be some sort of gravitational pull, or magnetic impulses, or something like that. It's the same with the sounds. There's some perfectly scientific explanation for it."

There was silence. Then the rustle of the bedding and the bedframe creaking as he lay back down. "Damn. You had me spooked there for a minute. Thought I married a crazy." He chuckled. "Night, honey."

"Night." I listened until his breathing changed to a sleeper's slow, deep inhales and exhales. I tried to focus on that, so I wouldn't hear anything else.

Provisions

I STOPPED THE Kia at a red light and scanned through some soft rock and some jazz, finally landing on the local public radio station. They were in the middle of one of their fundraising efforts, asking all listeners to call in and pledge money. I was just about to hit the scan button again when a live announcer broke into the canned pledge drive message.

"We interrupt our scheduled broadcast now with breaking news from Mercy Hospital in Bond. There has been a confirmed outbreak of Hacker's Flu with at least three deaths reported. Quarantine procedures are in effect at the hospital. A break-in attempt by relatives of one of the flu's victims has—" the announcer's voice is drowned out by the jarring sound of the emergency broadcast system introduction. I waited while it chimed through its dissonant tune and then a louder, gruffer voice reverberated from the Kia's tinny speakers.

"This is not a test. Repeat, this is *not* a test of the emergency broadcast system. Stay tuned for local updates after this announcement. The Center for Disease Control has declared that the outbreak of influenza type E7, otherwise known as Hacker's Flu, has been officially classified as epidemic in the United States. Citizens are urged to take all precautions to avoid contagion including the use face masks and of antibacterial hand wash after each instance of skin-to-skin contact with others. If possible, remain in your homes and avoid contact with others. If you have a fever or cough, do not leave your place of residence. Do not go to your doctor or the hospital. There is no specific medical treatment available for the flu at this time. Drink plenty of fluids and rest. Remain calm. Do not panic."

The emergency broadcast tones sounded again and then the local announcer started listing school closures and pick up locations.

Do not panic. Right. The light turned green and I started to pull out just as an ambulance sped past, siren screaming. I slammed on my breaks, instantly shaking. "Deep breaths, deep, breaths," I whispered to myself. Easing into the intersection, I was almost hit by a minivan that was right behind the ambulance. The woman driving pounded on her horn and stabbed her middle finger at me as she raced by. She looked scared.

"Do not panic." I looked both ways and hit the gas.

When I turned onto the main street heading for downtown it became apparent that many people were going right ahead with the panicking. There was traffic—way too much traffic for the middle of the day, and nobody seemed too concerned about the speed limit. I glanced at my jacket on the seat next to me, thinking about the cash under it. If I was going to have to stay cooped up in my house, I needed supplies—food, for one thing. Between being constantly broke and hating shopping, I never had more than a couple of meals' worth of groceries in the cupboards.

I pulled into the parking lot of the grocery store I usually stopped at on my way home. It was already packed with cars. People were *running* in; some were coming out with carts stacked high with canned goods and bottled water. I couldn't see a single place to park. I followed the line of cars ahead of me, inching along, all of us waiting for an opening. A man in a muddy Bronco behind me kept revving his engine, as though that would make some sort of difference. After a couple of loops around the lot, I just wanted to get out of there: all the faces I could see were strained, fearful. I heard muffled shouting and saw the man from the Bronco, halfway out of his truck, holding onto some women's loaded shopping cart. He was pulling it away from her with one hand, offering her what looked like his wallet with the other. She kept shaking her head and trying to wrest the cart back from him. A couple of people started towards them, but I didn't stay to see what happened. The car in front of me finally slid into a parking slot and I pulled back out onto the street.

Maybe groceries would have to wait. I had enough to make do until tomorrow.

I headed toward home, but then I remembered Tyrone. I had fed him the last of his dog food that morning. I'd planned to stop and get more after work. Shit.

"Pet Mart, here I come." I hung a left at the next light and drove to the strip mall that housed the pet store, questioning my momentary lapse of judgement that day at the animal shelter.

⁓ ⁓

It was strange—my decision to adopt a dog. Strange, because I was always comfortable being by myself; in fact, I preferred it. I was usually alone, but I'd never suffered from loneliness, not like other people I knew. After the divorce and my escape to Billington, the little house I'd managed to put a down payment on with my divorce money, the little house I was barely managing to hang on to with the meager salary Pete paid me, had become my safe haven. I loved being there, reading, listening to music, anticipating gardening in the tiny back yard when spring arrived, doing whatever I wanted to do, whenever I wanted to do it. I could take deep breaths there.

But I'd wake up some mornings and wonder why I was bothering. I had made some acquaintances in town, people I could join for a drink or see a movie with, but I kept everyone at arm's length at all times. It was hard for me to be around people in any meaningful way. It was too hard to try to puzzle out whether they could be trusted, and too painful when it turned out that they couldn't be. I'd decided when I moved to Billington that I was done with risk.

Still, I'd begun to feel like I needed a reason to keep breathing. I'd tried helping at the local mission, spending my Saturday nights passing out dinner rolls to the worn-out men who lined up for meals there, but I kept looking at them wondering what they'd done. To whom they done it. I knew I shouldn't be seeing what I saw in *all* of them; I knew they weren't all guilty. But I also knew that some of them *were*. I quit after a month.

Then, I'd stumbled upon an ad looking for volunteers at a safe-house for women and children who were trying to escape abusive situations. That had worked for a while. I'd felt like I was making a real difference, even if all I did was to show them their rooms in the house and explain the rules. But I couldn't keep it up. It was the children, especially the little girls. I recognized the look in their eyes. That scared look, sure. They all had that. But some of them had shame mixed up in that fear. Some of them looked up at me with eyes that said they knew they were already dirty, that it had all been their fault, that they were never going to be anything but bad. I knew that look too well. It had stared back at me since I was a child myself, from every mirror I'd ever looked into.

Driving home from the safe-house after my last day volunteering there, I stopped at a red light. There was a billboard at the intersection, with a picture of a fluffy puppy with sad eyes sitting next to a sweet, little kitten. **SAVE US – WE'RE WAITING FOR YOU** was emblazoned across the bottom in huge red letters. The animal shelter address listed was in the same part of town as the safe house, on the street I was driving on, in fact—and that struck me funny for some reason. "Note to city planners everywhere, just make sure to put all the stuff we don't want to think about or see in the warehouse district," I muttered to myself.

As I approached the next intersection, I saw the shelter on my right. I tried to imagine that cute little puppy from the billboard inside the squat, corrugated metal building, but instead, all I could picture was every abused animal commercial I'd ever seen, complete with angsty soundtrack. The light turned red, and I stopped the car, forcing myself to stare straight ahead.

"*No*, Julie," I admonished myself. Still, I snuck a look at the building, then snapped my head back toward the light, tapping my fingers on the steering wheel. One more peek, then back to the light. When it finally turned green, I sighed, defeated, swung the steering wheel and pulled into the shelter parking lot. "Well." I shut off the ignition. "Just one quick look."

"We're sure to find something perfect for you," the lady at the counter gushed, before handing me off to another employee. Before I knew it, I was being ushered into the kennel area. "Don't mind the noise," called the lady, smiling and waving me off. She said something else, but when the doors to the back swung open, she was drowned out by the cacophony of barking.

Tyrone was in the last kennel of the first aisle, huddled against the back wall, sitting in his own urine. He would grow to be a huge dog, was already at least fifty pounds at seven months. He was some mix of bloodhound and shepherd—black and tan, upright ears, sharp muzzle, saggy jowls. There was nothing soft or puppy-like about him. There was no way around the fact that he was ugly, and on top of that, he looked vicious.

All the dogs before him had either been running back and forth barking furiously or plastered against the front of their kennels, wagging their tails. He was silent. He watched as I approached, lifted a lip at me and growled softly. I backed away.

"He's set for check out." The shelter worker who was escorting me—he had a cloth patch on his coveralls embroidered with the name "Steve"—said the words with what sounded like a moderate amount of regret.

"Not with me," I said, misunderstanding him.

"No." Steve smiled. "I know he's not the kind you'd be interested in. I meant, he's due to be put down." He put his fingers through the chain link and waggled them at the dog. "Sorry, buddy," he whispered. He turned to me. "I think we have a nice Golden mix in the next row."

I was still watching the dog. When Steve had whispered to him, his ears had swiveled forward and he had looked straight at Steve, searching his face. "Is he . . . is he mean?" The dog switched his gaze from Steve's face to mine.

Steve hooked his thumbs in his coverall pockets. "I don't think so." He kept his eyes on the dog. I got the feeling he didn't relate to his human customers so well.

I stepped closer and read the sheet of paper that hung encased in plastic on the door of the kennel. "Owner surrender." I turned to Steve. "Someone dumped him here?"

He nodded. "They do it all the time."

I kept reading. "Five to seven months, male, mixed breed, Tyrone."

"Notice it doesn't say *biter*, or *aggressive*." Steve raised his eyebrows at me. "We would put that if he was."

"What about that growling?"

Steve looked past me to the dog. "I think he's just scared. I've taken him out once or twice to the yard and he's never growled at me." He looked back at me. "He's still young. I think he's got a good dog in him."

"Why is he . . . set for check out, then?"

"He's out of time. He's not cute and cuddly like the lucky ones. He's been here too long." Steve kept his expression carefully neutral, but his tone conveyed something else.

I felt myself wavering. I'd come with the idea of a small, fuzzy, sweet-smelling puppy in my head. Not some pee-soaked, snarling behemoth. "Tyrone?" I made a face.

"You could call him whatever you wanted." Steve's tone lightened a couple of shades. He made eye contact, assessing what he saw.

"Hmmmmmph." The low sound startled me. It wasn't a whine, or a whimper. It was something like a moan, and it came from deep in the dog's throat. Steve and I both looked at him.

"Tyrone?" I whispered the name. The dog stood, eyeing me warily. He took a step, then another.

I knelt in front of the chain link. "Come here, boy." I said the words as gently as I could. And Tyrone walked right up to the door of his kennel and pressed his nose against the chain link. He stared at me, stared right into my eyes just like Steve had and I could tell he was assessing me, too. I could also tell he wasn't so sure I was a good bet, but he knew, somehow, that I was the only game in town.

I took him home that same day.

⚊ ⚊

Pet Mart wasn't busy at all, strangely enough. There were a few cars in the strip mall lot, but nothing out of the ordinary. I parked as close as I could and tucked the bundles of cash in my purse. When I got about five feet from the entrance, I understood why the parking lot was practically empty. There was a piece of cardboard with a handwritten **CLOSED** on it, shoved between the handles of the double glass doors. I stood there, not sure what to do.

The pet store was the biggest place in the strip mall, but there were several other stores: a sad-looking hair salon, a smoke shop and a Dollarama. I went straight for the smoke shop and was almost surprised when the door opened. I walked through the heavy scent of incense to the back counter where the owner, an elderly Korean woman, stood behind a glassed-in display of fighting knives and ceramic pipes. She knew me; I came here at least once a week to buy cigarettes. I knew they would eventually kill me. But that had always been kind of the point. And once they sunk their sticky, nicotine claws into a person, they weren't easy to shake.

"Afternoon to you," she said in her Korean accent, smiling her gentle smile. "Your regulars?"

I nodded and she turned to get my carton of cigarettes. "Um, wait." I counted; there were fourteen cartons of my brand on the shelf. "I'll take them all."

She turned to me and frowned. "All?" Something in her eyes made me think I'd scared her.

"I have the money." I unzipped my purse and separated a few bills from one of the stacks, careful to keep my actions concealed. I put what I thought would cover the cartons down on the counter.

She stared at the money. "You win the lottery? Better things to spend it on than those."

I smiled. "No, no. I just got a . . . bonus. From work."

"Ah. I see. So, all those?" She looked back at the cartons stacked on the shelf.

"Yes. Please."

"Is too much." She nodded at the cash, even as she began to stack cartons on the counter next to it. "Ah, you need bags." She reached below the counter and got two plastic bags. Once she'd packed all the cartons in them, she took the money from the counter and rang up the sale. She tucked my bills into the cash drawer and began to count out my change.

"No, it's okay." I waved away the money in her hand. "Keep it."

I was halfway to the door when she called out to me. "Miss."

I turned around. She looked tiny, standing behind the counter. Tiny and worried.

"You hear of the sickness?"

"Yes. It's probably nothing, though, right?" I kept my voice light.

She shook her head. "I think it's something." She lowered her eyes, picked at the tape that secured the age verification notice on the glass counter top. "You keep safe."

"You, too." For a minute I didn't want to leave her shop—this woman whose name I didn't even know, this woman who didn't know mine, even though we'd shared a weekly transaction of money and pleasantry since I moved here. Suddenly I wanted to ask her what her name was, how she came to be the mistress of the shop, whether she had family in town. But I didn't ask any of that. I just waved as I left, then went to the car, unlocked it and put the bags of cigarettes inside.

There were still the same few cars in the lot, employees, I guessed, of those stores that were still open. I was about to get in the car when the sign for the Dollarama caught my eye. I'd never gone in there; it had always seemed like the kind of store people went when they needed party supplies or wedding decorations. I was a divorced, childless woman. I stuck to the smoke shop and the pet store. Still, it was worth a try.

The place was open for business. A teenaged boy slouched behind the cash register at the front of the store, looking uncomfortable in his red polyester uniform shirt, avoiding eye contact. Strains of instrumental-only pop music covers filled the air. There were only two other shoppers—a woman and her little girl, filling their cart with sparkly ribbon and birthday balloons. I took a cart of my own and started down the first aisle. Cheap socks, cloth baby diapers, hair combs in packs of three. Nothing there for me. Ah, but in the next aisle, toothpaste and tooth brushes. Every disaster movie I'd ever watched played back in my mind. Essential supplies. All the things people couldn't get any more when the world ended. "Apocalypse now" I whispered, grinning. "Who would have thought the bonanza was at the Dollarama." I threw handfuls of paste and brushes in the cart.

Every aisle revealed new bounty. Toilet paper, shampoo, soap, off-brand canned tuna fish—if nothing else Tyrone could live off of that for a few days and so could I. There was aspirin, hydrogen peroxide, granola bars, bandages, candles. The Dollarama had *everything*. I grabbed anything that seemed useful, feeling foolish and frightened at the same time. They had antibacterial hand wash, and in the hardware aisle I found face masks meant for dust protection. I took them anyway. Maybe they'd stop germs, too. I grabbed dozens of jumbo-packs of disposable lighters and fifteen tubes of topical antibiotic ointment. When I'd filled the cart to capacity, I pushed it up to the boy in front.

He stared at the mound of goods and then rolled his eyes. "Jeeze, lady. We're going to be here a while."

"Yeah." I narrowed my eyes at him. "Is that a problem?"

"My boss wanted me to close up as soon as possible. I only let *them* in because it's that girl's birthday tomorrow." He pointed toward the woman and the little girl, both still absorbed in the foil party hats.

"Why do you have to close?" I already knew, but I was hoping I was wrong.

"There's some freak-out about the flu. The boss is scared there might be looting, or something." The boy gave me a look; clearly he thought the boss was an old fart. "At least I get off early."

"Is everything really a dollar?"

The boy rolled his eyes again. He pointed to a sign above his head. It said DOLLARAMA EVERYTHING IS $1. "Duh."

"Huh." I considered the sign. "How many items would you say I have?"

He shrugged. "I dunno."

"Not five hundred, for sure, right?" I set my purse on top of the mound of stuff and unzipped it. When I had five bills separated, I took them out and handed them to him. "This will cover it, and then you don't have to scan it all right now. You can just grab something later, when you get back to work, and scan it five hundred times." I watched his face manifest the action of his brain, cranking slowly into gear. "Or maybe just four hundred times. You know, keep the change." I added another bill. "That should take care of them, too." I tilted my head toward the birthday shoppers. "But I need help bagging this stuff up."

All four cylinders of his brain finally started firing and the boy had my items bagged in no time. I thought about staying to make sure he didn't charge the woman for her birthday decorations, but I didn't. Out at the Kia, I shoved the bags into backseat and didn't bother returning the cart to the store.

"Living dangerously now, Julie, aren't you?" I couldn't help but laugh. I never left a cart in a parking lot; I *always* followed the rules. But it felt like today was not a day for following the rules. I opened the car door, but a shadow of movement behind the plate glass front of the Pet Mart caught my eye. Yes, there it was again—there was someone inside.

The sky looked even more foreboding then it had when I'd left work. Dark gray clouds loomed low, heavy with the threat of a downpour. I stood by the open car door for a minute, weighing my options. I could go home now and miss the storm, but the thought of Tyrone's empty dog dish stopped me. If this thing was real it might be a day or two before I could get him any food. He was a big dog; he would go through the canned tuna from the Dollarama in about a second, and then, with my bare cupboards, what would *I* eat?

I locked the car up and trotted to the Pet Mart front doors. Pressing my nose against the glass, my hands cupped at my temples, I peered inside. There was a man way in the back, lugging a huge bag of something down the shiny linoleum aisle. Pounding on the doors, I called to him. At first he didn't look my way, but I kept hitting the glass and he finally dropped the bag he was holding and walked to the front, shaking his head the whole way.

"We're closed," he said, his voice muffled by the thick glass. He pointed to the sign stuck in the door handles.

I recognized him. He was the one who had helped me register for Tyrone's obedience classes, the ones we were supposed to start on the weekend. "Hey, it's me," I said, pointing at my face as though that would help matters. I noticed his Pet Mart name badge. "Brad. It's me, Tyrone's owner, you know . . . the big dog? I'm totally out of food and we're supposed to shelter in pl—"

He cut me off. "You coughing?"

I shook my head.

"Fever?"

"No."

He looked over my shoulder, beyond the parking lot to the road. I looked, too. There was a lot more traffic out there. A couple of cars were pulling into the lot. When I looked back at him, I could tell he'd made a decision.

"Got a car out there?"

I nodded, eager, like some puppy about to be rewarded for doing a trick.

He jabbed his thumb toward the back of the store. "Pull it around. But make it snappy." Then he walked away.

I watched him disappear behind a display of aquariums. A drop of rain hit my ear, two more hit my face in quick succession. I ran for the Kia.

Behind the building, I parked next to a pickup truck backed up to a concrete loading dock. It was one of those off-road trucks, riding ridiculously high on huge tires. The canopy of the truck was open; inside it was filled to the top with bags of kitty litter and cases of canned cat food. Above the dock there was a big, roll-up door. Stairs along one side led to a smaller, metal door. I went up them and knocked on the smaller door tentatively, hoping Brad hadn't just been telling me what I wanted to hear to make me leave. But almost as soon as I knocked, the door opened a couple of inches. Brad held the knob from the inside, barely glancing at me before he scanned the area behind me. When he was sure I was alone he eyed my car, and sighed.

"Back it in and pop the trunk."

"The trunk . . . I—"

"Now." Brad took a step back and let the door close.

I tried the knob: it was locked. "Shit." I took the steps back down two at a time, pulled the car out and backed it in like the truck was, as close to the loading dock as I could get it. I unlocked the trunk and lifted it, ran back up to the door and knocked again.

The big overhead door rose, first just a few inches, then higher than my head. Brad stood on the other side of it, one hand resting on the handle of a flat cart loaded with bags of dog food.

"I'll toss them in, you stack 'em." He picked up a bag and swung it off the dock into my trunk.

"Thank you so much, Brad. Really, I really appreciate it."

"Better get down there and start stacking or I won't be able to fit many in." Brad grabbed another bag and aimed for the trunk.

"I'm sure that one will do—I mean, Tyrone's big but it's just until—"

"That won't be near enough, if I'm figuring it right." Brad gestured to the cart, stacked with fifty-pound bags. "Even this won't be enough, maybe." He looked grim.

That stopped me in my tracks. "Have you heard something new—something more than the broadcasts earlier?"

He looked at me, dumbstruck. "You need to hear more than that?"

He had a point. I went down to the car and started stacking bags.

By the time the trunk was full, we'd managed to get ten bags inside. Brad pulled the big door down and disappeared while I was stacking the last two. He came back out the small door with a plastic Pet Mart bag stuffed full of something. Leaning over the dock, he handed it down to me.

"Some stuff you might need for that dog. Tyrone, right?"

I took the bag from him. "Yes. Do you remember him?"

Brad shook his head. "Nah. Don't remember him or you." He straightened, arched his back as though it was aching. "I see a lot of dogs, working here. I'm more of a cat guy."

I wasn't sure what to say. "Wait." I ran to the car door. "I need to pay you." I retrieved several bills from my purse.

Brad snorted when he saw the cash. "Funny." But his expression was far from humorous. "The latest on the news is that cell phones and the Internet are down. That," he gestured to my cash, "is nothing but paper, now."

Well. My lack of a smart phone was finally moot. Whenever I had to admit I didn't have one, people always reacted as though I'd said I didn't have a liver. I only had bundled cable phone service at home—the cheapest route for my new, post-divorce life. There was nobody for me to text my riveting lunch highlights to anyway, so I'd never really missed being glued to that little screen.

A car pulled around the far corner of the building, going slow, heading toward the loading dock. Brad eyed it, hopped off the dock and slammed the truck canopy door shut.

"Better take off, now. Good luck." He got in his truck, started it and drove off without looking back. There was a pink sticker on the bumper with *I love my Purrrrsian* spelled out in glittery silver letters.

The other car drew closer, revealing darkly tinted windows—even the front window was dark enough that I couldn't see the interior. It stopped about fifteen feet from me, engine idling.

Suddenly, the Pet Mart loading dock felt like a very unsafe place for me to be, at least all alone.

I could see movement inside the car, and then the window on the driver's side opened a tiny bit and smoke wafted out of the crack. Someone flicked a cigarette butt out and the window closed. And then the car just sat there, running. I could feel eyes on me, though I couldn't see the driver. I got in my car as calmly as I could, locked the doors and started it. Just as I pulled away, the rain began in earnest, sheeting down the windshield, blurring the world for a moment. I turned on the wipers and looked in the rearview mirror. The car was still there.

When I turned the corner I put on speed, watching the mirror, feeling panicky. Nobody rounded the corner after me. "It was just some kid, Julie, just some kid smoking in a car." I kept telling myself that all the way home.

Home

I DROVE TO my house using the side streets. When I finally turned down my street it felt like I'd been on a long journey, even though according to my watch I'd left the office just over two hours before. My place was two blocks down a short, dead-end lane. One of the reasons I loved the location was the dead end: nobody drove down the street unless they lived on it, so it was quiet. It wasn't a great neighborhood; all the houses were old and most were a bit run-down. But the people on the street were nice enough, and I could afford to own a home there.

Home. My squat, tiny, 1940's bungalow never looked more welcoming. It took me two trips from the car to the porch to get all the bags from the front and backseats and one sack of dog food from the trunk unloaded. I was getting soaked by the rain, and I figured the rest of the kibble was safe in the trunk for the night. As I fumbled with the key to the front door, I saw a vehicle turn onto the street from the main road. The key wouldn't turn in the lock at first and I felt a strange panic until I recognized the car. It was a beat-up old Ford, worse even than my old Kia. It belonged to a couple who lived at the very end of the dead-end—Mark and Nancy, or maybe it was Mark and Darcy. I didn't know them well and could never remember. I watched as their car rolled toward me and waved when it got close enough that I thought whoever was driving might see.

It was Mark. He didn't wave back like he usually did. He slowed the car, leaning over toward the passenger window to see better, but he didn't give me more than a glance. What he did look at were the bags piled around me on the porch. Once he'd passed me, he put on speed again and

I watched until his tail lights turned off into his driveway. A glance up and down the street revealed no other sign of life. I got the front door open and started tossing bags on the living room floor as fast as I could. Once they were all in, I locked the door behind me.

Tyrone sat next to the fireplace, watching quietly. He never rushed the door when I came home—no frolicking-happy-tail-wagging puppy greeting from him. No barking, either—I'd never heard him do it. It wasn't that he couldn't; I'd had him checked by a vet when I adopted him. There was no damage to his vocal cords. The vet had just shrugged. "Some dogs just don't have a lot to say. Or at least, not a lot they want to say to *us*." But he was always there, waiting. I never came home to find him sleeping, or busy with a chew toy, or in a different room. He was always sitting by the fireplace, looking huge in my tiny living room, calmly watching as I made my entrance.

Usually, I called him over and fussed over him a bit before letting him out into the backyard. Today, I dragged the bags into the kitchen and held one of the French doors open for him without even giving him a pat on the head. Then I went straight back to the living room and shut the white metal blinds that covered the big picture window. Hooking a slat with my fingers, I peered out onto the street again. It was starting to get darker—the storm clouds were lower and the rain was still pelting down. I didn't see anyone outside, though a couple of the houses had lights on.

I checked the old laptop in my office; the Pet Mart guy was right—every webpage just came up with a *no connection* error. Back in the living room I grabbed the remote and flicked on my old television, pushed the buttons for CNN and sat on the edge of the sofa. The screen lit up, a news anchor's worried face in the center, scrolling text bands at the top and bottom.

"—appears that it may have been purposefully introduced by terrorists, using sophisticated biofabrication techniques. New intelligence suggests that 3D bioprinters in key laboratory locations were hacked by the terrorists, allowing the entire nation to be seeded at once with the virus. The name *Hacker's Flu* has stuck, in reference to both the way the virus was planted in our nation's bioprinters and one of the first symptoms—a violent cough—that characterizes infection. Here now is the last interview with Dr. Elizabeth Graham, the noted Chicago geneticist and biofabrication pioneer who was, we believe, the first person to contract Hacker's Flu."

The picture switched to a woman in a hospital bed, hooked up to an IV, wearing a protective face mask. The camera zoomed out to show the plastic isolation tent she was in, then zoomed back in on her face.

"The printer was in mid-operation when I came in that morning." The woman's blue eyes were the only part of her face visible above the paper mask. "I hadn't programmed any printing the night before, so I was shocked. I checked the logs, and no jobs were scheduled, so I waited for the printing to finish and then I . . . then I opened the—"

"You were infected at that time?" A reporter asked the question. The camera zoomed in even closer on the woman's eyes. They were brimming with tears.

"Yes. I didn't think, I just—"

The reporter interrupted. "And have they found any successful treatment, any vaccine or—"

The woman started to answer but she was wracked by a coughing fit. She covered her mask with her hand, her body thrown forward with each deep cough. When she took her hand away, the mask was covered with spattered blood, scarlet droplets blooming outward as they soaked the paper. The station switched back to the studio.

"Doctor Graham succumbed to the flu yesterday, one of the first victims of what is now believed to be a carefully orchestrated bioterror attack." The news anchor shook his head gravely, doing that *I'm deeply concerned* pantomime they all do when they're reporting bad news. "The President has now instituted national quarantine protocols. Citizens are urged to remain in their homes and to take precautions to avoid all contact—"

I cycled through channels, looking for local news. One station had a garish orange and blue graphic treatment of the word HACKER pinned to the bottom corner of the screen. The reporter, young and clearly frightened, obviously not the usual studio anchor, kept looking at the wrong camera, giving the impression he was speaking to someone off stage.

"—not certain yet whether the virus is transmitted only by direct contact or if it may be airborne. The one thing we do know is that the virus can be fatal within days. Symptoms begin with aching and fever followed by extreme coughing, blood in the lungs and ultimately, death. The Center for Disease Control and Prevention recommendations include using all precautions to avoid infection and quarantine if infection is suspected. There is no known antidote at this time." The screen split, the left side showing the reporter and the right showing a suburban street.

"As you can see from this live footage, some residents are already self-quarantining." On the right side of the screen the camera panned up and down a street of split-level houses, the kind of neighborhood families with two wage-earners and one-point-five kids call home. Then it zoomed to one of the garages, focusing on a crudely spray-painted letter **Q**, blazing orange against the tasteful beige garage panels. It looked like graffiti sprayed with some of that landscaper's paint they use to mark off new perennial beds; I had some somewhere buried in a cupboard, but mine was chartreuse. The camera traveled up the front of the garage to a picture window on the front of the house, where a man stood holding an infant. He stared down at the camera as though he expected help, held the baby up to show the news crew. Then he started coughing.

I switched off the television and realized I'd been holding my breath. My heart felt like it was beating too fast and I took a couple of deep breaths, inhaling through my nose, exhaling through pursed lips, like those people who loosely follow whatever Buddhist tenets they find convenient do in times of stress. Then I heard a thump from the kitchen and any Zen I might have been attracting fled. I froze. Listened. And again—thump. I looked around but there was really nothing that would suffice as an impromptu weapon. Edging to the kitchen doorway, I tried to think what to do. If I was fast, I could get to a knife. I could see the battered old bread knife in my mind, worn wooden handle, wicked serrated blade, third drawer to the left of the sink. I took another breath, crouched, as though that would make some sort of positive difference, and slunk through the doorway.

Tyrone sat, drenched, on the deck outside the French doors, one paw on a glass pane. He saw me and raised his paw, then let it hit the glass. Thump. Beyond him, dusk was gathering, deepening the rain-darkened sky.

"Aw, Tyrone." I'd completely forgotten he was outside. When I opened the doors he came in and sniffed at all the bags I'd strewn on the kitchen floor and then looked up at me, a question in his deep brown eyes.

"Don't worry, buddy, one of those has dinner in it. Let's get you dried off first, though."

After a brisk toweling, Tyrone ate the bowl of kibble I poured him, while I put away the Dollarama stuff. I stashed things in various places—socks in the bedroom dresser, toothbrushes in the bathroom linen closet, tuna in the kitchen. I opened the mystery Pet Mart bag to find years' worth of flea treatments. There were at least fifteen blister packs, each holding a six-month supply. I stared at them for a long time before I shoved them all in the dog food drawer.

The guy at Pet Mart thought there might never be a way to get flea treatment again.

There was a knock on the front door. Tyrone made his sound—the same *hmmmmmph* sound he made that first day in the shelter. He didn't seem worried, just alert. He followed me to the living room and stood at my side as I peered through the peephole in the front door.

It was Greg, the neighbor. He looked worried, his ever-present baseball cap pulled down low on his head. Greg was a good guy; a bit gruff, but he'd helped me with a clogged kitchen sink during my first week in the house. I'd knocked on his door hoping he could recommend a good plumber and the next thing I knew he was under my kitchen sink, ordering me to hand him tools. At first I'd been uneasy—having a strange man in my house is not my ideal scenario. But he'd been solely focused on the plumbing, not on me.

Greg was a bit of a conspiracy theorist; he and Diane, his girlfriend, had had me over for dinner before ski season had begun and he kept bringing up government plots and asking me if I had "prepared" for "the big one." It had been a strange evening, but the food was good, and Diane just shushed him when he got too animated. They were both very into skiing and I hadn't seen them much during the rest of winter, but I opened the door to Greg without hesitation.

As usual, he cut to the chase. "You hear the news?"

I nodded. Before I could say anything, Greg invited himself in and strode to the window, peeking through the blinds. "We're heading out tonight. Thought you might want to join us." He scanned the street. "We figure the ski cabin might be just the place to ride this out—I have it even better provisioned than the house. Diane is over there worrying that you'll be stuck here, being new to the area. I told her you probably have people somewhere, right?" Greg turned around. "But she won't be happy until I—"

My expression must have conveyed what I was thinking. I *didn't* have people somewhere. My mother was dead and I could only hope my father was; I hadn't seen him since I left home at seventeen. My ex-husband was definitely not *my* people. My best friend in the world was Gina Dearborn, but she was living in Tokyo. We'd been friends a long time, but her life was so different from mine. She went back to college, snubbed all the boys that wanted to marry her, and had a fabulous career as a global brand manager for a big software company. I went back to college, studied English of all things, and struggled to find employment after my divorce. Thank goodness I had taken accounting classes too.

Greg scowled. "Anyway. If you want to come, you should pack up a few things."

"I . . . I appreciate it." I didn't know if I actually appreciated it, but it seemed the proper thing to say. "But do you really think it's going to be so bad that we need to leave?"

"Hell, yes." Greg sputtered the words. "Have you seen what's happening back east? It's going to get nuts here, too, and soon. Diane and me are getting out while the getting's good. Only thing." He grabbed the bill of his cap and lifted it. After sweeping a hand over his receding hairline he reseated the cap on his head. "The dog can't come."

I'd been about to accept his offer. I was scared, and the idea of putting it all into Greg's hands, even if they were conspiracy theorist hands, of just riding in the back of his king cab pickup to some ski cabin, sounded good at the moment. "Why?"

Greg shook his head and sighed. "Diane's scared to death of him. I told her he was a big softie, but she doesn't like his looks." He hooked his thumbs through his jeans belt loops and shook his head again. "She got bit by a German Shepard when she was a kid. Never liked dogs since. You notice she hasn't been by to ask you to dinner? Course, we haven't been around like we were before ski season, but she told me I'd be the one asking once we were back in the neighborhood routine. She's scared to come to the door."

"I see." I looked down at Tyrone, who had stationed himself next to me when Greg came in the house. I couldn't really blame Diane—he looked like he could take an arm off of someone without too much effort. But I couldn't drive off and leave the dog to fend for himself. "I think I'll have to pass, Greg. But thank you."

Greg looked shocked. "Seriously, Julie. I know you like the dog, but this isn't the time to be a fool about a pet."

I nodded. "I know. But I can't just leave him here."

He shook his head, real regret in his expression. "I have to go. Diane's going to be wondering what's taking so long. You sure you don't want to rethink this?"

I followed him to the door. "Tell Diane I understand. No hard feelings." I hoped I sounded sincere. "I'll be okay." I watched him through the blinds as he crossed the lawn, heading back to his house. Then I locked the front door. After a second of thought, I threw the deadbolt too, just for good measure.

I eyed the phone, sitting on its charger. I wanted to call someone, but I had nobody to call. With the time difference, Gina would be at her job in Tokyo, probably in some important meeting, and I didn't want to bother her there. I thought of her as my best friend, but truly she was just my oldest. Sometimes, I thought about how we were different now, different than we had been when we first met. Nothing wrong between us, just time and distance and lack of attention fraying the fabric of true connection until it's nothing but a thin memory, still interesting to look at, but the pattern is so faded you can't make out the meaning of the images anymore. Most of the time I pushed that realization away. I think Gina did, too.

I felt strangely calm, and wondered if I was in shock. Maybe everyone was just overreacting. I switched the television back on, hoping for some confirmation that everything still made sense but it was just more of the same: half the stations sensationalizing as much as they could, half simply repeating the standard *stay-calm-shelter-in-place* message.

I wandered from the living room to the kitchen for a while, until I realized I was making Tyrone nervous. It was still early evening, but I was exhausted. Finally, I decided to brush my teeth and get in bed, but I left my clothes on—it felt like I might need to be ready to go. Though some childhood-like fear made me want to leave them on, it seemed safer somehow to have the lights off, as though my house might escape notice more easily—the idea of *whose* notice, I tried not to dwell upon. I left the porch light blazing though, and the back-deck light, too.

Several times during the night I awoke to the sound of car engines starting. The nearest neighbors to the north drove off at around two in the morning. I could hear them shutting the trunk of their car, trying to be quiet, and then the electronic whir of their ecologically sound car engine. I pictured them in my mind: a younger couple, always friendly in that *let's not get too friendly* sort of way. The woman was one of those straightened blonde, peppy types—I thought she was a nurse. I couldn't remember what the man did.

When my eyes adjusted to the darkness I could see Tyrone's silhouette on his dog bed, on the floor next to mine. He was lying down, but his head was up, and I knew he was alert. I listened to the sound of his breathing, trying to match my own breaths to his.

It was a long night.

The Morning After

THE MORNING SUN streaming through the blinds woke me. That, and the sound of Tyrone's nails clicking on the kitchen floor. The clicking stopped, silenced by the carpet as he entered the bedroom. He snuffled around to my side of the bed and saw that I was awake. After he made eye contact, he trotted back out to the kitchen. It took a moment for all that had happened the day before to seep back into my brain and once it did, I didn't want to move. But I rolled out of bed and followed him.

"You want out?" It was pretty obvious he did—he was already sitting in front of the cheap French doors that opened onto the back yard, looking over his shoulder at me. I opened one and Tyrone ran out onto the deck, but he didn't jump off into the yard like he usually did. Instead, he nosed at one of the terra cotta planters that lined the edge of the deck. When I bought the house, the planters had been filled with ornamental annuals—velvety russet pansies, some icy blue lobelia. They were dead now, frozen into brown lumps over the winter. I'd planned to make a run to the local nursery soon to replace them, now that the winter was over. But Tyrone wasn't sniffing at the flower carcasses. He was interested in something else.

There was a plastic bag on top of the dead flowers in one planter, a yellow bag with the name of the local newspaper printed on it in blue, knotted at the top. It hadn't been there yesterday. I stood in the kitchen, my hand on the door knob, slow dread creeping up my spine. I scanned the fence surrounding the back yard—six-foot cedar boards with a gate at the back and one at the side of the house. The gate at the back looked closed, but clearly, at some point during the night someone had opened it or the side gate and walked up onto the deck. I thought about how my bedroom window was a mere five feet from the flower pot.

Tyrone nudged the bag with his nose and looked through the door panes at me. Then he jumped off the deck and lifted his leg on the dwarf pine tree. He didn't seem concerned, didn't act as though anyone was actively trespassing. He moved further down the yard, nose to the ground, checking all his usual spots. I turned the knob and stepped through the door into the early morning.

The sky was dull, metal gray, low clouds so dense they looked like a ceiling. The grass was damp beyond the deck, heavy with rain from the night before. I stood, listening, but there was no sound save the birds, singing their sunrise song. I eyed the gates.

"Tyrone." I whispered the dog's name and he was instantly at my side. "Let's go." I picked up the plastic bag, holding it away from me as though it might detonate, and backed into the house, locking the door behind us.

Tyrone figured it was breakfast time, but I wanted to investigate the bag. It was light in weight, and when I worked the knot loose there was only a scrap of notebook paper and a small, silver key inside. I unfolded the paper and read. It was from my next-door neighbors to the south.

Hope you've been watching the news—we won't be coming back. Help yourself.
Greg and Diane

So they'd really gone, without me. I looked at the key, shining cool in my palm. Too small for a house key. I left it on the kitchen counter with the note and went to the living room to turn on the television. The first two channels I tried were static, but on the third, a grim-faced reporter appeared, mid-sentence.

"—travel ban since early this morning, and the governor says troops *will* forcibly stop any vehicles attempting to access freeways. Again, the public is directed to remain in their homes. Quarantine is in full effect in most counties and most hospitals are over-capacity, with no effective treatment options to offer." The camera zoomed in on the reporter's face, showing the dark circles under his eyes. "The latest information is that drinking fluids, staying warm and waiting for the virus to run its course are the only treatments for Hacker's Flu. Fatality rates are rising. Citizens are encouraged to mark residences with ill people inside to indicate quarantine and if not already ill, to avoid all contact with the infected. Federal authorities are investigating Internet outages nationwide, and while there is some cell service in areas across the nation, it appears that most areas are without service."

With each word the reporter said the fear and disbelief I'd wrestled down during the night resurfaced. It really *was* happening. I switched channels through more dead static, searching for better news. I only found one more station broadcasting, the reporter saying the same things the first had, complete with film of uniformed troops lined up across onramps pointing their rifles at minivans and RVs, and shots of various **Q**s painted on the outside of houses, some scrawled with spray paint, some neatly, carefully drawn on.

A crashing sound out front drew my attention away from the screen. I turned off the set and peeked through the living room blinds. Two cars were stopped in the street, one with its front bumper jammed into the back of the other. I recognized both of them as neighbors' cars, one from the house directly across from mine. I'd never learned the man's name who lived there—he worked nights I thought, and I rarely saw him. The other car belonged to an older woman who lived down a block or so. She got off work just after me, so I often saw her driving past, on her way home. Soon after she arrived in the evening she would walk a tiny black dog—one of those fluffy little things with three brain cells circling each other inside its skull—up the street.

I used to watch them make their way past my window, the woman walking slowly, bundled in a puffy polyester jacket, the dog waddling along in front of her, straining at the leash with its tiny body. She had gray hair, worn in a short style that proclaimed she'd given up preening, and she didn't try to hide the extra weight she carried with spandex or large prints. I thought of her as one of the *remnants*.

I don't know when I started categorizing people as remnants—it felt like I always had. One of the checkers at the grocery store I frequented was a remnant: a woman in her thirties—she was pleasant to all her customers, but there was something in her gaze, something hard and hurt. When pressed, she made small-talk about her cat. I imagined her going home after her shift to a small apartment, furnished with cautious neutrality. I could see her cracking open a can of "gourmet" canned food for the cat, leafing through the junk mail she got that day while the cat ate, then making some small frozen dinner for herself and eating it in front of her television. I imagined her telephone rarely rang, and when it did, it was her mother, or her best friend from high school, who had married and moved to another state years ago.

There were remnants everywhere: the postal clerk with the terrible scars on his face, which were eclipsed by his bitter, angry expression; the boy in my sixth-grade class, who lost half his leg in a lawnmower accident and whose mother never let him forget he was different. I remember watching him as he started believing it, watching as he withdrew from any overture of friendship. He was made into a remnant so young.

Sometimes, when I looked in the mirror, I knew I was a remnant, too. I saw it in my eyes, and when I reviewed my life, I saw it in the fact that I didn't try to form new relationships. Not anymore. Like the rest of the people I thought of as remnants, my life, my being, was made up of what was left of me. When I looked in the mirror I saw the remnants of my potential self; the pieces that were left after I was damaged beyond repair, after I gave up trying. After I stopped believing that love was available to all who sought it.

Outside, it looked like the neighbor across from me had been backing out of his driveway when his car got hit by the woman from down the street. I watched as both vehicles' doors opened and the drivers got out. My neighbor started toward the woman, his face concerned, his hand outstretched toward her. She stood by her open car door, holding it as though to steady herself. Before the man could reach her, she doubled over, coughing.

The man froze in place for a moment, and his expression shifted from concern to revulsion. He backed away, slowly at first, then turned and ran for his car. He slammed the door shut, gunned the engine and was gone before the woman could recover from her coughing fit.

I gave Tyrone the hand signal I'd been practicing with him—the one that meant *stay*, and opened the front door. I could hear shrill barking—the little black dog must be in the car. I started across the front porch, but before I reached the steps the woman saw me and held up a hand.

"Don't." She lowered her hand, transforming the gesture from a *stop* to a *please*. She looked embarrassed, as though she'd just snapped at a grocery store checker after a bad day. Ducking her head inside the car, she shushed the little dog, crooning until the shrieking barks subsided. Then she straightened and turned back to me, a great weariness in her movements.

"Don't come close." She tried to smile. "I have it." Another coughing fit overtook her.

I stayed on the porch. "Can I . . . can I help?" The words sounded useless to me, empty. I couldn't help.

She replied too quickly, the way people do when they're lying. "I'll be fine." And she looked at me, straight into my eyes, for the longest moment.

In her eyes, I could see so much wistfulness, so much regret. I wondered what life she was remembering, what lost chance. I started to speak, but she shrugged, gave another half-smile and got back in her car. She didn't look my way while she started the engine. I saw her lean toward the passenger seat, to pet the dog, I imagined. Then she drove down the street, toward the main road. I watched until her car disappeared. I wondered where she was going, dying, with her little black dog.

The neighborhood looked even more deserted then it had the night before. There were no lights on at any of the houses now. A couple of garage doors were gaping, left that way during hurried departures. The quiet felt oppressive, instead of peaceful. I looked up and down the street and saw no one, nobody at all. Greg's truck, which was usually parked on the street in front of his house, was gone. There were no other cars parked on the street at all except mine. There were a couple pulled into driveways; Mark's, and one farther down.

I went back into the house and walked past Tyrone to the kitchen, grabbed the car keys from where I'd dropped them the night before. When

I headed for the door again he stood, wanting to come, but I gave him the signal to stay put.

Travel ban. Remain in your home. *I have it.* This thing was happening, and I was in it. I shut the front door on Tyrone and stood, shaking, on the porch. I eyed the Kia, but only for a moment. I had nowhere to go.

Time to get the rest of the dog food out of the trunk.

Human Nature

I WAS UNLOADING the last bag of kibble from the trunk, trying not to look at the empty parking spot where Greg's truck usually was, when I saw Mark, the neighbor who had driven by without waving, walking down the street toward me. He had his head down, arms swinging at his sides. In one hand he held some sort of gun—a .38? All I could see was the blue glint of metal and the way he held it, like he wasn't used to it.

He got within twenty feet and stopped when he realized I was watching him. I stood there holding the bag of kibble, wondering what he had in mind. Waiting.

"What's that for?" Mark gestured toward the bag with his gun.

"What's *that* for?" I nodded toward the gun.

He considered the gun in his hand, lowered it, spat on the asphalt. "We wondered if you needed anything. Me and Nancy." Everything about him was tense, wrong.

"So you came down to ask with a gun in your hand?" I shifted the bag in my arms, hoping it hid the fact that my hands were shaking.

Mark's chin went up. He looked down the bridge of his nose at me. "Can't be too safe with everything going on." He took a step toward me. "I saw you last night, hauling bags into your house." He took another step. "Nancy's pregnant, due any day now. We've been close to the bone for a while now—the refinery's been cutting hours for months. There's not much in the house. I figured you could spare some."

"I have some cans of tuna, Mark. That's about it." I wished I was lying. I couldn't imagine what Nancy must be feeling right now, pregnant, housebound, with no supplies. *I* felt scared, and I wasn't worrying about a baby on the way.

Mark slowly shook his head. "I'll see for myself." He started toward me, raising the gun and pointing it squarely at my chest.

For a long, slow-motion moment, staring into Mark's empty eyes, I realized I was very probably about to die. A fucking man—of course—was about try to kill me. My body kicked into full-on biological survival imperative, sending strange waves of adrenaline through my muscles, transmitting klaxon screams to my brain: DO SOMETHING DO SOMETHING DO SOMETHING.

I didn't know what to do. So I started coughing.

I dropped the bag of kibble, doubled over and coughed as hard as I could. I didn't look up until I was completely out of breath, and by then Mark was halfway back to his house, darting looks over his shoulder as he went. I kept a fist at my lips, watching him go, and mustered up a few more coughs. When I was certain he'd gone back in his house, I grabbed the bag of kibble and ran for my porch.

Inside, I locked the front door and looked through the peephole. It showed me a fishbowl version of the front porch and not much else. I backed away and let myself fall onto the sofa. If I hadn't faked that cough, would I be dead right now? How much time had I bought myself? I felt a strange guilt for protecting my cans of tuna with a lie, mixed with rage at the idea Mark would try to take what I little had with a gun. But mostly I felt like crying.

Tyrone nudged my hand with his warm, wet nose. His worried brown eyes sought mine, softening when I rubbed his shoulders. Mark's desperation, his willingness to take, to provide for his family; none of it really surprised me. My own instant and instinctual reaction—to survive—surprised me a great deal. For as long as I could remember, life had been optional in my mind. Every day, every month, every year, whenever things got too painful, I weighed the cost of living against the simplicity, the relief, of giving up. It was a very close calculation sometimes, too close.

I never thought of myself as special in this habit. Regrettably, I knew I wasn't. I was just one of so many children who had the bad luck to have hope eliminated from our lives before we ever really experienced it. One of the used, the abused, the lost. Born to those who in all likelihood had had the misfortune to belong to the same forsaken tribe of which they made us, in our turn, members. Generation unto generation, misery passed along in one form or another, from lack of . . . what? Strength? Courage? Heart? I'd seen others, everywhere, all my life, some desperately numbing the pain with sex, or drugs, or the pretense of apathy. Some permanently dead inside. Some just plain dead, after too many years of trying to survive an existence filled with agony and grief. Others stumbled on, doing the same grim calculation I did—percentage of stamina left, minus grief still to come, equals live? Or die?

For me, sometimes the silliest thing tipped the balance toward perseverance: a new job, a sunny spring day after weeks of rain. Sometimes it was more substantial: a man who made me think, the idea that humans *could* love, the tenuous belief that it mattered. But it was always on the table, that calculation, always in play. I truly thought of myself as the remnant of who I might have been. I always wondered how long a scrap like me could carry on doing what it took a whole person to do properly. I didn't really want to commit suicide most of the time, but I'd come to be resigned to the fact that I probably would, someday. I knew in my heart that sooner or later, the balance would be broken and life—or at least the version of it I experienced—would fall clearly in the deficit column. Someday, I would just get too tired, too empty.

So my reaction to Mark's gun surprised me. Maybe it was simply instinct kicking in, maybe not. I only knew that I hadn't wanted to die there in the street in front of my house, over cans of tuna.

Tyrone hummed his odd little hum to me, signaling his desire for breakfast. I got up, lugged the bag of kibble from the living room to the kitchen and added it to the others in the pantry. I took a measured amount from the already opened bag and filled Tyrone's bowl, my hands still slightly shaky.

"You, my friend, are covered in the food department. At least for a while."

While Tyrone wolfed down his food, I rummaged through my utensil drawer and selected the sharpest paring knife I could find, ran a finger down its blade. As if I could ever use it against someone. Mark would be able to take it from me easily and he wasn't that tough. I let it clatter back into the drawer.

"Wait a minute." A thought struck me—the image of a can of spray paint. The top shelf of the pantry was where I kept all the odds and ends of my household life; a hammer, some bungee cords, some open, folded-over seed packets from last spring's garden, a few clay pots. Behind a stack of folded paper grocery bags was the can of bright green landscaper's spray paint I'd bought when I moved in, to plan some perennial bed outlines in my tiny back yard. I grabbed it and gave it a shake. Still a quarter of a can left.

I hurried to the front door and looked through the peephole again. Nothing. Cautiously, I opened the door and peered outside. The street looked deserted both ways. Out on the porch, I shook the can up and down, wincing at the rattle it made—the sound seemed to echo through the neighborhood. I raised the can and sprayed a huge circle on my front door. It felt illegal, somehow, as though I were vandalizing my own property. I sprayed over the first circle again and then made a line through the circle, forming a **Q**. From a couple of steps back it didn't look too bad.

When I stepped off the porch onto the front lawn, I realized my first **Q** wasn't visible enough from the street. The siding beside my front picture window beckoned, a canvas awaiting my duplicitous art. I made the second **Q** as large as I could, retracing it four times. When I was done, the **Q** was impossible to miss, bright green rivulets of paint dripping from it like alien blood.

Back in the house, I slid two fingers between the slats of the blinds and surveyed the street. If anybody was out there, they weren't showing themselves. I wondered if Mark and Nancy were the only two people left on the street besides me. Tyrone shoved his head against the back of my knee, wanting attention.

"Not now, buddy." I switched the television back on, skipping through the static until I found a picture. Another uneasy reporter, this one an older man in shirtsleeves, shot in a slightly-out-of-focus close-up.

"—apologize again for the lack of our usual quality broadcast, friends." The man loosened his tie. "As I mentioned earlier, we are operating on a skeleton crew here at KQRN, with just a camera operator and myself at this point. We do still have contact with our national network and will be bringing you the latest bulletins as we receive them. So far, we've heard that the travel bans across the country are still being enforced. The incident in New Hampshire where four members of a family, including two children, were reportedly shot by National Guard troops for—"

The screen went blank. For a moment it remained an opaque gray-black, but then static buzzed into place. It was the same with every channel I tried. I stared, a feeling not unlike the electronic snow on the screen creeping along my skin.

I turned the volume down, but left the television on, the static a flickering reminder that outside my house something awful was happening. Tyrone nudged me again and I sat down, letting him lean against my leg while I scratched his forehead. He sniffed at my fingers, interested in the smell of the spray paint. I needed to get myself something to eat, needed to change out of yesterday's clothes, needed to figure out what to do. But all I did was sit there, staring at the television.

A Goodbye

THE PHONE RANG.

The electronic trill of it cutting through the silence of the room made me jump. I sprang to my feet, grabbed it from the charger and managed to hit the talk button just before it clicked over to voice messaging.

"Hello?"

"Julie?" It was Gina. She sounded far away. And worried.

"Is it happening there?" I tried to picture her in the Tokyo apartment she'd sent me pictures of, sitting on her creamy, minimalist sectional in front of the biggest television I'd ever seen.

"Are you okay?" Gina's voice cracked—I could tell she was crying. This was not good because, like me, Gina never cried.

"Are you?"

"So far." Gina paused and I heard her light a cigarette. She'd quit two years ago, but she kept a pack in the freezer in case something horrible happened. I used to laugh at that, but it didn't seem so funny anymore. After she took a drag, she continued. "They're not saying much on the news. What about there?"

"There *is* no news. Just static. At least right now."

"Shit. We lost Internet and cell, but we still have television. I'm calling on the land line. It feels so weird—like the 1950s or something." Another drag, and then the soft sound of her exhaling. "Are you . . . do you have enough food? Is there a place to go, a hospital, or a military base or something?"

I grabbed my cigarettes from the end table and drew one out from the pack. Gina must know more than I did if she thought I should be heading to a military base. "What time is it there?" I tried to calculate the time difference—it had to be the middle of the night.

"It's the middle of the night. Well, closer to morning, actually." Gina groaned. "I'm exhausted, but I can't sleep. I've been trying to get through to you, but this is the first time I've been connected—the calls just keep dropping."

"So it hasn't hit there—the flu?" I didn't like how vague Gina was being.

"Oh." She tried to sound off-hand. "It's here. I've been stuck in the apartment since yesterday. They're telling everyone to shelter in place—"

"Same here. They have a ban on travel—I heard they shot a family."

Gina was silent. I listened to her smoking, knowing she would talk when she could. Finally, she whispered my name.

"Jules? You know all those crappy novels you like so much?"

I had to smile. I met Gina in college, both of us adults going back to try for something better, both of us amazed at the silver-spoon kids sitting next to us in classes, oblivious to the chances they'd been given. We ended up in a poetry class together. She'd bummed a smoke off me during a break and we'd been friends since. I'd never told her about the murmurations—I wished I'd been as smart with Roger—but she was the person who knew me best in the world. She'd been through the same sorts of things I'd been through in childhood. Even if we'd been coasting on history in recent years in terms of our friendship, we *understood* each other. But she'd always given me grief about my penchant for dystopian fiction. *Read something decent*, she'd say. Her idea of decent was usually the latest self-help guru touting the newest recipe for happiness. Or some fad philosopher who promised to make sense of the whole world, maybe even the universe, in three easy steps. Still, different as we were in some ways, distant as we'd become, we were made of the same stuff.

"Yeah, Gina? What about them?"

"I think maybe they're going to come in handier than I thought." She exhaled again, a long smooth breath. "They're still broadcasting here, but it's crap. At first, they were covering what was going on there, but then it hit Tokyo and now they're just showing file tape of cute pet stories."

"Seriously?"

"Seriously. Fucking cat videos." Gina laughed a little, but quickly sobered. "I'm right by the airport, remember? And nothing's coming or going. I haven't heard a jet since last night."

I didn't know what to say. For a few moments we just smoked together, thinking our thoughts.

"Listen, Julie." Gina broke the silence. "Even if . . . even if we make it through this, I don't—"

She sobbed, the suddenness of it shocking. "I don't think we'll ever see each other again."

"Of course we—"

"I don't think we will. I don't think there will be flights. I don't think there will be enough people left to keep everything going." Gina was dead serious. "So, I want you to know that I love you."

"Oh, Gina, come on—" I didn't want to think about what she was saying. I stubbed my cigarette out in the fireplace and sat on the floor, my back against the sofa.

"No, Julie. I mean it. I think this is it—I'll try to call you again, but the way the calls are dropping I don't know if I'll ever get another chance to say this to you. And I want you to know I love you. Always have, always will."

She was smiling when she spoke her next words; I could hear it in her voice. "You better read up on those survival techniques in all those awful, end-of-the-world zombie stories you like so much and kick some ass, woman."

I couldn't help smiling myself. I thought of all the times we'd each talked each other off some high cliff or other, how many times we'd given and received understanding that no other person could provide. I knew I had to say how I really felt. Gina knew I loved her, but the words should be spoken. No flippant phrase, none of my usual *back-at-ya* euphemisms would suffice right now. I took a deep breath. "Gina."

There was no answer. Just a hum from the handset. "Gina?" The hum got deeper, cut out for a moment, then resumed. I sat holding the handset to my ear, listening.

"Gina," I whispered. But there was nothing.

I glanced at the flickering screen of the television, watching the static as the telephone's hum filled my ear. I thought I heard a whisper of something—a word? Straining to hear, I cupped my hand over the handset and my ear, hunched in front of the sofa. The whisper faded in and out, an indecipherable message, a phantom on the line. Tears spilled hot from my eyes, and I finally let the handset fall and buried my face in my hands. Tyrone crept over to me and licked at my hands until I pushed him away. I turned my back on him and curled up like a baby on the floor, weeping until I fell asleep.

Tyrone's worried stare was the first thing I saw when I awoke. He stood towering over me, his jowls drooping, watching me as though he feared I would never stir again. When I blinked, a low grumble came from deep in his throat.

"Oh, Ty." I reached up and patted his head. "I'm okay."

He pushed in as close as he could get, huffing at me, so I petted him until he seemed a bit less anxious. Judging from the angle of the light breaking in through the slits of the blinds, I must have slept only a short while. The television screen still sizzled with salt and pepper static. I picked the telephone handset up from the floor and held it to my ear. Dead air, no sound at all. No Gina. Pushing stiffly to my feet I stepped closer to the blinds, peeked through just in time to see Mark walking past the house toward his own, hauling a garbage bag filled with something. He stared at my house as he passed, and instinctively I froze, leaving my finger between the slats. Mark's face displayed a mixture of emotions: I saw anger there. That didn't surprise me. But I also saw what I could only think of as . . . patience. He looked like someone who would be back, all in good time. I waited until he was out of sight before I moved.

Tyrone grumbled. I looked down at him, wondering what in the hell I was supposed to do.

"I guess we'd better get it together and try to kick some ass, boy."

The key was still where I'd left it on the kitchen counter. I examined it to see if it held any clues to what it might unlock. It was small, silver, unmarked. From its size, it looked like it must fit a padlock of some sort, or a locker. After rereading the note from Greg and Diane, I threw on a jacket, grabbed my house keys and the mystery key and walked to the French doors. The panes of glass that I'd always thought of as so lovely because of the light they let into my kitchen suddenly seemed dangerous—weak spots, easily breached.

The yard beyond the panes was empty and the gate at the back looked closed. I cracked one of the doors and listened. Birds chirped, but there was no other sound. Usually on a weekend there would be cars driving down the alley on the other side of my back fence, children laughing while they played. Today all was silent. I slipped out onto the deck and locked the doors behind me. Tyrone watched mournfully from the kitchen as I crossed the deck and stepped down into the yard. I knew better than to bring him; I wanted to be as stealthy as possible and a huge, shambling dog probably wouldn't be helpful.

I stood still in the middle of the yard, listening again, trying to see through the spaces between fence boards. After a moment I continued to the gate, opened it as quietly as I could, and peeked out. I looked toward Mark's house, but it was too far down the alley to tell if he was out back. After a minute or so, I decided it was as safe as it was going to get. I stepped through the gate and closed it behind me. Then I ran toward Greg's house.

He had a big, detached garage with large, roll-up doors that backed onto the alley and I skirted it, hugging the walls like I was in some spy movie. The back door to his house seemed far away, the expanse of lawn between it and me an impossible distance to cross. I stopped at the corner of the garage and listened. After a few seconds of silence, I sprinted for the back porch, took the two steps in one leap and plastered my back against the door. I kept my eyes on the alley and felt for the door knob. Locked.

"Shit." Fumbling in my pocket for the tiny key, I tried it in the knob even though I already knew it was too small.

It *was* too small. "Shit, shit, shit."

Gravel crunched from the alley and I froze. A car. Coming down the alley from the main road. I dropped to the cement floor of the porch and lay as flat as I could get. All I could hope was that if I was still enough, whoever was in the car wouldn't notice me.

The sound got louder as the car got closer and finally it appeared, moving slowly, swerving to avoid the worst of the potholes in the poorly maintained alley. It was a sedan, green and boxy, not a car I recognized, but there were a lot of people from the next street over that used the alley to park at the back of their houses. I couldn't see inside the tinted windows, couldn't tell if a face turned my way. But the car didn't pause as it came abreast of Greg's yard and in just a moment it was past the garage. The sound of the gravel beneath its tires faded into nothing, replaced by the sound of my ragged breathing. I lay with my cheek pressed against the cold cement, clutching the tiny key in my hand, until my heart stopped racing. It felt like all the warmth in my body was seeping into the porch floor, as though if I lay there long enough my limbs would stiffen, my blood would thicken, and finally my heart wouldn't be able to pump anymore.

I could hear the damn birds, chirping away as though nothing was wrong. A tiny spider appeared on the cement in front of my face, black, with intricate white striping on its back. It scuttled along on its daily business, unaware that everything had changed. It froze in place when I blinked, waited a moment until it was sure that no threat was present. I tilted my head up to watch as it continued on its way until it encountered an obstacle in the form of a small galvanized metal box that was bolted to the porch floor, against the wall of the house. The spider reached up and tapped the side of the box with one of its segmented legs, backed up a bit, then approached and tapped again. I watched as it tried to climb the sheer wall of the box, with no success. It finally tapped its way along the bottom edge until it rounded the corner of the box and disappeared.

I hadn't noticed the box before. It had a latch on the lid, secured with a padlock. From my vantage point on the floor I could see the bottom of the padlock, with its jagged little key slot. I reached up over my head, key in hand, to give it a try.

The key fit. I sat up, popped the lock open and lifted the lid. Inside, the box was empty except for another key, this one a dull gold metal, larger than the silver one Greg had left me. This one looked like a house key. I plucked it off the dusty bottom of the box. Slowly I stood, my legs stiff from the cold, and tried the key in Greg's back door. It slid right in the lock. I let out the breath I hadn't realized I was holding and grabbed the knob with my other hand, ready to open the door. But the key wouldn't turn. No amount of jiggling made it fit, no matter how many times I removed and re-slotted it.

The sound of a car door from far down the alley made me drop to my knees. After a moment, a second door slammed shut. Then came the faint whine of an engine starting. I ran down the porch steps to the garage, stopped to listen, trying to gauge whether I could make it back to my gate before the car came down the alley. It sounded too close—I could hear the gravel crunching clearly as the car approached. There was no place to hide; all I could do was stay on the far side of the garage hidden from whoever was about to drive by. I flattened myself against the garage door and waited, breathing fast, listening. The car drew nearer and nearer, until it must have been directly on the other side of the garage.

And then it stopped. I heard the click of a door latch, the squeak of unoiled hinges, the sudden blare of the radio. Some anthem from the '80s that made me picture young men with big hair and heavy eyeliner.

"—just see if he's there. I'm telling you, he showed me this magazine all about preppers." The voice was rough, a man, fairly young.

"Even if he does have supplies, what makes you think he'd share?" Another man's voice.

The first man laughed. "Who says we'll ask? Come on. Let's pay him a visit."

They were less than fifty feet away. I turned and tried the door of the garage. Locked. One car door slammed, then another. Shaking, I shoved the key in the door lock, turning the knob with no real hope.

It opened.

As silently as I could, I slipped inside the door. The two men walked past just after I pulled it toward me. I left it cracked, afraid they would hear if I shut it, and I could see them through the slim opening. One wore a puffy red ski coat, the other a denim jacket. The one with the ski coat lifted the back of it as he walked, tucking a gun into his pants. They moved out of sight but I could hear them when they got to the back door of the house. One of them knocked on the door.

"Looks like nobody's home."

"Try again."

More knocking, then silence. The sound of the door knob being jiggled. One of them chuckled.

"You actually thought it might be open?"

"Well, *this* will be in just a minute."

There was a crash, followed by the tinkling sounds of glass falling to the cement. Pulling the door toward me as gently as possible I let the knob turn so the latch fell into place. Directly above the door knob was a deadbolt lock and I slid it home softly. Pressing my ear against the door, I tried to hear what they were doing, but I couldn't make anything out. I heard only my own raspy breathing, my own heart pounding so hard that I was afraid it would explode.

Trapped. I was trapped inside the garage with those men right outside. I saw that there were two more deadbolts, one at the top of the door and one at the bottom, and I engaged them as silently as possible.

I turned around. It was dark inside the garage except for the glow of a nightlight plugged into an outlet near the door. There were no windows and I could only dimly see a high, raftered ceiling. As my eyes adjusted to the murky light, a workbench built along one wall came into focus. It stretched the length of the garage, as far back as I could see, rough two-by-four construction with a yellow laminate top. The place was huge, easily a triple-car garage. And it was filled to the rafters with neatly arranged barrels and boxes, save for a narrow aisle next to the workbench.

An orange light blinked about a third of the way down the workbench. I grabbed the edge of the bench and felt my way along, pawing through various hand tools—screwdrivers, hammers, wrenches—all precisely placed on the bench top. The light was coming from a laptop, closed, but obviously powered up. An electric cord snaked out the back up to a wall outlet. I opened the top and the screen glowed, then lit up, displaying three grainy, black and white images. As I studied them, I recognized the roll-up doors on the backside of the garage in one, with a section of the green sedan's back bumper captured. The second frame showed the front door of Greg's house. In the third, the two men were standing on the back porch, clearing jagged pieces of glass from the frame of the window next to Greg's back door.

It was a surveillance system. The feed was jerky, but it was exactly what I needed. A way to know when I could safely let myself out of the garage and run back home. On the screen, the men climbed through the window, lifting their legs carefully over the window frame. They disappeared into the darkness of the interior.

At first, I stayed glued to the laptop, hoping the men would reappear quickly and leave. But five minutes went by, then ten, with no movement on the screen. I noticed more tiny lights further down the workbench and decided to investigate. There were two power drills, sitting in front of a bank of five drill batteries plugged into outlets on the wall. The green lights on each indicated a full charge. Some lumber was stacked against the wall next to the end of the bench: various sizes of plywood sheets, some veneer scraps, a couple of treated-wood fence posts. Then came piles of two-by-fours, a wheelbarrow, some shovels, and a rake.

I returned to the laptop to check the camera feed. Still nothing. It was beginning to feel like I might be stuck in the garage forever. I found a flashlight hanging on the pegboard above the bench and decided to investigate the containers Greg had stacked up so neatly. There were barrels, boxes, and lidded, plastic tubs, many with printed stickers labeling them. One stainless-steel barrel in the front had a sticker with H_2O on it. It was raised up on cinder blocks and fitted with a heavy-duty spigot. Not enough water to last very long, but better than nothing. A stack of tubs next to that had **RICE, PINTO BEANS** and **SUGAR** labels. Behind the tubs were shelf units filled with canned fruit and canola oil, sealed glass jars filled with salt, and foil packets of freeze-dried stuff. After a glance back at the laptop, I walked further down the narrow center aisle. There were so many tubs. I spotted a long, low wooden box with a hinged lid in the front of one stack, labeled **TRADE**. Inside were four cartons of regular cigarettes and four cartons of menthols, six bottles of whiskey, a case of red wine, some chocolate bars and some boxes of ammunition. I rifled through the contents to see if there was a gun to go with the bullets, but there wasn't. I closed the lid and stood, looking around in awe.

Greg must have been a full-on prepper. One of those doomsday guys, the kind who thought that the end was coming and planned to be ready. I remembered his conspiracy theory comments during that dinner, months ago, when he and Diane had me over; his questions about whether I was "prepared." I had dismissed them as so much prattle at the time. I tried to envision the interior of their home, tried to recall some clue I'd missed that would have told me then, while I was eating their pasta and drinking their wine, that they were serious preppers. I couldn't come up with anything. I remembered a standard-looking home, granite countertops in the kitchen, pillow-back couches, a flat screen television on the wall over the fireplace. Diane's collection of seashells displayed on glass shelves in a cabinet Greg made for her. It was strange to think that all this time, right next door, my neighbor was stocking his garage for Armageddon.

It was a goldmine. My Dollarama haul seemed paltry when compared.

A muffled thud from outside sent me rushing back to the laptop. On screen, the man with the puffy ski coat was already outside on the back porch. There was a pile of stuff at his feet—it looked like clothes, mostly—and the man in the denim jacket was handing him a backpack through the opening of the broken window. Ski Coat started stuffing the clothes into the pack. I could see that they were talking, but I couldn't hear anything from inside the garage.

"Come on, leave," I whispered. I could feel sweat dripping down my back, though it wasn't especially warm in the garage.

Ski Coat straightened and lifted the back pack by a strap, while Denim Jacket stepped through the window frame. The camera feed showed a spasmodic version of their progress toward their car. Just as I breathed a sigh of relief, a frame on the surveillance video caught Ski Coat jutting his chin at the garage door, and less than a second later the door knob rattled, softly at first, then violently. I froze, staring at the knob, less than five feet from me. Another try at the door, a muffled conversation and then silence. I stood unable to move, afraid to make a sound.

Two dull thuds—car doors shutting—released me, and I watched as the sedan disappeared from the laptop's camera feed of the back of the garage. They were gone.

I kept an eye on the surveillance feed for a few more minutes, but all I could focus on in my mind were the shards of glass on Greg's back porch. I thought of the huge picture window in my living room, of my French doors, of Mark walking down the street with his gun, of Ski Coat and Denim Jacket coming back for more of whatever they could find. I turned and leaned against the work bench, surveying the garage.

I'd have to check out the food later; what I needed right now was protection.

Fortitude

IT TOOK ME forty-five minutes to gather everything I thought I might need by the door and almost twice as long to haul it all from Greg's garage to the living room of my house. Tyrone greeted me worriedly with each trip, but after the first admonition he didn't try to follow me when I went out for another load. Some of the plywood panels were almost impossible to maneuver by myself but I got it done, scared every step of the way, listening and watching for any sound or movement, wondering if the green sedan would pull back down the alley. By the time I had the last two-by-four inside my house I was shaking. I hadn't eaten all day and I knew I had to get some calories inside me before I started my project. I opened one of my Dollarama cans of tuna and forked it into my mouth standing over the kitchen sink. After that I drank two glasses of water, all the time thinking of the box labeled **Water Catchment** I'd found in Greg's garage. I hadn't had time to check it out, but I planned to as soon as I could. For now, I had work to do.

My first concern was the living room window. The largest of the plywood panels covered the whole thing, but getting it up proved more difficult than I had thought it would be. I ended up propping the bottom of the panel on the arm of a chair and lifting the other side up on the wall while balancing on my stepstool. Once I got the first corner screwed into the wall with one of Greg's drills, the rest was relatively simple. Before I covered the window I'd closed the blinds and drawn the curtains, hoping that would make it less obvious from the street that the house was fortified.

The French doors were next. I needed to be able to open them, so I wanted to cover just the glass, leaving the doors functional, but there was only one piece of plywood the right size for a single door. There was a table saw in Greg's garage, but I had no clue how to use it, nor did I want any noise attracting attention to my activities. The drill seemed bad enough; I was banking on the idea that the noise it made was muffled outside. In the end, I decided one functioning door was enough. There were no blinds or curtains on the French doors and the plywood, which would be clearly visible from outside, seemed like an announcement to me. *Someone is inside this house.* I didn't want that. I wandered from room to room, trying to think of some solution. The sheets on my bed—my best set—provided it. They were floral, sort of curtain-like, I thought. My other sheets were plain, and didn't give the same effect. Ripped in half, the floral ones would fit nicely between the glass and the plywood on the French doors.

I attached a plywood sheet to the door meant to open first, after tacking up the half-sheets over the panes. It fit just right, covering the glass but allowing the door to open and close. The only piece of plywood that would work for the other door was so big that it covered a large portion of the wall next to the door as well, but that didn't matter; I only needed one door to open and the overlap might actually add some strength. I stood back and surveyed my work. Nobody would be able to break through the glass, but the lock on the French doors troubled me. It was one of those cheap locks, the kind *I* could probably kick in if I really tried. Rummaging through the items I'd brought from the garage, I found just the thing: metal brackets—the kind used to hold two-by-fours to keep barn doors closed. A couple of sets of those and some hand sawing to an eight-foot two-by-four to get it to the right length and I had a barricade it would take some doing to get through. It seemed like a good idea to add the same kind of brackets and a two-by-four to the front door. It was steel, but the locks, though better than the set on the French doors, still looked easy enough to kick in. I put two sets of brackets and braces on it for good measure.

By the time I finished the front door, I was exhausted. I'd planned to get to all the windows in the house, but it would have to wait. I walked from the kitchen to the living room and back again, evaluating my efforts. The place looked like some sort of poorly made bunker. The plywood was crooked and the ends of the two-by-fours were raggedly cut, but I'd drilled so many screws into it all that I thought it would hold up.

Tyrone rumbled at me and I realized it had been hours since he'd been outside to relieve himself. The window above the kitchen sink revealed darkness; it was already night. After peeking through the window to see if the backyard seemed safe, I lifted the bar off the French doors to let Tyrone out. He ran off the deck to the grass and lifted his leg immediately, holding it up for so long I felt guilty. I stepped out onto the deck to wait while he found a place to take care of the rest of his business.

The night sky was clear, no sign of the rainclouds from the last few days. The stars were out in full force and the fresh, spring air smelled wonderful. If I ignored the strange silence of the neighborhood outside my fence, if I didn't turn and see the bold floral sheets disguising the plywood behind them on my French doors, I could almost pretend nothing was wrong. Almost, except for the sharp edge of fear that seemed to be becoming a permanent fixture in the back of my mind.

I clicked my tongue at Tyrone, who leapt to the deck and clattered into the kitchen, wanting his dinner. After I lifted the two-by-four back into its brackets across the doors, I scooped some kibble into the dog bowl, and while Tyrone ate, I opened a bottle of wine and poured myself a glass. I knew I should eat, but I was bone-tired.

In the living room, the television still buzzed with static. At least I didn't have to worry about the light coming from its screen betraying my presence in the house; none of the interior lights would get through the plywood covering the picture window. I collapsed onto the couch, feeling a certain satisfaction at the bars across the front door. Tyrone sat at my knee, watching my face, ears pricked. Picking up the remote, I flicked through the channels, not really expecting to see anything but the same static on all of them. But three clicks in, a picture came into focus. It was the local cable channel, and a man was standing at the podium in the center of a bank of seats used for city council meetings. He was not, judging from his appearance, a city council member. He wore a flannel shirt, had an unkempt beard and shaggy hair and slouched forward, leaning his arms on the desk as though he was too tired to stand upright. His face was pale with deep, bruised-looking circles under his eyes. I sat forward and turned up the volume.

"—so that's it, really, folks." The man shrugged, and smiled, or at least his lips curved upward. "Sorry about the static shot, but Danny left about twenty minutes ago and he was the last one who knew how to work the camera." The man stopped talking and stared at the podium surface for a long time. Too long. His upper body rocked, ever so slightly, back and forth. He picked up a gavel, idly turning it in his hands. Finally, he looked back up at the camera. "As I said before, your best bet is to head for the hills, at least according to everyone I know. The cities are just breeding grounds for the flu, and most of the services are gone now, anyway. Some places still have power and most still have water, but that's not going to last long." The man tapped the gavel on the podium, experimentally at first, then with more force. "So, head out my friends. Get while the getting's good." He banged the podium one last time. Then he looked straight at the camera once more and his face changed from a mask of bravado to naked pain. "And if anyone has seen Amy Pritchard, tell her to meet me at the place we first kissed. I'll be waiting there, for a couple more hours." He dropped the gavel and stood, every move betraying his weariness. And then he simply walked out of camera range.

I stared for the longest time at the screen, at the empty council room, the seats flanking the podium, the flags drooping on either side of the dais. I kept thinking the man would come back, but he didn't. Finally, I turned the television off, let Tyrone out one more time and crawled into my bed. I lay trying to sleep, but even though I was as tired as I could remember being, sleep didn't come. When the furnace kicked on, its hum and thrum rose in the darkness. I listened for the murmurations and they came. I let them in—old friends I'd been too busy to pay any mind to for some time now. I was too tired to try to understand them, but the murmurations soothed my mind, let me drift just enough to let go of the image of that man in the flannel shirt, of the hope and the desolation mingled in his eyes.

"It will be better in the morning." I whispered the words in the dark, a prayer of sorts to a god I'd never been able to believe in. I hoped with all my heart the prayer would be answered.

Darkness

IN THE MORNING the lights didn't come on. I went from the bedroom to the kitchen to the living room to the bathroom and back again, flipping switches as though there must be some mistake.

But there was no mistake. Tyrone followed me from room to room with a creased forehead and worried eyes. Once I realized the lights were truly not going to blaze to life just because I willed it, another thought crossed my mind. I ran to the kitchen sink and lifted the faucet handle, filled with dread. But water streamed from the spigot just as it always had. I wondered how long that would last.

I checked the back yard, let Tyrone out and then got him some breakfast. No lights meant no refrigerator, so I decided to go through its contents to see what I might be able to consume before it spoiled. There was very little to worry about; less than half a quart of milk, three lemons, already shriveled from sitting in the produce bin for a week. I couldn't remember why I'd bought them. There were a couple of apples and an orange as well. Mustard, ketchup, three sticks of butter. The freezer was empty except for one frozen single-serving entrée—a vegetable lasagna. I left it there, in the hope that the electricity would come back on soon.

After I ate a bowl of cereal on which I poured all the milk left in the carton, I flipped the light switch by the kitchen sink one more time, just to check. Nothing. Good thing Greg's drills were battery-powered—the first battery had lasted through both the picture window and the French doors, so I thought I'd have plenty of juice to finish the rest of the house. I piled plywood sheets near the bedroom door—there were two windows there, one in the office, one in the kitchen. I'd have to be careful to rig some sort of peepholes or I wouldn't be able to check before opening a door to let Tyrone out. I'd have to—

My racing thoughts dwindled to nothing then and I sat down on the floor. Tyrone sat next to me, watching my face. I realized I was rocking slightly, back and forth, and my breathing was so fast I was almost gasping. Tyrone shifted his front feet and yawned, a wide, nervous yawn, while he stared at me. I reached out, put a hand on his shoulder. "We're okay," I said, softly. From where I sat on the kitchen floor, I could see my bedroom, the door to the bathroom and on through the doorway opening to the living room. It was so dark in there—one thing I hadn't realized when I boarded up the living room window was just how dark it was inside with no lights and no daylight coming in through the glass. Once I finished the rest of the windows, I would need some sort of illumination if the electricity didn't come back on.

If the electricity didn't come back on.

I thought about the man on the local cable channel. *Head for the hills,* he'd said. I didn't know anything about the hills. I didn't know anything about anything. I shook my head, pushed myself up off the floor. I just couldn't think about it anymore. It felt insane to be drilling holes in my walls, barricading my windows and doors, but it felt just as insane to remember Mark, coming toward me with his gun. To hear the shattering glass as the men from the green sedan broke into Greg's house. I couldn't wonder if I was right or wrong, or try to predict whether this little house would end up being my kingdom or my crypt.

I picked up the drill and got to work.

It only took me about four hours to get the rest of the windows done. I was guessing, because my alarm clock and the clock on the microwave were both out of commission, but it seemed like late afternoon when I checked the light outside. I was pretty proud of my handiwork; for a non-power-tool person I felt like I'd done a great job. After some digging through Greg's drill bits, I found a jagged-toothed circular one with a drill point in the center. It looked like I could drill holes through my plywood sheets with it, and with a little practice on scraps, that's just what I did. Before

I mounted the plywood on the rest of the windows I drilled peepholes. I screwed small squares of wood over the holes, leaving the screws loose enough that I could swivel the covers over the peepholes when I wasn't using them. I had to make matching holes in the sheets I'd already used to camouflage the plywood on the French doors, which compromised the look a bit, but from afar I thought it should be undetectable.

After I finished each window I checked the lights, just in case the electricity had been restored. It was pitch-dark in the house without light from outside; I had to scrounge up a couple of Dollarama candles to finish my work in the bedroom and the office. The only pair of candle holders I had were ornamental; pretty crystal things meant for romantic dinners rather than illumination—a holdover from my marriage. I rigged a safer option by dripping some hot wax inside two coffee mugs and sticking the candles in—I could set them anywhere and not be afraid they would get knocked over or drip. They provided enough light to get the job done.

After driving in the last screw I slumped down to the floor in the office, drill in hand, exhausted. Tyrone appeared in the doorway, a dark silhouette against the murkiness of the living room beyond.

"Come on, boy." I felt a little guilty; I hadn't given him a thought in hours. He walked over and sat next to me, watching my face. "What do you think? Think it will hold?" Tyrone snuffled, his eyes shining in the candle light.

I don't how long I sat there in the dim light, absently stroking Tyrone's head. I was stiff from my day's labor and uncertain what to do next. The house was silent in a new way; no hum from the computer, no buzz from the refrigerator, no soft rush of air from the heat registers. At some point Tyrone lay down alongside my outstretched leg and slept. My thoughts wandered. I thought of Gina in her tiny, Tokyo apartment, tried to imagine what she was doing. I thought of the woman from a couple of blocks down, the one with the brainless black dog. I wondered if she was still driving, or if she'd encountered some impassable freeway ramp, cars stalled in a line, nowhere to go. I wondered if she was dead yet. I tried not to think of her dog, panting in the passenger's seat, whimpering at her stillness, licking her hand now and then. Watching her face.

A gunshot rang out, an explosion out of nowhere, and then another. Tyrone and I both jumped; he began growling instantly, the fur on his spine rising stiffly. I couldn't tell what direction the shots originated from but they were close. I ran to the front door and squinted through the peephole, but the convex view of my porch revealed nothing. I stood there, alternating between peering at the street and pressing my ear to the door. Once, I thought I heard muffled screaming, but I couldn't be sure. Tyrone stopped growling, but stayed close to me, hackles up. I backed away from the door finally, shaking. I realized I'd been waiting for sirens; confirmation both that something bad was happening and that help was on the way. But there was only silence.

I didn't know what to do. Something bad *was* happening and help *wasn't* on the way. Nobody in a uniform was coming to investigate. Nothing was how it used to be. So I focused on what I *could* do, inside my house. Back in the office, I gathered the drills and carried them and a candle mug out to the kitchen. I stashed the drills in a cupboard and quickly returned to the office for the second candle, nudged by a new awareness of flammability. I fed Tyrone and considered the frozen lasagna entrée, but I couldn't bring myself to eat it raw, so I threw it in the kitchen trash can. There were several piles of sawdust on the kitchen floor by the French doors, where I'd sawed the two-by-fours for brackets. I opened the closet to get the vacuum out and had it all the way over to the mess before I realized it was a pointless endeavor. No electricity, no vacuum. Instead, I swept up the sawdust and emptied the dustpan into the trash can, then stood considering that receptacle.

Trash. How would I get rid of my trash? I could burn some of it in the fireplace. Or could I? Would the smoke coming from the chimney be a beacon to anyone looking for . . . whatever people would be looking for now? I thought of the cache of food and supplies in the garage next door. Would someone come find it? Try to take it? The dark kitchen seemed chilly with no heat and it wasn't even winter. What would happen when the temperature plummeted? Every question was followed by another question in my mind.

Someone knocked on the front door.

It was a non-threatening, door-to-door salesman kind of knock; it didn't raise a single hair on Tyrone's back. I walked to the doorway of the kitchen and stared at the front door from there.

Maybe it was just my imagination.

Someone knocked again.

Tyrone stayed by my side, looking up at me as though waiting for some sort of signal. I held an index finger to my lips as though he would understand and crept as quietly as possible to the door, trying to imagine who was on the other side, staring at my sloppily spray-painted quarantine symbol. I let out the breath I hadn't realized I was holding—the police! Finally? I envisioned men in swat gear holding assault rifles, checking houses to see if there was anyone to evacuate. Who else would approach a quarantined house? My hands were on the first two-by-four brace, ready to lift it out of its brackets, when I remembered the news story about the National Guard shooting some family. Were the police here to help? Or to dispatch the last of the infected?

Leaving the brace bracketed, I leaned in as quietly as possible and peeked through the peephole. There were no police outside. Instead, lit by the slanting rays of the late afternoon sun, I saw Mark's wife, Nancy. She stood about four feet back from the door, hands behind her back like a school child, tear streaks glazing her cheeks. She was wearing a stretch cotton sundress and the fabric was taut across her swollen belly. From the looks of it she had to be close to term. While I watched, a fresh stream of tears began to slide down her cheeks and her face crumpled in anguish. It was strange to see her standing in daylight—the darkness inside the house made it feel like permanent night.

The gunshots. Mark must have shot someone. Or maybe, someone shot Mark. He must be hurt, or worse, and his wife had come looking for help. I gripped the first of the two-by-fours again, feeling horrible for leaving her out there as long as I had. As I lifted the bar I heard her mumble on the other side of the door, a collection of words I couldn't quite make out. I looked once more through the peephole, the two-by-four balanced in my hands. She sniffled, and brought an arm forward from behind her back to wipe her nose with her wrist. With her wrist—because her hand was busy, holding a gun. I imagined it must be the gun Mark had earlier. Her wrist left a watercolor smear on her face; a saltwater wash of blood mixing with her tears. She stared at the blood on her wrist for a moment and then seemed to realize the gun was in view. Quickly, she tucked it behind her back again. She looked out toward the street and then leaned in toward the door. My view from the peephole was obscured as her head covered the opening and I realized she was listening.

Silently, I lowered the two-by-four back into the brackets. I pressed my ear against the door, picturing her doing the same thing on the other side. She was mumbling some sort of prayer. Then silence. I listened for a moment more, then peered through the peephole. She was standing back from the door again, but this time she had the gun in front of her, pointing straight at the door. The look on her face scared me as much as the gun—I should have dropped to the floor and crawled away. But I didn't. I just stood there, transfixed by the awful, naked feelings flashing across her face—fear and anguish and desperation. A glint of light on the gun drew my attention—she'd begun to shake, but the barrel was still pointed straight at me. I stood on the other side of the door, frozen, wondering if I was going to die.

She didn't pull the trigger. Instead, she let her arms drop, the gun dangling from one hand. I heard her gasp for air as though she was choking. Then she slumped off the porch, out of my sight.

I couldn't follow her progress from the living room window. I hadn't thought it would be wise to add peepholes to the plywood there, since it was right on the street. All I could do was strain to hear—a scream, a moan, the crack of a gunshot. I heard nothing. I waited a long time, wondering if she had walked away down the road to some other house, or if she was just outside, waiting to see if I would open the door.

It was all out there. The new world. Right outside my house was the absence of everything I'd taken for granted all my life. Police, grocery stores, ATMs, medical treatment, harmless neighbors. I looked from the boarded-up window to the barricaded front door, the gloom of the living room mirroring my state of mind. What would take the place of the world I had known until now? Did I even want to be here to see?

A low moan from Tyrone heralded a practical issue: he had to pee. Again. He walked nervously from the living room to the French doors in the kitchen and back again, eyeing me with sad, brown eyes. The last thing I wanted to do was open the door, even though Nancy was probably already on the main road heading . . . somewhere. But there wasn't much choice. Reluctantly, I followed him into the kitchen where the coffee mug candles provided dim light.

Tyrone sat in front of the French doors expectantly. I swiveled the plywood peephole cover and squinted out at the yard. It looked deserted. The back gate, of which I could see only a part, was closed, as it should be. After removing the bars from the doors, I unlocked the deadbolt and slowly turned the knob. I opened the door just a bit and light and fresh air poured in. Tyrone nosed at the opening but I nudged him back with my foot and listened. Nothing. I opened the door wider and peeked out. The yard was empty, so I stepped back and let Tyrone through. He ran to the end of the deck and leapt off into the grass and lifted his leg. Then he ran around the perimeter of the yard, nose to the ground, doing his usual quick check of the property. When he was done, he began his more serious surveillance routine, the one where he closely examined each bush and fence post for new scents, but I cut it short, whispering his name until he leapt back up on the deck and squeezed through the door.

It wasn't until the bars were back in place across the doors, shutting out the light and the unknown, that I realized I was shaking. I clasped my hands together trying to still them, but they seemed like creatures in their own right, convulsing in fear against my chest. I tried to think about Gina, sitting in her apartment a world away, but all I could imagine was never seeing her again. Was she alone and afraid, like me? Was she even still alive? If this was happening in Japan, where else was it happening? Was the whole world in the same mess? I swallowed, my throat as dry as dust, and looked around my dark kitchen. Suddenly I was as weary as I had ever been. My legs felt numb, but I forced them to move, to carry me step by leaden step to the bedroom. I knew I should be doing something more—assessing my food stock, figuring out how to get water once the plumbing stopped working, how to heat the house. I should be planning for the future. But it felt like there was no future. And all I wanted to do was sleep.

I didn't think there was any way I *could* sleep, but I crawled into my bed just the same, hoping for oblivion. I stared up toward the ceiling, which I couldn't see in the dark, and ignored the worried huffs Tyrone was making from where he sat next to the bed. I thought about how I had planned to learn Spanish someday. How I had meant to look up the etymological origins of the phrase *beyond the pale* on the Internet. How Gina and I had promised each other that we would plan a vacation to Greece some year when I was less poor and she was less busy. How instead of attending dog obedience class, I was barricading myself inside my house.

And then I fell asleep.

Monday

I **AWOKE TO** silence. No humming furnace, no faint traffic noises from the main road, no alarm clock blaring. I lay still, not wanting to give Tyrone any indication that I was conscious. Not yet. I needed to think.

The only thought I had was *how do I find a gun?*

The answer to that question was one I dreaded. I'd have to go out and get one.

But not yet. I would have to wait, at least a few days. The silence I'd awoken to didn't guarantee that everyone was gone. *Dead, Julie,* I corrected myself, *you mean dead.* I tried to remember what the newscasts had reported about the length of time it took for the virus to kill: a few days I thought, but I wasn't positive. The longer I waited, the less chance I would run into someone like Mark, or the guy with the ski coat. There were things I could do while I waited—a serious inventory of supplies in the house, a more critical look at my fortifications.

And maybe I was wrong about everything. Maybe in the next few days the power would come back on and the television screen would be filled with jubilant news reporters detailing rescue efforts and a possible vaccine. Maybe it would all work out.

I rolled off the bed and felt my way to the kitchen where Tyrone sat, barely visible in the darkness, by the French doors. I fumbled for one of the candle mugs on the counter. There was a pool of hardened wax in the bottom of each; I'd left both of them burning last night. So much for safety-consciousness. Thankfully I'd left a package of candles on the counter so I didn't have to rummage through the cabinet in the dark to find them. Once I had one lit and anchored in a mug, I carried it to the doors and peeked through the peephole to the back yard. The morning light revealed nothing out of the ordinary. Tyrone pushed against my legs while I removed the barricade and the moment the door was open, he ran through it. I poked my head out, listening more than looking, but again, there was only silence. Feeling reassured, I stepped out onto the deck.

Tyrone looked up briefly but quickly returned to finding the perfect spot to pee. That in itself made me feel better—surely he would be on high alert if anyone was around. Emboldened, I ventured down the two steps to the yard.

It all seemed so normal. The grass was heavy with spring dew, the sky was that unbroken, pale blue that only happens in early April, cloudless and calm. Birds chirped in nearby trees and I could hear a tree frog croaking somewhere not far off. I could almost imagine that nothing was out of the ordinary. That I could open the back gate and walk out into the alley and see cars zipping by down on the main road, nod hello to one of the neighborhood children running after an errant ball. But I knew neither would happen. There was none of the faint, ocean sound of traffic on the main road. There was no laughter from children or scolding from parents. There was nothing ordinary out there.

Tyrone wandered over to me and I knelt to pet him. I was still wary about being outside, but I didn't want to go inside just yet—the fresh air and light were so wonderful. Tyrone rolled in the wet grass and then stood and shook dew all over me, making me smile. I was reaching to pull a blade of grass away from his eye when we heard it.

A scream, one scream, cut off before it reached its crescendo. Not far away—perhaps a block. Tyrone was instantly rigid, his hackles up in a spikey display. I crabbed my way, low to the ground, to the deck, moving without thought, instinctually, and got us both inside the house. I kept the door slightly open, straining to hear. The scream had sounded like it came from a woman, but I couldn't be certain. Minutes passed, I don't know how many, with no other sound, while I stood holding the door knob, shaking. Part of me wanted to close the door and bolt it but the other part was afraid to shut out the information I might receive if I kept listening.

The shouting decided me. Two men, maybe more, having some sort of disagreement. Over the screamer? I didn't wait to find out. Quietly, I closed the door and set the two-by-four back in its brackets. I carried the candle mug onto the living room and sank down onto the sofa, insulated from the sounds outside. Tyrone settled next to me on the floor, ears still pricked, alert. I focused on the candle flame in my mug, trying not to think about the woman out there, about what might be happening to her. There was nothing I could do to help.

After a while I set the mug on the side table and picked up the telephone from where it lay on the sofa cushion next to me. The push of a button produced nothing—no dial tone, no frightening void—just dead air. I ran a finger down the sleek, shiny surface of the handset, felt its heft in my palm. A useless hunk of plastic, now. And yet I still had the feeling it could ring at any moment, that Gina could call, tell me she was fine, and to turn on the news. I did just that pointed the remote at the television and clicked, but it was a useless hunk of plastic now, too, its blank screen dully reflecting the candle flame.

I wondered then, why wasn't I sick, or dead? Certainly I'd been exposed to enough people during my trip home Friday, and before that, even. Who knew how long the virus had been floating around Billington? Was I immune to the virus? Or would it just take a few more hours for me to show symptoms? I was tired, hungry, a bit numb, but I didn't feel sick. I thought of all the people I'd been in contact with Friday; the cigarette shop lady, the Dollarama mother and child and the teenaged cashier, the Pet Mart guy. And what about Pete, and Greg, and even Mark. Any of them could have been contagious. I wondered if Pete and his wife had made it to wherever they were going, if Greg and Diane had made it to their ski cabin. I wondered if they were all dead. It would probably be easier to be dead, right now.

But I wasn't dead. My lungs kept inflating, my heart kept beating, all without consulting me. It would take a razor or a knife to stop them, unless it turned out that I was infected. I thought about what I had in the house, razor and knife-wise. It would have to be a knife unless I could take apart the disposable razor I used to shave my legs. I'd always planned on pills when I thought of suicide. Nothing messy or painful; wanting to die didn't include wanting to suffer. In fact, it had always represented the promise of the opposite; an end to the suffering.

Tyrone picked that moment to shove his wet nose into my hand. He puffed his jowls at me while I stroked his muzzle, watching me with his brown eyes. If I killed myself, he would be on his own. I could let him out, hope for the best, but I could imagine how that would go. The image of him loping along a deserted street, ribs visible, coat matted, fear in those sweet brown eyes, came to me. I couldn't let that happen.

I shoved myself up from the floor, limbs stiff from sitting. I tried to touch my toes, unsuccessfully. Tyrone rose too, still watching my face. I couldn't help but smile at his expression. He seemed to know I had made a decision.

"I got your back, buddy. I guess we're in this together." I didn't feel silly talking to him; I never had. He was good company. Maybe all the company I would have from now on.

I was going to keep breathing. I was incredibly lucky in terms of having food at hand, and I would figure it all out. The world outside my house could go to hell as far as I was concerned. It already had.

———   ———

I spent the next four days inventorying and organizing supplies, first in my house and then in Greg's garage. The Dollarama had yielded a surprising amount of useful stuff; more practical things than I remembered throwing into my cart. I had enough toothpaste to last for years, and toothbrushes to go with it. Hydrogen Peroxide, antibacterial ointment, shampoo, nail clippers. I shelved these in more orderly rows than I had initially, checking expiration dates, wondering if they would come to matter. Then I went through the rest of the house, counting blankets and sheets and sweaters and coats, folding and refolding them in neat piles. Every pair of socks seemed precious now, every shirt assessed for warmth and durability. I had a feeling I wasn't going to be able to just go out and buy new ones.

It took me a day and a half to get through the stuff in the house. Each morning I flipped the light switches, hoping they would work. Then I'd try the phone, and finally the television. For the moment just before I flipped a switch or hit a button, there was hope; I could imagine the can lights in the kitchen ceiling blazing, or the cable booting up on the television screen. Every time that nothing happened I felt a little jolt of surprise, a disbelief of sorts, that this was all real. The faucet *did* work; for now at least, we had water. I didn't know how long that would last and my first impulse was to look it up online. I was actually halfway to the computer before I realized, yet again, that there was no Internet anymore.

Tyrone ate well enough from the store of kibble we had, but my menu was limited at first to the canned tuna from the Dollarama and the fruit that I'd had in the house. I ate one apple a day, saving the orange for later, thoughts of scurvy dancing in my head. If Greg hadn't been a prepper I would be out of food in a week. Not just food, either. I was going through candles at an alarming rate in order to sort things in the darkened rooms of the house. What had seemed like plenty at the Dollarama turned out not to be so much when I was staring at forever. I hoped an inventory of Greg's garage would ease my worries about more than food.

On the morning of day three, I fed Tyrone and let him out in the yard. Once he was back inside, I ate a can of tuna and then peeled my orange, doing it slowly, trying to appreciate the smell of the oil beading on the skin, examining the sticker that identified it as a navel orange from Florida. Florida. If things were as bad as they seemed, that might as well be China. Perhaps I'd never see another orange again. I sectioned the fruit and ate it, feeling nostalgic already. Then I donned a jacket, took the key to Greg's garage from the cupboard I'd hidden it in and knelt by Tyrone.

"I'm going next door, buddy." I scratched the spot behind his ear the way he liked.. I'd considered taking him with me but decided in the end to leave him in the house—less chance of trouble. He watched as I removed the bar from the door and cracked it, and pushed his nose forward to snuffle the fresh air. I listened for long minutes and when I was satisfied nothing was amiss, I slipped through, locking the door with my house key. Crouching, I shuffled off the deck onto the grass and got to the back gate. There I paused, listening again. Birds, chirping. Nothing else. No

crunching gravel from the alley, no distant screams. So far, so good. I un-
latched the gate and stepped through, latching it as quietly as I could. The
alley was empty in both directions. The main road at the end was quiet. I
scooted around the back of Greg's garage past the rolling doors and ran
along the side to the smaller door, key at the ready.

I was relieved to see that the door was intact. I'd wondered if the two
guys who broke into Greg's house might have returned and broken into
the garage, but they must have assumed there was nothing of value inside, that or they'd moved on or died of the flu. The key slid into the lock
smoothly and I was inside. I shut the door and engaged the deadbolts, and
then realized it was pitch black. No nightlight glowed on the wall anymore.
I remembered the flashlight I'd found on the pegboard—I groped along
the wall until I felt the barrel in my hands. I switched it on and a beam of
light illuminated the space in front of me. Moving down the workbench to
the unlit laptop, I opened it, hoping somehow that despite the electricity
being out it might boot up anyway. To my surprise, it did, using its battery
charge, but there was nothing to connect to and no camera feed.

From there I moved straight to where I'd seen the box labeled **Water
Catchment**. It had been on my mind daily; I had no idea how long the
pipes would keep flowing and no way to find out. I did know that a source
of clean water was going to be one of my first priorities in order to survive. The box was where I remembered, a large cardboard container with
a shipping address from Phoenix, Arizona. The packing tape on the seams
had already been sliced through. Flipping back the cardboard flaps, I directed the flashlight beam inside, holding my breath.

It was empty except for packing materials. I pawed through it, but all
I felt was the bottom of the box. I was just about to give up when I felt
the corner of a booklet and fished it up through the packing scraps. It was
an instruction manual, printed on cheap white paper. Paging through it, I
saw various warnings and cautions in the front, followed by diagrams of
what looked like half a house with a plastic tarp extended on the roof. In
cross-section, the diagram showed a large tube attached somehow to the
tarp, extending down into the house. At the end of the tube was a barrel,
with sections marked off and labeled *gravel* and *charcoal* and *sand*. Another

section of tube came out of the barrel and ended in a blank space with the words *Receptacle—stainless recommended.*

I stood and went to the front of the garage where I'd earlier found the stainless-steel barrel marked **H_2O**. There was a spigot on the front—a quarter turn and water dribbled from it. Moving a few of Greg's tubs of supplies, I cleared the way so I could get behind the water barrel. There, on an even higher platform of cinder blocks, was another barrel like the one pictured in the diagram, attached to the first with tubing. It was fitted with swing-out sections, each labeled; gravel, sand, charcoal. The flashlight beam revealed more tubing that went from the barrel's top up to the ceiling. I could picture the tarp on the roof outside, just as it was in the diagram.

"Thank you, Greg." I uttered these words like a prayer. It wouldn't be the first time I said them. As long as the system worked, I wouldn't have to worry about my water supply. And given the stacks of supplies Greg had collected and the care with which the garage was maintained—everything was organized and practically dust-free—I had a feeling the system would work. I stashed the instruction manual on the work bench and began my inventory of the rest of the supplies.

It took me all day to inventory Greg's garage. There was plenty of food; rice and flour and egg powder and beans and dried fruit enough to last me for at least a year in my estimation. Glass jars filled with juice, tins of fish in oil, canned vegetables. There was dried beef, too, that I hoped I could use for Tyrone. I'd been a vegetarian for years, before deciding that being a pescatarian was good enough. I'd stick to fish and beans, if I could.

There were five halogen flashlights in addition to the one I had found on the pegboard, with plenty of batteries. There were kerosene lamps and gallons of kerosene to go with them. There was a portable contraption like a camp stove, but fancier, that came with a 40-page manual. Greg had a huge stack of pressed logs I imagine he'd planned to burn in his fireplace come winter. They would work just as well in mine. He'd even compiled a small library of books—all titles like *How to survive Nuclear Winter* and *Canning for Beginners.*

The one thing he didn't have was a gun.

I searched every place I could think of, but I came up empty. There was only the ammunition in the wooden **TRADE** box. The boxes were labeled *40 S&W,* whatever that meant, and I added them to the pile of items I was taking to my house. It took two trips with the wheelbarrow to get what I thought I might need immediately, and I dumped all of it in my office. I only took about two weeks' worth of food during those first trips, along with the stove, the flashlights, the kerosene lamps and ten gallons of water, just in case. I wanted enough to get by while I tried to plan my next steps, but I was scared to make too many trips back and forth. It seemed deserted on my street, but I couldn't be sure.

I got the wheelbarrow back into Greg's garage, locked it up and sprinted for home. Before I went back in the house, I stood on the deck and scanned the roof of the garage. Sure enough, there was the outline of the water catchment tarp. Greg had purchased one near the same color as his roof, and it wasn't easy to make out unless you knew to look for it. I wondered how long it would last. How long would it *have* to last?

The day had gone by while I was in the garage. Dusk was falling, and the stars were just beginning to glimmer in the sky, so much brighter than when they were competing with suburbia's electric glow. I was tired and hungry, but I remained on the deck for a few moments, listening to the utter silence in my neighborhood. Not even the birds were chirping now. Tyrone, whom I'd let out to pee, sat next to me, the only living thing in the area besides myself as far as I knew. As I stood there, the wind began to pick up, moving through the trees. I let the sound in, closing my eyes, letting it fill up everything, and soon enough the murmurations began. Softly, barely there, conveying something I couldn't quite catch. The sounds felt sad, tonight. I listened for a while, comforted even by the vague sadness, comforted that they were still there, whatever they were. That I could still hear them. A part of me wanted to crawl inside them, to let them carry me away from this place. Another part of me wanted to live, and that part unlocked the door and went inside.

After I bolted the door, I fed Tyrone and then myself. I had planned to sample something from Greg's stores, but I was so tired I simply opened another can of tuna. The faucet still produced a steady stream of water and I finished three glasses standing at the sink. I carried a candle mug to the living room, too exhausted to figure out the kerosene lamps. I'd already flicked the light switches in the kitchen to no effect, and I tried the television remote and the phone with the same result. Nothing, nothing, nothing.

The wind was gusting outside now—I could hear it through the walls of the house. Just a spring storm coming in; tomorrow would be rainy and gray. I wanted nothing more than to shut down my brain, so I trudged to the bedroom and climbed into bed. Tyrone settled next to me on the floor and I reached down to pat him, whispering his name. Then I snuffed the candle in the mug and lay back, pulling the covers up high around my neck. Staring up into the blackness, I listened as the moans of the storm enveloped my little house. Slowly, I began to hear the patterns, the murmurations within the wind. I let them speak, trying to understand at first, but soon enough fatigue dragged at my mind and I closed my eyes, drifting, until I fell asleep.

At some point, I dreamt—a dream of the sky, a vast blue canvas, stretching on forever. In my dream the entire sky was covered with tiny specks, each like a single grain of pepper, all moving together toward me. As I watched, the specks began to coalesce, uniting in strange patterns, undulating and changing like sheer fabric folding in upon itself, deepening in opacity, unfolding again and becoming transparent, flowing like liquid. It was a murmuration, only I didn't think the specks were birds. I couldn't tell what they were. It was hypnotic and beautiful and left me again with the sense that something was being written, written on that sky. Something I couldn't read. I wanted to stay in the dream, stay and watch the patterns unfold until I could understand.

The Neighbors

I **THINK** I lost two days. I'll never know for certain, because there is no way to tell what the date actually is anymore. Perhaps it was my body, exhausted and requiring rest, or perhaps it was my mind, finally overwhelmed and protecting me by keeping me from consciousness for a time. All I know is that I slept. I slept without waking, except to stumble to the bathroom and back to the bed. When I finally opened my eyes and kept them open, the darkness in my bedroom reminded me of everything that I would face when I rose from the bed. I found the candle mug and carried it to the kitchen where I'd left the lighter. The smell hit me before I could get the candle lit; the flame revealed Tyrone, who was watching me anxiously, tail between his legs. He had left quite a mess next to the French doors. The sight made me sad—he'd had no choice. I imagined him making nervous trips from the bed to the door, wondering why I didn't get up and let him outside.

"It's okay, buddy." I knelt and he came near, trembling. "You couldn't help it, Ty, you couldn't. It's okay, we'll just clean it up."

I mopped up what I could with paper towels. Then I let Tyrone out for a bathroom break he clearly didn't need, and when he came back in I fed him. The television and lights and phone were all dead, as usual. The faucet still worked though, and I needed a shower. I'd been too busy to worry about more than brushing my teeth for days and I smelled like it. I didn't remember that the water would be cold until I was already in the shower. For just a moment I wanted to jump right back out, but the water heater was not going to magically heal itself, so I forced myself to lather up, shampoo my hair, and rinse off. I think it was the fastest shower in history, and not just because of the cold water. I had a mission.

It was time to go find a gun.

Once I was dry and dressed, I dug out my old backpack from the closet. Then I got one of the dust masks from the Dollarama out of its plastic packaging and stretched the elastic over my head, letting the mask hang at my neck. I stowed two more, along with one of Greg's flashlights, in the backpack. After a quick survey of the flatware drawer I selected a short paring knife. It felt like no protection, simply because I could picture someone easily overpowering me and taking it. Then, my gaze fell on the pastry roller Gina had sent me for my birthday one year—it was more or-namental than practical—oversized, carved from a beautifully patterned hardwood. I never baked, so it stayed in its display hanger on the kitchen wall, a decoration. As a weapon, it might do. I lifted it from the hanger and felt its weight, took a practice swing. I could knock someone out with it if I had a chance, with more distance between me and them than a knife allowed.

Tyrone had been watching my preparations quizzically and I consid-ered taking him with me for a moment, but discarded the idea almost im-mediately. I couldn't predict what he would do out there, and I didn't want to be fettered by a leash.

"Sorry, Ty. You're staying here this time." I lifted the bar off the French doors and let myself out, locking the doors behind me, hoping that would be enough to protect the house while I was gone. Then I set out for my first supply run.

Avoiding the roads seemed like a good plan, so I struck out across the alley and straight through the backyard of the closest house, hugging the side of it. When I reached the front corner of the house I stopped and scanned the area; this street looked as deserted as mine did. There were no cars visible, which made me think about the Kia, still parked out in front of my house, a flag to anyone who noticed. I'd need to move that as soon as possible. Across the street, one I'd walked Tyrone down several times since I adopted him, two houses had quarantine marks painted on their front doors. Crouched by a bush, I listened and watched for a long time, but I heard nothing, saw no movement at all. It was as though the entire block of residents had simply disappeared.

I decided that the house I was leaning against was as good a place as any to begin. I crept along the front to the porch in order to ensure there was no quarantine sign painted there. There wasn't; just a red front door with a brass handle. Two shiny red ceramic planters flanked the door, planted with spring flowers; deep purple pansies and delicate blue lobelia. I'd admired this house on my walks with Tyrone before the flu hit—it was a well-maintained, craftsman-style home; a style I'd always loved. One time, the owners had been outside, the husband edging the perfect lawn while the wife planted the pansies. I remembered returning the friendly wave the husband offered, and I wondered where they were now. Pulling the dust mask up over my face, I pinched the metal band on it so it was snug over my nose. I didn't know if it would protect me at all, but entering even a house with no quarantine marks on it made me nervous.

It felt like I should knock first, before I tried to enter, so I did, a very hesitant, quiet knock. Of course, there was no answer. I tried the door knob, already looking around for an appropriately-sized rock with which to break the front window.

It was unlocked.

Slowly, I opened the door, poking my head inside. It was odd walking into some stranger's home, uninvited. I shut the door behind me as quietly as possible and after a moment's thought, engaged the deadbolt above the knob. It felt safer—at least whatever might be outside would stay out. I walked to the window and parted the lace curtains, surveying the street for any movement: nothing.

The front entrance opened right into the living room of the house. There was a fireplace, much nicer than mine, with a heavy wooden mantle, covered with carefully arranged framed photographs. A large sofa, clad in light blue upholstery, faced the fireplace, and two cream damask, wing-backed chairs flanked it, forming what interior design magazines called a conversation area. The walls were painted an elegant café au lait color. There was no sign of any hasty departure here—the whole room looked perfect—a little too perfect, as though nobody ever used it. I skirted the window and crossed to the fireplace photographs. In one photo, a man—the man I'd exchanged a wave with—posed in a formal shot next to the woman who had been planting spring flowers. He was about 45 years old; she was at least ten years younger, holding a small bouquet of lilies. Their wedding day? Perhaps a courthouse ceremony, I thought, judging from the attire; he wore a suit and tie and she was in a simple dress. More photos of the two of them and a young girl, perhaps ten years old in the first shot of the three together, about twelve in what looked like the most recent photographs. The man and the woman smiled carefully in all of the photos. The girl was smiling only in the earliest of them.

After I checked the rest of the downstairs rooms—a kitchen/family room combination, a home office, and a bathroom—I climbed the stairs to the second floor, pastry roller at the ready. On the small landing at the top of the stairs I stopped, listening for any sound from the rooms. A single hallway with three doors opening off of it lay before me. The first door revealed the master bedroom, and here there were signs that the family had left quickly. Drawers hung open, emptied, in the long, low dresser under the window. The bed was unmade and covered in discarded clothing, some still on hangers. There was a door, open, to the left of the bed, and I approached it cautiously. The room beyond was dim; little of the daylight the bedroom window let in penetrated past the doorway.

As I neared the door I saw movement from within and immediately panicked. Brandishing the pastry roller like a light sabre, adrenaline pulsing through my body, I lunged forward and screamed at the shadowy figure in front of me. I saw a weapon, a raised arm and all I could do was try to cover my head and cower, waiting for the blow to land. I stood trembling, arms over my head, pastry roller dangling uselessly from one hand for what seemed like forever, but no blow came. Finally, I peeked through my arms and saw why.

The door opened into the master bathroom. There was a mirror mounted over the double sinks; the mysterious attacker was my reflection. Mouth open, heart still beating too quickly, I stared. The image I saw was startling. A woman, frazzled hair pulled back in a haphazard pony tail, wearing a carpenter's dust mask askew on her face, who looked as haggard as a beggar. I had lost weight, and I could see dark circles under my eyes, disappearing behind the dust mask. I looked exhausted, so much so that it frightened me. I gazed for a moment longer at my reflection, taking deep breaths to steady myself. The bathroom was in disarray; towels spilled from a linen closet and the medicine cabinet was open and had been, for the most part, cleaned out. There was a bottle of aspirin and an electric toothbrush left. I put the aspirin in my backpack.

The next door in the hallway was another bathroom. There was a curling iron on the counter, and the medicine cabinet here had nothing but a bottle of acne wash and some fingernail polish. The cabinet under the sink held two bottles of shampoo and some rolls of toilet paper. I shoved all of it into the backpack. The third door was the girl's room. An unmade canopy bed with soft pink ruffles, walls covered with movie posters. Three stuffed bears, looking as new as the day they were purchased, sat in a chair by the window. A quick sweep revealed nothing useful that I could take with me. I was on my way out the door when I saw it.

On the floor, propped up against the wall right next to the door, was a book. A scrap of folded notebook paper lay in front of it. I picked up the book—it was a diary, the kind bound with fake red leather and a cheap gold lock on the front. The notebook paper had a key taped to it, and written inside the fold, in rounded cursive, were the words *For the police*.

Still holding the diary and the note, I peeked out the bedroom window, down at the street. Still deserted. I walked to the pink bed and sat down on the corner and reread the note. Why would the girl have left this diary, this note, so carefully placed where a quick glance inside her room wouldn't reveal it, in the middle of what I was certain must have been a chaotic situation? I could imagine her parents shouting down the hall to her: *hurry up, grab what you can, we're leaving now*. I reread the note, tore the key from the notepaper and unlocked the diary.

Flipping through the pages I saw they were about half filled with the same rounded, childish script. One page was dog-eared, the corner folded down so that the diary naturally opened to it. The entry was dated almost a year prior.

June 7

I tried to tell Mom today. He's been gone since Thursday night on one of his business trips and we had three days without him. It felt like it used to, before they got married, before he was even around. We watched movies and cooked whatever we wanted to eat and we stayed in our pajamas until way past noon on Saturday. Mom was almost like she used to be. She laughed, and she wasn't scared, and she never told me to be quiet even once. Her eyes smiled when she smiled.

I knew I was going to tell her this morning. It just felt like my last chance, like maybe if she could remember how it used to be, she would be brave enough to get in the car and just go. Like maybe she really didn't know what he does, and that once I told her she would get really mad and strong and we would leave, just leave and go where he can't find us.

I was scared to do it. But he won't stop—he told me he wouldn't. He told me he can do what he wants and if I say anything, he'll make me pay. He comes in my room almost every night now when he's home. He told her we need story time, time with just me and him so we can bond. And she just lets him, now. So I knew I had to try, today, before she went to get him. And so after lunch when we were checking the tomato plants in the garden to see if they had any flowers yet, I told her. I told her what he does. I couldn't look at her while I said it—I just kept looking at the tomato plants. And when I was finished she didn't say anything for a long time, so long that I finally looked up.

She was staring at the tomato plants, but not really. And she wouldn't look at me. And she stayed quiet for a long time. When she finally spoke, all she said was "I'll ask him about it when he gets home."
She'll ask him about it.

She left to pick him up just now. They'll be back by dinner time. She said to make sure my room was cleaned up before they get back—he likes things just so. I'm scared, because he meant what he said. He'll make me pay. I just don't know how yet.

I closed the diary and placed it on the bed. Until the tears slipped past my dust mask, I didn't realize that I was crying. I wiped at my cheeks with the sleeve of my sweatshirt, angry and sad at the same time. That nameless girl. Hoping that the end of the world might be her salvation, that the good guys would come rolling in and find her diary, arrest her asshole of a stepfather and take him away. That girl, believing that she would be returning to this house, of course, that the flu would pass and all would be well, and the police would save her. Her and her mother.

I knew that story too well. Some part of me hoped that girl was dead, that the flu killed her quickly and mercifully, because it *would* be a mercy, compared to what she would have to endure if she lived. At least if the asshole lived, too.

When I left that house, I looked back at it from the street, taking in the beautiful planters and the lace curtains at the front window, remembering that man waving at me, remembering that woman planting flowers. Remembering how I wondered, as a child, why people walk by, just walk by every day, house after house, child after child, never knowing what goes on behind the facades, never dreaming what a house, or a child's face, can hide. Never *asking*. Just like I had done not so long ago, walking Tyrone on a brisk spring day, right past hell, waving at the devil.

— —

I explored two more houses that day—both on the same street—before I decided to head home. I skirted the ones with **Q**s on the doors and the two I went into weren't much help. I did get an air mattress, still in its packaging, from the first one, but there was not much else of use in it unless I wanted to cart home some really beautiful area rugs and furniture. It looked to me like a rental house that didn't have a tenant. The second house was slightly better; I found two cans of green beans and an unopened package of dried prunes in the kitchen cupboards. There were clothes in the master bedroom closet that looked like they might fit, along with plenty of extra blankets in the linen closet that I could come back for when I needed them. But no gun. I'd have to keep looking.

It was on the way back to my house that I found a real jackpot. I was tired, and nervous about being outside my fortified bunker of a home any longer than I had to be, so I was cutting through backyards to get to the alley when I saw it. Inside a six-foot wooden fence surrounding the yard next to me, the top of a greenhouse was visible. I went to the side gate and opened it, checking the yard carefully before I entered. The house itself wasn't one I had checked out yet. It had a large sunroom addition—the kind made of panels of glass set together, curving at the top to form a roof—built onto the back, and I could see no sign of occupancy through the windows. There was a door onto the deck from the sunroom, and I decided to check inside before looking at the greenhouse. Climbing the deck stairs, I donned my dust mask and tried the door. It was unlocked.

The temperature inside the sunroom was oppressive, even this early in spring. Sunlight shone through from every angle, heating the room like an oven. I moved through quickly to an interior door, opening it as quietly as possible. On the other side was the kitchen, a rather nice kitchen, newly remodeled from the looks of it. Every surface had an unused sheen and all the usual clutter of a lived-in room was missing. I didn't bother looking for any supplies—I really just wanted to ensure the place was empty, so I cruised through each room quickly. I found nobody, just as I had expected. On my way back through the kitchen a note pinned under a magnet on the refrigerator caught my attention. The magnet was a red enameled heart, and the note it affixed was written on pink paper.

> *Solly,*
> *You will always be my favorite Valentine.*
> *Even though you snore.*
> *Love you, Jenna*

I stood and stared at the note on the stainless-steel door. Not that long ago—mid-February—this house had been home to Solly and Jenna, and all they were thinking of was love. I wondered what they gifted each other for Valentine's Day. Was it traditional chocolate? A dinner out together? I wondered where they were now.

Back outside I descended from the deck to check out the greenhouse. It wasn't a huge greenhouse—it was one of those smaller, garden-in-the-suburbs kind of things. But Solly and Jenna had clearly taken that sort of agriculture very seriously; the greenhouse was filled with row after row, shelf after shelf, of plant starts. Everything was carefully labeled—beans, peas, two kinds of tomatoes, squash, carrots, and various cooking herbs. Right outside, freshly dug and ready for planting, was a huge raised garden bed, just waiting for warmer nights so the plants could be set out. I pushed an index finger into the spongy potting soil surrounding a bean start. It was crumbly and dry—too dry. It had been too many days since these plants had water.

There was a green garden hose neatly coiled on the deck off the house, attached to a faucet. I turned the water on to just a trickle and dragged it to the greenhouse. Some of the seedlings seemed too far gone, papery and wilted, but I watered them all, hoping that they might recover. There were plenty that would be just fine. It was a perfect setup, really. I'd been thinking about my own tiny backyard garden, my half-empty seed packets from last year. I'd figured I'd have to try to grow some food to augment Greg's supplies—they would last so much longer that way, and I'd have the nutritional benefit of fresh produce. But I'd also been thinking about how to avoid drawing attention to my house. A thriving garden in the back yard wasn't going to do anything to hide the fact that I was living there, and I had a feeling that keeping my presence hidden was going to be necessary. The idea of having the garden in a neighbor's yard, close, but not too close, appealed to me.

When I got back home the murky interior of my house surprised me yet again—being in houses where the windows weren't boarded and daylight was enough to get around had felt so normal. I dug the flashlight out of my backpack, ignored Tyrone's eager greeting and went straight to the living room for the car keys. Moving the Kia felt urgent—I couldn't believe I'd overlooked it. It seemed safer to approach the street from the back yard instead of opening the front door, so I turned and went back out the French doors, locking them behind me. I stopped at the side gate in the backyard, listening for any sound from the front. The gate creaked when I opened it; I left it open after I slipped through in order to avoid more noise.

Nothing seemed changed on the street; the houses were all empty, the driveways vacant. I walked to the Kia and unlocked the driver's side. Once I was in, I locked the doors and turned the key in the ignition. The engine sounded thunderous compared to the silence surrounding me—if anyone was around there was no way they'd miss it. I put the car in gear and pulled out, not sure where to go. I didn't want to go too far because I'd be walking back home. In the end, I simply drove down to the end of my dead-end street and parked in front of the last house. I passed Mark and Nancy's place: the front door hung open, but the house looked deserted. This end of the street was the same as my end; no sign of life anywhere. I tried the radio—static across all stations. The gas gauge showed half a tank.

The idea of getting Tyrone and few supplies and just driving away had been in the back of my mind for some time, but as I sat there listening to static on the airwaves, I could envision the trip; I'd get out on the main road just fine, and onto the nearest freeway ramp, and maybe a few miles down that four-lane highway until I encountered a huge traffic jam of abandoned vehicles. Snippets of the last news announcements I'd heard played in my mind: troops trying to block on-ramps, shooting at vehicles, a massive, panicked exodus. Even if I could get further than I thought I might, where would I go? What would I do to survive when whatever supplies I could pack in the car were gone? I checked the rearview mirror and turned off the car. There was really nowhere to go but back to home.

When I got out of the car, a dark smudge in the sky a few blocks to the east caught my eye. Smoke. As I watched, it formed into a column, light gray and fluffy at the top, darker and billowing further down. I stood transfixed; someone's house was burning down. The smell of smoke drifted to me and I watched as the column of smoke grew and grew, wondering if the fire would spread. There wasn't much wind, but the houses around here were close enough together that it could easily happen. I thought it was too far away to reach my house—at least I hoped so. Some part of me was waiting to hear sirens, to see firetrucks racing toward the neighborhood. But there would be no sirens. The house would burn to the ground, and all I could do was watch. I didn't want to watch. I didn't want to see any of the things I was seeing. I turned away and headed home.

I scanned the backyard carefully before I entered and shut the side gate as quietly as possible. Once Tyrone had a bathroom break, I locked and barred the French doors. Using the flashlight to navigate inside the house, I unpacked my scavenged items from the backpack and tried the lights and the telephone and the television again. Nothing.

That's when I started shaking.

It was actually real. It was all real. Seeing all the deserted houses, all the signs of panicked departure, it all hit me at once. Tyrone followed me to the sofa where I sat, in shock. I stared at the television; a mute, blank box that seemed to symbolize everything that was lost.

For a long time I just sat there, my arms wrapped around myself, crying. I thought about what my life would be like now, however long it might be. There was still the chance that I would catch the virus and die quickly, or maybe I would survive for a while, maybe even years, and die some other way. Whatever happened, I realized that I was probably going to die alone. But what I also realized, maybe for the first time with total clarity, was that I was going to do that anyway, pre-apocalypse. I was going to die alone, without any actual friends, except long-distance ones like Gina, because I had never been able to trust anyone. Not truly.

I considered this. I heard Gina's voice in my head, telling me, as she always had, that I was being too black and white. *You trust me*, she would have said. And that was true. Long-distance or not, I had always trusted Gina. She knew the same world I did, had suffered some of the same cruelty, so she and I had a sort of shorthand; we could understand each other in ways "normal" people wouldn't. But I'd refused to trust anyone else, especially after my divorce. I'd pushed any chance of entanglement away, kept all my relationships on the surface, because it felt safer that way. And I honestly wasn't convinced I was wrong. I'd seen too much of the weak, stupid, selfish, cruel side of humanity to want much to do with it in general. So, I would have died alone no matter what. This whole end-of-the-world thing just made it more difficult to avoid thinking about that.

Tyrone, in his wonderful *hey-I'm-here-what's-wrong* way, nudged my hand, and I leaned forward to give his soft nose a kiss. He was such a presence in my life after such a short time. Since that day in the shelter when I first saw those soft brown eyes, I'd loved him. He was *safe* to love. He just loved me back, no questions asked. I felt a fierce protectiveness for him, the kind I imagined parents, at least normal parents, must feel for their children.

The day was almost over—at least over enough for me. I was tired, and the thought of just getting the kerosene lamps filled and lit and coming up with some sort of dinner was all I could bear. Tomorrow I would go water the seedlings and keep looking for a gun. Tonight, I just wanted the comfort of my dog.

Learning to Fly

AFTER GETTING TYRONE straightened away for the day, I gathered my pastry roller and flashlight, along with two gallons of the water from the ten I'd hauled from Greg's garage. A lucky thing I had hauled them over to the house; when I tried to fill Tyrone's water dish I discovered the plumbing had finally stopped working. The faucet bucked with explosions of air and water which subsided to a trickle, then nothing. I would have to haul the jugs to the greenhouse to refresh the seedlings.

Clouds hung low in the sky as I made my way to the greenhouse; more spring rain would be coming soon. I crept along the sides of houses, watching and listening as always, but the neighborhood was silent. When I arrived, I found many of the seedlings plump and strong, restored from drought by yesterday's watering. Only a few had died. I rationed drops to each little pot, wishing I had more, wondering how I would manage hauling what I needed even a couple of times a week. Looking around, I found a whole stack of empty plastic buckets under one of the benches and had an idea. I could set them out to catch rain water and use that to irrigate with when I came. I lined them up on the far side of the greenhouse, away from the gate.

As I left the yard, I turned back to survey the place. Thankfully, there was a stone path leading up to the gate, and from the gate to the greenhouse and up to the back deck. My comings and goings wouldn't be detected from foot trails in the grass. Of course, if anyone was really looking, if they actually came through the gate, they would see the plants thriving in the greenhouse and know that someone was coming here. Later, they would see the garden I hoped I could grow in the raised bed. But I couldn't do much about that.

I only hit one house that day; I knew I had to get back to mine and move some more water from Greg's. The house I chose was three blocks down, on a street I hadn't walked Tyrone down before. It was a ranch-style house, unassuming in its medium-suburban-ness. There was no **Q** on the door, though I still donned a fresh dust mask just in case. The front door was locked, but the side door into the garage was open and so was the kitchen door inside the garage. It looked as though only one person had lived there, though I was guessing. The main bedroom was well-lived in and the other bedroom looked like it had been used as an office. There was a desk and several bookshelves and not much else. The books were ordered by genre—I only knew this because each section of shelves had a label. There were books the owner had categorized as *Historical*. There was a *Romance* section, and a *Biography* section, and a *Science Fiction* section. I saw a lot of books I'd read—those good old dystopians—in the *Science Fiction* section, and imagined having a spirited discussion with the owner about whether they were appropriately shelved. One oddly-labeled section caught my eye: *Reality*.

This shelf held titles like *Knitting for Beginners*, and *The Human Body: Anatomy of Change*. It also had a paperback called *Thinking Through Death: Volume I*. I slid this book from the shelf. The cover was light blue, with images of clouds floating behind the title. The editors were a man named Scott Kramer and Kuang-Ming somebody—the cover was torn and the last name of the coauthor was obliterated. I flipped through the pages, stopping at the introduction to read a snippet.

> As our knowledge is delimited by the paradox of death, all other aspects of our lives—emotional, volitional, managerial—are surrounded by frustrating ambiguities and uncertainties. An unexamined death makes for an unexamined life, which is not worth living. How we interpret death provides us a perspective on what life is; how we understand death determines how we should live.

Death. Life. A little light reading. Closing the book, I reexamined the cover. Where was Volume II? A quick search of the shelf didn't reveal a copy. Still, I popped Volume I in my backpack. I took the anatomy book and a science fiction novel as well.

The rest of the house yielded some canned corn and a prescription bottle of tetracycline with 30 pills inside. I had no idea what tetracycline was used to treat but I knew it was some sort of antibiotic. The bottle label said the patient was a Fred Carver, and that he was supposed to take two pills per day with food. The expiration date was three months out.

It looked like Fred had left in a hurry—his breakfast dishes were still on the table. He must have been a bachelor, because his refrigerator contained soy sauce and ketchup packets and a jar of pickles. I would have taken the pickles but the jar looked less than appetizing, with several tide-lines of hardened pickle juice dried at different levels inside. I wasn't certain they were still okay to eat. I left the condiment packets behind, too. I didn't have a clue whether condiment packets went bad. It didn't seem like there was much chance Fred had a gun, but I looked everywhere I could think to look before I called it good and left the house.

Back at home I unpacked, gave Tyrone some attention and then made three trips back and forth between the garage and the house, hauling water. I found some blue plastic, ten-gallon buckets under the workbench in the garage and brought three of them, too. I'd been thinking about the toilet. I wasn't certain how sustainable it was, but I'd seen on some television show that you could flush a toilet by pouring water into it. I set one of the buckets, half filled with water, next to it and wondered about how I would handle my waste if it didn't work. Urine wouldn't be much of a problem—I could simply pee in a bucket and take it out each day. But the thought of having to haul more substantial waste out each day and find a place to put it wasn't something I looked forward to doing. Thankfully, the bucket trick worked. So whenever I needed to flush the toilet, I could just pour a quarter of a bucket into the bowl and it would whoosh away down the drain. I tried not to think about what might happen when the sewer pipes reached capacity.

For the next few weeks my days took on a strange, new routine. I spent the mornings watering the greenhouse plants and looking for a gun. It rained enough that I didn't have to haul water very often—usually the buckets I'd lined up outside yielded plenty to get the job done. The seedlings grew stronger, varying shades of green, some plants squatty and stout, some elegant, with vining tendrils grasping for support. I tried to gauge the temperature each night during Tyrone's last bathroom break, wondering how long until I could safely set the plants out in the raised bed. I wasn't certain anymore what date it was; I'd neglected to make any sort of recording of time passing in the first days and now I was only guessing.

Once the nights seemed to be mild enough, I spent a whole day moving the seedlings into the raised bed. Silently thanking whoever it was who had plowed the soil so early in spring, I tucked each plant into the ground. I'd planted gardens before, at least simple salad gardens, but this one felt different; the survival of each tomato, each bean bush, was crucial. Every one of the transplants got a careful dousing and some of the fertilizer I'd found in a bag under the greenhouse shelves. I could only hope my scant knowledge would be enough to bring forth a harvest in the coming weeks. When I was done, I stood up and surveyed my work. The garden was impossible to camouflage; anyone who opened the gate to the yard would know someone was in the area, that someone came to this place often. It would be easy enough to set up an ambush. All I could do was hope that things were as they appeared to be; that the neighborhood was abandoned and people had fled in the first days or moved on soon after. Or died.

As my garden grew, I continued my search for a gun. I only went to one house a day; it still felt extremely risky to be outside the relative safety of my house. I heard gunshots twice, far off, and once I saw another column of black smoke, about two miles away, that rose into the sky all morning long. It made me think about fire again—I was already being careful with the kerosene lamps and candles but after that day I was neurotic about it. Luckily, one item I found often on my supply runs was household fire extinguishers. Most homes had one somewhere, usually stashed under the kitchen sink. I brought all of them back to the house and placed them strategically, afraid to test them, hopeful I'd figure out how to use one if the occasion presented itself. The instructions printed on them looked pretty simple. I found a variety of other things to haul home; more painkillers, a few more antibiotics prescriptions bearing the names of the people who used to inhabit the houses I entered, clothing and books and shoes. Lots of canned goods and toilet paper. I took anything I thought I could use.

I'd ventured four blocks from home by then, and was trying to be more systematic about my supply expeditions. On a crude map of the neighborhood I'd penciled on a sheet of paper, I marked each house I visited, filling in streets as I covered them. Tyrone was locked in the house for all my forays until the day I found the cat. It was the third house on the block, another ranch-style, painted green with purple shutters. I had to gain entry by breaking a window; I'd become adept at wrapping my pastry roller with a towel to muffle the noise a bit. I still wore my trusty dust masks, in case Hacker's Flu had a longer shelf life than I thought.

Inside this house were the usual signs of hasty flight; dishes on the table as though someone had been eating, drawers pulled out, still holding items deemed less useful to take in an emergency. I walked through looking for anything I might need, making note of items I might want to return for later. The cat—the tag hanging from a pink collar revealed her name was Nadine—was at the back door of the house. She lay, almost as though she were asleep, with her pink nose nearly touching the bottom of the door. She had died waiting for someone to come back through that door, waiting for someone to refill the water dish I found in the kitchen, dry as a bone, or the food dish next to it. She had used the litter box in the laundry room all the way to the end; I found no messes anywhere else in the house, though the box was filthy. She had starved, or died from lack of water, waiting for her people to come home.

I buried her in the back yard of that house. While I dug her grave, I wondered why I hadn't found more like her. Perhaps most people took their pets when they fled, or the pets were released outside. I had seen plenty of dog doors in the houses I'd been in; that might have explained it, except I hadn't seen any stray dogs. I made it a practice from then on to open a door in every house I passed—too late for most if they were trapped, but still, an attempt. I also took Tyrone with me everywhere I went from that day on. The thought of him waiting for me to return, sitting patiently by the French doors . . . if something happened to me while I was on a supply trip, or tending the garden, he would die waiting.

I was lucky in that Tyrone was naturally quiet; I still hadn't heard him bark once since the day I met him in the shelter kennel. He seemed to know I wanted him to remain at my heel. I leashed him for our outings at first, but soon enough I didn't need to; he stuck by my side, rarely tempted by a squirrel or a bird. I understood he wouldn't provide any protection—even if he looked vicious, he just wasn't that sort of dog—but I felt better knowing that if he wasn't locked in the house, he would have at least a chance of survival if something happened to me.

Even if Tyrone *had* been a guard dog, he wouldn't have had much work. I saw no one in my travels through the neighborhood. The smoke I'd seen and the shots I'd heard were the last true evidence I'd had of survivors. I never even saw a body, though if there were any I assumed they were inside the houses with **Q**s on the doors, and I never entered those. Still, I was filled with a sense of danger every time I ventured outside my house. Images of Mark's face when he came after my supplies; of his wife, shaking, near madness, ready to kill me; of the two men who had broken into Greg's house—all these kept me fearful. There might not be any people near now, but there could be soon. I had no way of knowing if everyone had migrated to the cities, or to the hills, or where they had gone.

The days passed. I worried sometimes when it didn't rain for a while, but Greg's water system held up, the tarp funneling even dew to the barrel. I read the directions I'd found in the packing box over and over, learning how to check the filter compartments to ensure they weren't clogged or in need of replenishment. I spent the evenings working on obedience commands with Tyrone, or reading by lamp light—I'd amassed quite a collection of books from my supply runs. Sometimes I read about how to preserve the vegetables I hoped would result from my gardening efforts. Other times I wanted nothing more challenging than a silly historical romance.

So many things quickly became normal that never had been: before, I showered daily, shampooing my hair in a luxuriant stream of warm water.

Now, I stood in the bathroom tub, and used a bucket of room temperature water to scrub and rinse my body. My hair went unwashed for days. I'd lugged the camp stove I found in Greg's garage over to my kitchen counter, and after reading the lengthy manual I learned how to use it to cook rudimentary meals from Greg's stores; I'd rigged a venting system for it through the existing stove vent in my kitchen, but I was never certain if I was going to asphyxiate myself. Using it to heat enough water to wash my hair was an hour-long process. It wasn't a permanent solution; sooner or later I would run out of the propane tanks that fueled it. I kept thinking about the fireplace and how I would need to heat the house when winter arrived. Greg's pressed fire logs would work, as long as they lasted, but the smoke they would produce bothered me; I would be advertising my presence far and wide.

Sometimes, because I had no great answers, I just stopped thinking about all of it.

I lost weight, but it was fat my body replaced with muscle. Physically, I was probably in the best shape I'd been since I was a teenager; lugging water and walking everywhere proved more effective than any Zumba routine, not that I'd have been caught dead doing Zumba before Hacker's Flu.

Time became very different. My activities were dictated by the sun. I never knew what clock-time it was; I only knew it was time to get headed toward home before the sun set too low. I didn't go outside the fenced yard at night, and once darkness fell, I only went outside the house to allow Tyrone to relieve himself, listening, always listening, in case someone was near. Inside the house the same dim lamp light marked day and night; the boarded windows let nothing of the sun in and at first, I lost valuable daylight because there was nothing to wake me. I slept through many mornings before I found a mechanical alarm clock on one of my supply runs. After establishing "early morning" by the sun, I set it for what I designated as 8 AM, in order to wake in time to get outside and do what I needed to do before dark. My 8 AM might have been 9, or maybe it was 6. I had no way to tell. I found it didn't matter in the least. In a way, my newfound freedom from the exact time was a wonderful feeling—I didn't worry about being late for anything, or how long something might take.

A task took as long as it did. I was never in a rush anymore; there was no reason to hurry.

Something else changed during this time: the murmurations. It didn't happen suddenly; it was a subtle thing, so gradual I almost didn't notice at first. But one day, when I was kneeling in the garden plot weeding between my tomato plants, I realized that I was hearing them all the time. I hadn't been seeking them out, and there was no wind that day, no stream nearby, no faucet running, no car engine to channel them. Yet there they were in the back of my mind, a constant refrain. And they sounded, to my ears, mournful.

I thought about it—this change, in both frequency and tone—during my evenings at home. When the garden was tended, I'd packed away any supplies I'd found that day, and Tyrone and I were settled on the sofa, my attention would drift from whatever book I held under the pool of light from kerosene lamp and I'd ponder again, like I had when I was a child, what the murmurations meant. What *were* they? Was I just mentally ill? Had I always been? Did the increase in frequency and the change in tone simply signal that my mental state was deteriorating? Was it the quieter world I existed in now that let murmurations come through to me all the time? Why were they sad? Why did I think of them as a "they"?

It felt like the murmurations did come *from* something else, from something bigger than my own mind, but what that was I didn't know. Sometimes on those nights, I actually wished I had someone to talk with about it. The first time that thought occurred to me, I laughed out loud. Me, the loner, the person who had always shunned all humans as untrustworthy, wishing for a friend. Ironic, now that all world had left to offer were people who would rather kill me for my supplies than chat with me about my freakish internal soundtrack.

The Gun

THE GUN WAS hidden in the back of a desk drawer in a house I hit mid-summer. It may have just been forgotten rather than hidden; it was under a sheaf of dusty tax records, bumping up against miscellaneous pens and rubber bands. It was a black handgun, the kind with a clip that inserted into the handle. There was a small box of bullets with it that looked exactly like the bullets in Greg's stash. I picked it up, cool and heavy in my hand, and turned it this way and that. I couldn't tell if it was loaded; I saw that the safety was on though, so I had to assume it was. Holding it, I felt a deep sense of relief that was, upon reflection, silly. I hadn't the first clue how to use the thing. There was no YouTube video at my disposal and no manual in the drawer. It was going to be trial and error to learn how to use the gun. But I finally had one. I finally had the one thing that could save my life if some nut like Mark or his crazy wife showed up at my door.

I spent two days at home, ignoring the garden, teaching myself how to work the gun. I'd never even held a gun before and my hands shook as I figured out how to remove the cartridge, unload the bullets, reload them and snap the cartridge back in place. I kept my fingers far from the trigger. But finally, I began to feel more comfortable with the weight of the gun in my hand, more adept at handling it. I knew I had to actually learn to shoot it, but I also knew that I'd have to find a place far from my house; the noise would attract anyone who might be near.

One morning, I packed the gun and some bullets in my backpack and Tyrone and I went to the garden. Two days without tending hadn't done any harm; there had been a light rain and all the plants looked good. Pale

blossoms dotted the tomato plants like yellow stars, and the early leaf lettuce was big enough to pick and eat. I pulled a few weeds, ate some lettuce, and watched Tyrone enjoy exploring the yard the garden was in; he
thought of it as his now and did the same patrolling of the perimeter he
did in our yard. When he had sniffed every corner, I called him over and
leashed him up. I was going to walk farther than we had in some time and
I didn't want to take any chances losing him.

There was a park about a mile from my house; Tyrone and I had walked
through it several times before, when walking in the park was a normal
activity. From what I remembered it might be a perfect target range. It
had a small playground in the middle of a clearing, which would allow me
to see anyone who might approach. I thought I could walk there, practicing firing the gun a few times once I'd ensured nobody was around, and
vanish quickly back into the suburban tracts before the noise drew any
potential interest.

We cut through yards and side streets on the way in order to avoid
the main road. I found a sort of orchard in one back yard; there were two
apple trees, a pear tree and what I thought must be a plum tree. They were
all setting buds, and I made a note of the location so I could come back
to gather some fruit when it was ripe. There were more **Q**s on the houses
here than in my neighborhood. Most were spray-painted on crudely in
various colors, like the one I had done, but some were black, stenciled letters. The military? Some official clean-up crew for certain, from the looks
of it. The silent streets were already showing signs of desertion: a recycling
bin that had blown into the middle of a street remained tipped on its side,
undisturbed. Bits of paper and plastic littered the sidewalks, drifting in
corners like strange snow. The lawns were shaggy, the flowerbeds filled
with a healthy crop of weeds. It was a sunny morning, one that normally
would have brought everyone outside to wash their cars, or mow their
lawns. Instead Tyrone and I were the only two living beings present. At
least I hoped so.

The park was just as I remembered it. A play set—three red rubber
swings, a yellow plastic slide and some low climbing bars—sprouted from
an area covered with recycled rubber chips, designed to soften the falls of

playing children. Except there were no children playing today, no small groups of parents watching their kids slide or climb on the bars. The red swings hung motionless from their chains and a fine film of dirt already coated the slide. Around the desolate play area, long and unkempt lawn stretched away in uneven waves until it met the surrounding trees; plenty of space for me to feel relatively safe from undetected watchers.

I crouched by the first clump of bushes I came to and stayed there for several minutes, watching and listening for any sign of company. When I was certain I was alone, I ventured out and crossed the lawn to the play set. After tying Tyrone's leash onto one of the metal poles supporting the climbing bars, I unslung my backpack and unpacked the gun. Tyrone gave me a look that clearly expressed his dubiousness about being tied to the pole, but I wasn't sure how he would react to the gun shots and I didn't want him to bolt. I couldn't imagine trying to catch him once he got going.

The gun didn't feel as strange to me now, after having practiced handling it, but I wasn't sure what to expect from shooting it. All I could remember from movies and books was that I needed to be ready for it to kick back at me once I pulled the trigger, and that it would be really loud. Looking around, the best target I could see was a metal sign posted by the Parks Department urging residents to bag up their dog poop. It was about fifteen feet away, mounted on a post about six feet tall. I moved away from Tyrone, who watched me with increasing worry. Spreading my feet apart and bending my knees, I straight-armed the gun out in front of me and squinted past it at the picture of the poop bag on the sign.

"Deep breaths, deep breaths," I counseled myself. My arms were shaking a bit, so I adjusted my stance, steadied my aim and pulled the trigger.

Nothing. At first I simply stood there, dumbfounded, pressing on the trigger over and over. Finally, I realized I still had the safety engaged. I looked around, embarrassed, until I realized there was, of course, nobody to see my ineptitude. Clicking the safety off, I took my stance again, aimed, and fired.

The blast of sound shocked me more than the kick. It was terrifying. It felt as though my right arm had been struck by a club. It also felt like I had just announced myself to any and every other survivor for miles around.

And when I looked, the poop sign was unscathed. Muttering to myself I took aim again, being very careful to focus on the center of the sign. Then I pulled the trigger again.

Same blast, same kick, but this time I was prepared. And this time, there was a satisfying hole in the metal sign. I couldn't help but smile. Tyrone, who had practically leapt out of his skin the first time I shot the gun, now simply cowered, shaking, next to the climbing bars.

"It's okay, Ty." I felt awful that he was so frightened, but I had to prac- tice. "Just a few more shots."

I fired three more times at the sign, and two of my efforts hit home. It felt oddly transformative, as though I now possessed a power I hadn't before. I was getting ready to try again when all my newly-formed confi- dence was shattered.

From somewhere east, someone answered my gun shots with their own. Two shots, about ten seconds apart. A definite signal. Immediately my heart began to pound and my face flushed hot; I felt instant fear, as though I had sighted a grizzly bear at the edge of the park, loping toward me, putting on speed. I ran for Tyrone and untied his leash from the pole, remembered to click the safety back on the gun and then tossed it in the backpack. Grabbing the pack by the strap in one hand with Tyrone's leash in the other, I ran for the trees.

I hunched down low in the tree line, catching my breath. The shots hadn't sounded close enough that the shooter could reach me in minutes, but it was hard to tell exactly how far they were from the park. All I could do was try to get back to the house without being seen, so as soon as I stopped gasping, I stood, shouldered my backpack and started off. Staying as close to houses as possible and sprinting when I had to cross a road, I made my way home. I couldn't stop shaking, even once I was inside and the French doors were barred.

There were others out there. Still. I had begun to believe I was the only one. My daily trips to the garden and my house-foraging had become a sort of normalcy, untroubled by threat, so while I had remained cautious, I had also started to feel safer, more relaxed. I wasn't starving thanks to Greg's supplies; I knew I had some time to try to solve the problem of long-term survival. And to be honest with myself, I had begun to settle into the solitude, even to enjoy it. It was as if a weight that I had carried every day, a weight I wasn't even conscious of, had melted away. People were not, to me, easy. My history had branded me with distrust, and not having to try to negotiate relationships felt so . . . simple. I didn't *miss* people. I hadn't trusted them before, and not having to try to decipher their action and evaluate their motives was a huge relief.

I realized I *wanted* to be alone. And those gun shots confirmed all my feelings. Now, there was no questioning that people, at least those who were left, were something to be avoided.

Solitude

IN THE DAYS that followed the gunshots, I was extra cautious with all my routines. I listened at the cracked door longer prior to opening it to let Tyrone out; I listened at the back gate before going through it to get supplies from Greg's or tend the garden. I scouted every house I chose to enter thoroughly, watching and waiting before I entered, clearing every room with the gun out in front of me before searching for bounty.

The gun. I took it everywhere. I slept with it on the night stand next to me. I practiced loading and unloading it until I could do it so smoothly and quickly it was like I was born doing it. I practiced pointing it a lot, in the evenings when I was done with my work and bored with my books. But I didn't dare practice shooting it again. The chance that I would hear those answering gun shots, this time too close to run from, was too great.

The summer days passed. I spent my time working on the garden and I still visited houses sometimes, but much less often. I had most of what I would need in terms of clothes and fire extinguishers and blankets for some time to come. I did count all the edibles in Greg's garage, dividing the stock by days as exactly as I could, in order to know precisely how long I had before I ran out of staples. As I catalogued all the items, I appreciated Greg more and more. I owed him my life. Without his garage, I would have died within a few weeks if what I'd read about how long it took to starve was true. Greg had calculated carefully and it looked to me as though he had planned to have enough calories to sustain two people for a year. When I factored in my garden, even sharing with Tyrone, which I would have to do once his kibble was gone, I had a slim but solid year and a half, minimum. After that, I didn't know what would happen, but I tried very hard not to think too much about it.

Instead, I focused on trying to become more self-sufficient. The garden was a huge start; despite my lack of experience, the vegetables grew well and I had tomatoes, squash, beans, lettuce, carrots, and, hopefully soon, potatoes. I also had an abundance of pears, apples and plums, ready to harvest, on the trees in the mini-orchard I'd found on my way to my ill-fated target practice session.

I'd been thinking about all my tomatoes, and about the fruit trees, for some time. I knew that if I couldn't find a way to preserve my harvest much would go to waste, and though I had studied Greg's *Canning for Beginners* from front to back many times, I didn't think I was up to the challenge. He had some canning equipment in the garage, but the idea of botulism scared me enough that I hesitated. I kept rereading the section on beans and how easy it was to can them incorrectly and then die a horrible death. It wasn't lost on me that I would probably die a horrible death in any case, but I tried to keep that thought at bay.

It was on my way to water the garden one day when I had a better idea. A window screen had fallen out of one of the windows in a duplex—one of those cheap metal frames with flimsy screening stretched taut. So many signs of decay had begun to overtake the neighborhood surprisingly quickly. All the windows were coated with grime; the few cars that remained had the same dusty film and some of them had flat tires. Panels from fences had blown down during early spring storms and lay where they fell, weeds and grass peeking up through the boards, nature slowly reclaiming the wood. I stopped to pick up the window screen, which was in perfect working order save for the fact that it was screening nothing at the moment. And suddenly I thought about dried fruit.

Looking around, I saw window screens everywhere—the duplex had six on the ground floor, and more in the upstairs windows. In my mind, I could see rows and rows of hanging screens, doubled and filled with slices of fruit, baking in the sunroom off of Solly and Jenna's house. It was perfect. The fruit would be protected from the weather, and the heat would

speed the drying process. It could work for my tomatoes, too. I could preserve the food I grew in summer, and eat it all winter long.

I started gathering screens right away. With some rope, some duct tape
and some work, I had the sunroom strung from one side to the other with
lines awaiting screens in just a couple of days. As tomatoes and apples
and pears ripened, I spent hours slicing them and laying them on screens.
Once I had a full screen, I lay another on top to secure my slices in place
and duct-taped the two together. Then I hung the screen like fresh laundry
from the rope lines, and let the heat of the sunroom do its magic. It was
a room-sized dehydrator and it worked like a charm. Soon, I had canning
jar after canning jar from Greg's stash filled with crinkled, leathery slices
of dried fruit and vegetables.

Working on the garden, trips to the orchard, slicing up the fruit I
hauled back, bringing more supplies to my house from the garage; all this
kept me busy during the long summer days. As I went about my business,
the smell of death—a sweet, stomach-wrenching scent—hung heavy in
the warm air. I noticed it most strongly around the houses with quarantine marks, and it explained a lot to me. I'd been wondering why I never
encountered a corpse in my house searches. And why, given the neatly
stenciled **Q**s I saw on some homes on other streets, which to me indicated
some sort of official presence had been in the neighborhood, no one had
pounded on my door offering help.

Clearly, the military, or whoever had stenciled those doors, had not
been looking for survivors in order to offer aid, or relocation. They had
simply been, for as long as the poor fools lasted, identifying homes where
people had died, or were going to die. If they saw a house with a quarantine symbol already painted on the door, as mine had, they simply passed
it by. The houses they marked must have had the sick or dying inside, and
instead of trying to help, they simply labeled the doors and moved on.

Perhaps there was nothing else they could have done. Perhaps the
deadly course of Hacker's Flu's was so rapid there would have been no
point in anything else. Or perhaps the plan was to identify people who
needed help and then come back, but there was nobody left to come back.
I imagined the scene at some command headquarters, not unlike the

deserted newsrooms in those last television broadcasts, where the best-laid plans fell apart as everyone who was charged with executing them died. Everyone in my neighborhood who could leave on their own did, and those who couldn't perished in situ.

In any case, the stench of death lingered all summer, a reminder of what was inside many of my neighbor's homes. I gave those houses wide berth and wondered how long the smell would take to dissipate; it was just another thing I could no longer look up on the Internet.

Death didn't take *all* the living things in the neighborhood. As summer passed, I began to see evidence of what had happened to all the pets—at least the ones who weren't taken along when their owners fled. There were cats, everywhere, it seemed. Colonies formed and kittens appeared, peeking at me from under hedges. They wouldn't come near because of Tyrone and I was relieved, because I knew I'd want to try to save them all. I remembered reading some article about how cats bred prolifically, and judging by the number I saw that first summer, it was true. They seemed to be fending for themselves well enough; the ones that survived must have adapted quickly to hunting rodents and birds.

There were chickens, too. Backyard chicken coops had been all the rage for years, and now the hapless birds were roaming the neighborhoods, squawking and pecking at the lawns. Some were a bronzy-gold color, some were iridescent black, and I spotted a couple of traditional, snow-white ones. They didn't tempt me because I was not a meat-eater, and luckily I had enough food not to have to test my resolve about that, but Tyrone was interested in them. I had to keep a close eye on him when we were out and we worked on renewed obedience training every day. I suspected their numbers would dwindle quickly, as they were picked off by the coyotes who lived the suburbs.

I still never saw any dogs. It made me wonder at first if dogs had been susceptible to the virus, though it could have just as easily been that they all got picked off by the coyotes early—they would be viewed as not just tasty, but as competition from a coyote point of view. Tyrone wasn't sick, but he might not have been exposed to the virus, just like me. Still, if the dogs had died from the flu, I thought I would have seen bodies. I put my money on coyotes as the reason for the dearth of dogs.

I spent many evenings reading, though it was an indulgence to use up my kerosene that way, so I limited it to a short session each night. I revisited the death book—that was how I referred to Volume I of *Thinking Through Death*—often, trying to digest what Scott Kramer and Kuang-Ming whoever were trying to say. The book was an edited collection of philosophical treatises on death, from Eastern and Western perspectives. It seemed like a very topical issue, but I didn't make much headway. I was usually too tired to read for very long anyway.

Sometimes I tried to figure who had been responsible for the flu—what country, or for that matter what radical group from our own country, was behind the bioprinter hack. I remembered the increasing uneasiness in the country before the flu hit, the newscasts covering protests over the most recent presidential election. There were rallies and demonstrations all over the country, and in other countries, too. On the day of the election, I remember Pete was shouting updates from his office as the television news reported state election totals. A guy walked up and down the street outside the office that day, wearing a literal tin-foil hat crimped on his head and screaming about genocide, until Pete called the police.

There was the weird weather—inches of snow in areas where snow rarely fell, torrential rain, arid summers in places where lawns had never required watering to keep them green. And the terrorism: attacks in France, Ireland and Oregon. The overthrow of Israel, and Jerusalem burning. It was all reported on the news; we all listened to it over dinner. And then we loaded dishwashers and set alarms and reviewed our mental lists of things to do, and the frightening and strange news stories became a part of the everyday routine for most of us. We groaned about the water bill or the fact we could only turn our sprinklers on for thirty minutes on even-numbered days because of shortages. But we went on with our routines, oblivious. And finally, somebody decided that it all had to end and sent a line of code into the ether.

Maybe they didn't mean to kill the whole world; maybe they hadn't—as far as I knew it could be business as usual in Germany, perhaps even in Connecticut. But here, no planes flew overhead. No cars drove by, no telephones rang, no street lights clicked on as dusk fell. Tyrone and I were entirely alone, save for the smoke in the distance and the gunshots that had answered mine. Lately, there'd been no evidence at all, of even distant human life.

The murmurations were ever-present, though. They were my background music, something I learned to tune in or out as I wanted, always there, always, I was more and more convinced, communicating *something*. I grew more adept at isolating tones—sometimes sorrowful, sometimes simply neutral. They never sounded happy, and I thought there had been times in my life when they had: When I was still a child and made a friend at school, or when I met Gina, or during my early days with Roger, before things went bad. Even as recently as when I adopted Tyrone, they had sounded almost joyful at times. But now, all I got from them was sadness or ambivalence.

I tried again to correlate them with some aspect of my life: the weather, the success or failure of a tomato plant in the garden, how I felt physically, how I felt emotionally. Nothing really matched up. I watched Tyrone when they were especially strong, seeking some indication that his dog brain picked them up, but he never betrayed any sign that he was aware of more than what was in front of his nose.

Finally, as I had when I was a child, I just took comfort from them, the same way I took comfort from Tyrone. Well, not exactly the same way. Tyrone was wonderful, and there was no substitute for his warm eyes, the simple sound of his breathing, next to me in the night. He was another living being. But the murmurations made me feel connected to something larger, and sometimes, even though I wasn't lonely, I had to admit that I didn't want to feel entirely *alone*.

I made a sort of holster for the gun, out of a leather belt and some duct tape from my scavenging. I never left the house without putting it on. When I went on my occasional house hunts, I still cleared the rooms like some television cop. Anytime I started feeling stupid about it I reminded myself about the shots I'd heard in the park. I had a list of things I'd like to find: additional canned goods, more kerosene, more books. I'd never been a big sweets fan, but chocolate was high on my list. The menu during an apocalypse is not varied and every time I scored a chocolate bar, I said I silent thanks to whoever had left it behind.

For the immediate future I had all the necessities required to live, but as the weather cooled, I became more concerned with how I would heat the house without being detected. I could wrap up in in any number of blankets, but the nights were going to be freezing once winter came, and though Greg's pressed fire logs would warm the living room, they would also produce telling smoke. I finally decided that when the time came, I would burn them only once night came. The smell would still be there, but the smoke from my chimney would be hidden in the dark.

The rest of the summer was uneventful. I worked the garden, dried fruit and vegetables, read and ate and slept. Solitude was almost blissful once I got used to it, though Tyrone's warm, affectionate presence meant a lot to me. He was always by my side, ready to play with a tennis ball or sit for hours next to me on the deck of Solly and Jenna's house, while I sliced produce and loaded it onto screens. His breathing at night was a comforting sound and each morning he awaited his breakfast with a goofy, dog-faced grin. There were days when I almost forgot that the world had ended. Days when everything seemed . . . simple. Until the day that boy, so desperate he was willing to kill my dog, reminded me that as long as there were people in the world, things would never be simple.

Rashad

HE SAID HE'D been watching me for three days. He'd come down from the mountains above Billington to seek winter lodgings where the weather might be kinder, figuring he might hole up in a house somewhere in the lowlands until spring. And by chance, he'd seen me on one of my trips to the garden. He'd followed me, observing me to see if I was safe, while I brought the last of my potato harvest back to the house. Just when he'd decided he might approach me, he saw the man and his son sneaking into my back yard.

"You ought to try to eat some more." Rashad—he had introduced himself as soon as I regained consciousness—swept his wool cap off his head and ran a hand over his scalp, barely disturbing his closely-shorn hair. His skin gleamed through in some spots, as though he'd barbered himself without the aid of a mirror. He was sitting on the side of the bed, having brought me a glass of water and a pain pill from the stash in the cupboard. "I worked hard on that reconstituted whatever the hell it is." He grinned, and gestured to the plate of food he'd brought in earlier, which I had set on the night stand next to the kerosene lamp, uneaten.

I didn't smile back. I wasn't sure how long I'd been sleeping, but it had been long enough for him to get pretty familiar with the pantry. I put the water glass on the night stand next to the plate, wincing—moving much at all caused pain. I felt under the sheets; there was some sort of bandage around my abdomen.

"You're lucky. He didn't hit anything important, I don't think. And I found these." Rashad dug in a pocket of his jacket and retrieved one of my salvaged bottles of antibiotics. "I think you have a bit of a fever and that worries me. These ought to help." He eyed the label. "Looks like one pill every four hours." He handed the bottle to me and leaned down to pat Tyrone, who was sitting next to the bed. "As long as you don't get—"

"Where's my gun?" I tried for tough-sounding-bitch and to my surprise, I think I came close.

Rashad looked up, eyebrows raised. "Why thanks, Rashad," he said, in a voice an octave higher than his normal range, which was suddenly tinged with a southern accent. "No, no *really*, thank you *so* much, for taking that chance, for dragging my ass inside and locking up the house, for patching me up and hauling me to the bed and tucking me in all nice and cozy and feeding my damn *dog* on top of it all." He stared at me indignantly, clearly offended.

I stared back. Rashad was a Black man, about my age, I thought. He had smile lines at the corners of his eyes. He looked tired. And hungry—his cheekbones were a little too prominent. In some other context, I would have found him attractive, but here in my house, in the middle of the apocalypse, I found him nothing but frightening.

"Where is my gun?"

Rashad held my gaze for a moment, then shook his head and looked down at Tyrone. "It's in the kitchen on the counter," he said, quietly. He sighed. "I'm not here to hurt you. Like I said, I was looking for a place to hole up for the winter, that's all. If I wanted to hurt you, I would have already done it."

I considered that. He had a point. And maybe he was harmless. He said he'd been a Finance professor at the university in town before Hacker's Flu hit. He'd headed for the mountains—a cabin somewhere—with some friends the moment the news started "looking sketchy," as he put it. But I still didn't trust him. Nor did I want him in my house. I threw the blanket off and swung my legs off the bed. I had planned to stand up, but the twisting motion caused daggers of pain in my abdomen and I doubled over, waves of dizziness overtaking me.

The next time I awoke I was alone in the bedroom. The kerosene lamp was trimmed to a dim glow, but I could see my gun on the nightstand, next to a glass of water and a bottle of pain pills. I stretched to reach it and checked the magazine—the gun was loaded. The safety was on, but it was loaded. I listened and didn't hear anything from the other rooms in the house. There was light coming from the kitchen; a lamp must have been left lit there, as well. I whistled, but I already knew Tyrone wasn't in the house—he would have been right by my side. Immediately I felt his absence, felt how much his quiet, brown-eyed presence had come to mean in my daily life.

I sat up, slowly, testing the pain. It was still there, though less intense than before. I had to get up—get going. I felt tears welling in my eyes—Tyrone was all I had. If Rashad had taken him, I would go after him. I would find him, I would find him, I would find him. I whispered the words aloud. Once I got my legs over the side of the bed, I had to stop to catch my breath. Before I made it any further, I heard the rattle of the lock in the French doors, then the door opening, then the sound of Tyrone's nails on the floor. In seconds, he was in the bedroom, front feet on the bed, ecstatic at seeing me awake. I tried to greet him and quiet him at the same time, straining to hear what was happening in the other room. Someone closed the door, and I heard the two-by-four brace being thumped into the brackets. Heavy footsteps then, covering the few feet between the French doors to my bedroom door, and Rashad poked his head around the door frame.

"You really need to stay in bed and let that hole in your gut close." He started to help me get my legs back up on the bed, but backed off, hands up, when I looked at him. He was right—just the effort of trying to stand had made me realize how weak I felt. I inched myself back into bed, each movement more uncomfortable than the last, keeping a grip on my gun. Once I was finally settled, I signaled Tyrone, who had been attempting to jump on the bed, that he should sit. He did, immediately.

"How long have I been out?" I noticed Rashad had a rifle, slung by a strap over his back. I gripped my gun a little tighter, and clicked off the safety, though I didn't raise it. He lowered his hands a bit, gestured toward the rifle.

"I'm just gonna take this off. Okay? I took Tyrone out for his last bathroom break is why I have it on." He waited for my permission.

I nodded and he looped the strap up over his head, slowly lowering the rifle and leaning it against the wall. "You've been in and out for two days now." He shook his head. "Had me worried, but I think the fever is down a bit. How are you feeling?"

Tyrone squirmed and harrumphed up at me, impatient for some attention. I reached down to touch his head and he wagged and grinned. He looked good—healthy and as though he had been fed well over the last two days. Obviously by Rashad. "I feel okay."

"You need this?" Rashad gestured toward a shallow Tupperware container on the dresser. I stared at it, trying to figure out why I would need it. And then I saw the roll of toilet paper next to it, and realized it was a makeshift bedpan.

"*No*, I don't need that," I said, stiffly. I wanted to die of embarrassment.

"Hey, we all need to pee." You've been in no shape to make the trip to the bathroom.

There was a very awkward silence.

"Um, you hungry at all?" Rashad moved to the end of the bed and took a seat. "I took the liberty of cooking a couple of those potatoes and they are pretty darned good. I cleaned up the rest and bagged them up in some pillow cases. They need to be stored someplace cool if you want them to last through the winter. I think the cupboard under the sink will probably do—it's on the outside wall and this place isn't insulated very well, so it feels pretty cold. Anyway, want some? You've only had broth the last days."

"You talk a lot." I was a little overwhelmed by the barrage of words. It had been just me and Tyrone and the murmurations for what felt like a long time.

Rashad laughed, a huge, roaring laugh that came from somewhere south of his chest. "Sorry." He looked sheepish. "It's been a while since I've been in talking distance of someone—at least someone who isn't trying to shoot me." Then he looked pointedly at my gun. "You willing to call it a truce? I won't shoot you, you don't shoot me?"

I shrugged. But I didn't let go of the gun. He raised his eyebrows, but stood and headed for the kitchen. "Dinner coming up," he said, over his shoulder.

When he was out of the room, I patted the bed and Tyrone jumped up next to me, carefully, as though he knew it would hurt me if he jostled me. He arranged himself alongside me and laid his head on my thigh. Then he heaved a deep sigh and closed his eyes. I couldn't help smiling; I was so happy to see him alive and well. I could hear Rashad making cooking noises in the kitchen—he must have acquainted himself with the cook stove. I didn't like the idea of him rummaging around in my house, but at that moment I was too tired to care.

I'd fallen asleep again by the time he came back with the potatoes, but Tyrone's tail wagging against my arm woke me. He seemed happy to see Rashad, which I took as a good sign.

"Here we go." Rashad cleared some space on the nightstand to set a plate of food. Then he added a pillow to the one already behind me so I could sit up comfortably, and handed me the plate. "My special recipe for spuds with no butter." A fleeting, mournful expression clouded his features. "Damn, I miss butter." He sat on the foot of the bed, watching me expectantly. After a minute or so of watching me hold my fork without taking a bite, he cleared his throat. "Well?"

"Are you . . . going to watch me eat?" I had expected him to leave the room after he brought the food.

He forced a puff of air out of his nostrils—that sound people make when they're exasperated. "Yeah. Well. We need to talk and now is as good a time as any. Winter's coming, and if I'm staying here, there are things to be worked out about this house. The fireplace, for example—"

"Staying here? You're not staying here." I lowered the plate to my lap and surreptitiously edged my free hand closer to the gun—I'd laid it next to me when I took the plate from Rashad. He saw my move and shook his head as though I was an errant toddler.

"Really?" Rashad scowled. "You're gonna be like that? I mean, I know you don't know me, but clearly, again, if I meant you harm I've had ample opportunity to *do* you harm." He leaned back against the footboard of the bed, assuming a nonchalant expression. "I mean, I can go somewhere else. I can go hole up in one of the other houses." He studied the bedroom wall as though the pattern of the texture applied to it was fascinating.

"That would be perfect." I watched him, waiting. He was a big man— over six feet tall. I wouldn't be able to do anything but shoot him if he went for me. We stayed like that for what seemed like a long time. Finally, Rashad looked at me. The lamplight accentuated the weariness on his face.

"Look, I'm going to be real, here. I mean, I *could* go hole up in some other house, but that would mean figuring out a whole new game before winter really hits, and it looks to me like you're ahead of things by a stretch." He pointed toward the kitchen. "You have some sort of food supply—I know I'm another mouth to feed, but I can pull my weight in other ways. You've also got a good start on fortifying this place to keep it safe." He took a breath. "I don't know how much you've been out and about." He waited for my answer.

"I've stuck close to here." I couldn't see where admitting that would hurt me.

Rashad nodded. "Then you don't really know." He thought a moment and added a correction. "You don't know the whole thing, anyway. I mean, you must know that most people are dead. Right? And the ones who are left, at least around here, are mostly just like that guy who was ready to kill you for some canine flank steak." He lowered his head and rubbed his eyes, and when he spoke again his voice was low, as weary as the rest of him. "I just don't think I have it left in me to start over. Not before winter hits." He looked back up at me. There was no plea in his eyes, not exactly. But there was something close. "You seem like a decent person. And those are few and far between, now. It's like, the world, what's left of it, has turned savage. People out there will as soon shoot you as look at you, now." He held my gaze and it felt like he was looking for something—something specific I couldn't name. "I'm tired, I'm just damned tired. And I wouldn't mind spending the winter in the company of another decent person."

Tyrone made the decision, really. At that moment, he stretched and turned around on the bed to face Rashad. Then he raised a paw, awaiting a high five. Rashad grinned and gave him one. As I watched that simple interaction, I thought again of the people I'd encountered since the flu took over. Of Mark, and his wife, and the men who broke into Greg's. Rashad was like a Disney character compared to them. At least so far. Despite my misgivings, I couldn't bring myself to turn the man away. I owed him.

In the back of my mind was another thought: I might not have a choice. Just because he was asking me permission to stay didn't mean he'd take no for an answer. I was in no shape presently to defend myself against him if he decided to get ugly.

"There's an air mattress in the other room. It's still in the package." I picked up my plate of potatoes, suddenly hungry. "You can set it up in there."

"Fabulous." Rashad stood and head toward the door, but he turned back. "Listen, are you Gwen, or Sandra or Jean?"

"What?" I wondered if he was a little off.

"Well, those pill bottles all have different names. I've been trying to guess which one belongs to you."

For some reason I didn't want to give him that—my name. But I did. "I'm Julie."

"Well, Julie." Rashad did a mock bow. "It's a pleasure to meet you." Then he headed for the office to find the air mattress.

— ～

It took me another week to really recover, mostly because of the infection I'd suffered. Rashad had cleaned the wound well, but it still became inflamed. He pushed antibiotics at me with the fervor of an alarmed grandmother, and as the days passed the angry redness faded from the puncture and my temperature dropped back to normal. I started getting out of bed every day, just to walk around the house a bit and build up my strength. I even took over Tyrone's bathroom breaks. Rashad fussed about it but I shut him down.

"He's *my* dog."

Rashad gave me a look when I said it like I was the coldest thing he'd

ever encountered. And he was right, in a way. I should have been thanking him for saving my life, and for feeding Tyrone while I was ill, and
for not raping and killing me, but instead I was still focused on keeping
my boundaries. On letting him know he was no more than a temporary
housemate, and one I didn't want, at that.

It wasn't really about a housemate, though. It was about people.
Hacker's Flu had solved all my problems with people because it removed
them from my daily life. I didn't have to struggle with the idea that I *should*
have more friends, or I *should* try for another relationship, or I *should* work
on the damage my childhood had wrought, because I had no options. I
didn't have to grapple with whether or not to trust people. There were no
people, or at least, the ones that did exist were *clearly* to be avoided. There
was just Tyrone, and I knew I could trust him implicitly. Somehow, over
the summer, I'd become comfortable with my solitude. It was so black and
white; a respite from all those grays that had made up every day before.
Rashad was ruining it for me.

He did cook well, at least better than I could. And he had all kinds
of ideas about the house—good ideas. One morning I found him in the
middle of the living room, holding a lamp low to the floor. The look on
his face made me wonder if he'd found something dead.

"What is it?" I peered at the circle of floor lit by the lamp.

"We should rip this carpet up." He leaned down, brushing at the low
pile shag. When he straightened, he held out a handful of Tyrone hair,
along with some string and lint. "There's no way to keep this clean anymore. If we rip it up we can at least sweep the subfloor." He scowled at the
wad of hair in his hand. "I mean, this is just gross."

"I haven't had much time for housework." I was slightly insulted. I
tried to keep the place decent, but he was right—there was no way to clean
the carpet anymore. Over the summer dirt and dog hair and all kinds
of flotsam had found its way into the corners, and there were darkened
trails where I walked the most. We spent two days ripping up the carpet
and padding and hauling it away, and I had to admit it felt much nicer
afterwards.

Rashad just shook his head and made tsk noises when I showed him my toilet flushing routine. "That's not going to last forever, you know. I mean, yes, for urine, but we can't be doing our . . . number twos that way. That shit will back right up in the house before too long."

I just stared at him.

"What, a little extra work scares you? I mean, we just find a bucket with a lid that seals well for in here. Then we haul the stuff outside." He shrugged. "I'm not trying to offend you—"

"No, it's not that." I had to grin. "It's that a grown man just used the term 'number two' right before he said the word 'shit.'"

Rashad stared back at me for the longest time. "You know what's even more astounding then that? It's that I *think* you just made a joke. I mean, ice-queen-has-a-sense-of-humor-who-woulda-thunk-it?" He swiveled and exited the bathroom, humming some tune under his breath.

Once I felt strong, I showed him the garage. I'd thought long and hard about it but there wasn't really a way to hide it from him; I'd have to get more supplies eventually and he'd find out about it then. I made a point of strapping on my holster and tucking the gun into it before we left, just in case he decided to kill me once he saw the stores. Rashad kept watch while I unlocked the door and after I pushed it open, I gestured for him to enter first. I fired up two of the flashlights I left on the workbench for my supply trips and handed him one. His eyes widened in awe when he saw the garage.

"Good *lord*." Rashad shone his flashlight over the stacks of supplies, pausing on labels, skipping around, trying to take it all in. He smiled, a huge smile that lit his face, but then it crumpled up before my eyes into something else, and before I knew it he was doubled over, one hand covering his mouth. He dropped his flashlight and started making retching noises.

"Rashad!" I knelt next to him, trying to support him, wondering what was happening. "Are you sick? What—"

It was then I saw the tears. He wasn't retching—he wasn't sick. He was sobbing, deep, wracking cries shaking his frame. I didn't know what to do, so I simply stayed there, next to him. He struggled to bring himself under control, swiping angrily at his cheeks, avoiding my gaze. He took a shuddering breath, then another. Finally, he picked up his flashlight and stood.

"Sorry." Rashad looked at me, eyes red, pain still twisting his features. "Well. What should we be hauling back to the house?"

"Do you want to . . . talk—"

"I don't want to talk about it." He walked toward the end of the work-bench and then back my way, noticing the laptop as he came. "Who was your neighbor?" Rashad flipped open the laptop, punched the unrespon-sive keyboard, flipped it closed again. "Prepper, huh?"

"I guess." I wondered what had caused him to break down. Nothing in his manner thus far had prepared me for it.

"So. How far do you think this will take you?" Rashad waved a hand at the stacks of supplies.

"At least a year." I hesitated. "Less, for two people, I think. I was only counting for one."

Rashad didn't look at me, but walked slowly down to the end of the ga-rage again, stopping in front of the wheelbarrow. He grabbed the handles and swiveled it around, rolling it to a stop in front of me. "I say the fewer trips the better, for now. And the more of this we get in the house, the less might be stolen. Let's load up and get back."

Brutal Truths

WE HAULED AN assortment of things back to the house: more rice, some water, a covered bucket Rashad said would do for latrine duty. He was happy to see the pressed logs—the temperatures at night were dropping quickly—and agreed we could burn them only after dark to hide the smoke. I dug around in the **TRADE** box and found the chocolate—I'd eaten all I'd found scavenging—offering it up in hopes it might break the strained demeanor he'd taken on since he broke down crying, but he barely nodded at the sight. Once we locked the wheelbarrow back in the garage and Tyrone had his run in the yard, we barricaded ourselves inside the house and Rashad began dinner.

"More potatoes, huh?" I watched him slice them into a pot he'd filled with water.

"More cigarettes, huh?" Rashad curled his lip as I lit one. The first time he'd seen me smoke he was horrified. I just laughed and said I wasn't too worried about my health, given the circumstances.

"No, man," he'd said. "I mean, in the house? Who smokes in the *house*?"

I had reminded him at the time that it was *my* house, and that smoking outside seemed like more of a health hazard these days than the risk of cancer. Since then he'd given me a hard time about it every time I lit up. And I ignored him.

We ate together, as we'd gotten in the habit of doing. Before Rashad showed up, I ate on the sofa in the living room most of the time, or simply stood over the sink in the kitchen with an open can of tuna or beans.

But he'd decided we should set the small kitchen table, and eat 'like civilized folk.' Our conversation usually felt awkward to me; it was like having dinner with some distant relative in town for just one night, exchanging comments about how cold it was getting, or how silly Tyrone was being, or whether the potatoes would keep over winter. I'd grown accustomed to solitude and sometimes the sound of another human voice felt like an overwhelming intrusion, but I did my best to hide it. There were moments when it was too much for me, moments when I withdrew into my own world, tuning out his voice and tuning into the murmurations, just for a little respite. I didn't think he could tell.

But he *could* tell. And on this night, Rashad stopped eating halfway through his plate of potatoes and rice and set his fork down. I hadn't been listening to his words for a few minutes, but this caught my attention. Rashad liked his food. I looked up at him, quickly shutting out the tones I'd been focused on. He was looking right back at me, with a puzzled expression.

"Julie. What *is* that?"

"What?"

Rashad gave me a look. "I've been talking for five minutes and you've been off somewhere . . . where?" He leaned back. "You do that a lot, like you're on some other planet. What's going on in your head right now? Are you even listening to me?"

I'd been listening, but not to him. I'd been listening to the murmurations. They'd been in my head all day, as usual, but they'd been surging to the forefront of my awareness more then they'd had all summer. I hadn't realized I got so lost in them—I'd have to be more careful. "Sorry. I guess I was just thinking."

"Yeah. Well." He looked skeptical, but he let it go, and changed the subject. "You've never asked me about . . . before I showed up here. I mean, I told you the basics, but . . ."

"I figured you'd tell me what you wanted me to know."

Rashad picked up his fork and pushed at his food, but he didn't take a bite. "Yeah. I kind of figured the same thing with you. But I guess I might be waiting a while for that."

I refused to take the bait. "Not much to tell, on my end." I didn't need to fill Rashad in on my life before. Our agreement was that he would stay the winter, no more. I didn't see why he would need to know anything more than he did about me. And frankly, I didn't really want to know about him, but I had a feeling I was about to anyway.

Rashad put his fork down again and crossed his arms. "Like I told you, when the flu hit, some friends and I headed for the mountains. One of my colleagues at the university had a cabin; he said it might be a good place to hole up, so the four of us—him and his partner, me and mine—headed there. His name was Joel, and his wife's name was Sherry. So, it was them, and me and Anthony." He paused, assessing my reaction. "That going to be a problem?"

At first I didn't know what he meant, but then I did. "You being gay?"

"Yes."

"Actually, that sort of *solves* a problem for me." I'd slept with my gun in my hand since Rashad arrived. I knew I still would, especially now that he knew about the supplies, but at least sexual assault was probably out of the picture.

Rashad smiled. "You are a lovely lady, Julie, but not my type. No worries about me hitting on you."

"Maybe I'll put the safety on the gun at night now," I joked.

His smile faded. "Oh. You thought I would *rape* you?" Rashad recrossed his arms and leaned even further back, away from the table. "And now you know I'm gay, you think that means you're safe." He shook his head, frowning at me. "If I was the type of man who would rape a person, it wouldn't matter if you were my flavor. We don't live in that world anymore." He narrowed his eyes, contemplating something I couldn't see. "Maybe we never did."

"Sorry." Rashad was right, of course. I thought about my neighbor Greg, and Brad, the guy at Pet Mart, hell, even my old boss, Pete. They were all men, just like Roger had been, just like Mark with his gun, but they wouldn't have hit me or raped me, before, and I didn't think they would now, if I met them again. They had all, in their ways, tried to help me. "It's not you—it's just me. I don't trust easy."

Rashad snorted. "No kidding." He continued his story. "We had some supplies, but we'd figured we'd just be up there a few days, avoiding the worst of it. When we left, we didn't even know it was fatal—just that it was incredibly contagious and that the news reports were getting scary. On the ride up we even had a good time, sort of treated it like an impromptu vacation. We had the tunes going in the jeep and everybody but Joel—he was driving—was drinking beer. So we get to the cabin, we build a fire in the fireplace and we settle in to listen to the radio Joel had—one of those crank-type things that works without electricity. And the first night passes, and the second, and the news gets grim and then it just stops." He stares at me, astonished at the memory. "It just *stopped*."

"Here, too." I remember how it felt to see the blank screen on the television; to press the call button on the telephone and hear nothing at all.

"After a couple of days of that we realized it wasn't a short-term scare. Joel wanted to go back down the mountain, check it out, but Sherry wasn't having it. They argued for a couple of days, but finally Joel won. He pointed out that we only had enough food to last the four of us another day or so, and that if things were as bad as they had sounded before the news stopped, we'd need to get some more supplies up to the cabin anyway." Rashad studied the lamp flame, watching it flicker, but I could see he was remembering his friends.

"You and Anthony stayed behind?"

"Yeah. Anthony didn't want to go back down to Billington until we knew more and I couldn't blame him." A trace of a smile flickered on Rashad's face. "We'd been together four years by then." He looked up at me. "You from here? Billington?"

I shook my head. "Just moved here recently, before it happened." I didn't add any details.

Rashad's smile got bigger. "Don't worry; I won't ask." He returned his gaze to the lamp. "I'm not from here either. Just came for the teaching gig—tenure-track *and* in a semi-liberal town. I met Anthony my first weekend. I was walking downtown, just trying to get my bearings, and I wandered into a wine shop. He was the shop sommelier. And he was fine." Rashad grinned again. "The kind of fine you think *nah, that's not for me. That's for somebody else.* But Anthony walked right up and started talking, and I could tell he wasn't really talking about wine. We were together from that day on."

I was almost afraid to ask the obvious question. "Where is Anthony now? Is he—"

"As far as I know he's alive." Rashad didn't look at me. "Joel and Sherry didn't come back. We gave up hoping on them after about a week—I don't know if they got sick, or if they got in a wreck on the way down the mountain, or if somebody wanted their jeep. By then we were in deep shit at the cabin; we'd only packed enough food to last the four of us for a few days, and even though Anthony and I rationed it, we ran out fast. We had water—plenty of snow to melt. But the food was gone."

Rashad paused. His expression cycled through several emotions, so quickly I couldn't track them enough to discern whether he was sad or angry or a bit of both. With some effort he composed himself, arranging his features into a blank façade that betrayed nothing.

"They showed up when we'd been out of food for almost a week. One of them knocked on the cabin door, didn't let on about the others until he checked us out. Once he knew we were unarmed, his buddies showed up. Four of them. They were well ahead of us in terms of what was happening, in terms of what it meant." He sighed. "Ahead of me in ways I hope I'll never catch up on.

"One of them put a rifle on Anthony and me and the others rummaged through the cabin looking for food. When it became clear we had none, I thought they were just going to leave. But they had other ideas."

"What about your rifle?" I wondered if he'd been too afraid, or just too surprised, to use it.

He chuckled. "I found that old thing on the way down the mountain. It's loaded, but I'm not exactly sure how to shoot it. But I *wish* I'd had it then."

"These guys were hunters—that's why they were up there in the first place. But they were hunting out of season—poachers. They were good old boys—the kind that live out in the county, the kind I left Alabama to avoid. They informed us that they were going to be taking over the cabin.

The leader said we could stay if we joined them, but one of the others said something in his ear that changed that."

Rashad was silent for a long time. When he spoke again it was in a whisper—a hoarse, rasping whisper filled with pain. "*Faggot.* That's what he said. He pointed at Anthony and said *faggot.* And the leader—I still don't know his name—he looked at us and asked, almost politely, if we were faggots. *Because we can't have none of that,* he said."

"And Anthony—" Rashad's voice broke. He swallowed and continued. "Anthony, the love of my life—Anthony looked him straight in the eye and said, *if I was it wouldn't be with some coon.*" Rashad looked at me, a hard look, tears shining in his eyes. "He didn't skip a beat." He shook his head, as if he could shake off his feelings.

The lamp sputtered and I adjusted the wick. The kitchen seemed very small, just then, very small and unable to contain the kind of awful truths it was filled with at that moment. I felt Rashad's anger, his disappointment, his loss. I'd experienced that same loss—the loss of belief in my fellow humans. I felt close to him then, closer than I'd felt to a human being, besides Gina, in a long time.

"They all laughed, looked at me like I should be joining in, but I just said I didn't think having rifles pointed in my face was so funny. They backed things down a bit, the whole bunch acting like I was just being a poor sport. The leader said they'd rest up for the night, said they'd be heading out to hunt in the morning and we could *decide things then.*

"I thought Anthony must be just trying to throw them off until we could get out of there. So I waited, I waited until it was dark and they all seemed asleep, and then I signaled him to follow me to the kitchen. I said we had to go right then, that we'd leave any gear we had behind and just slip out—hike all night to put some distance between us and them.

I watched his eyes, and they told the tale. "He didn't go with you."

Rashad lowered his head. He said nothing.

"I'm so sorry, Rashad." Stupid words, but all I had to offer him.

"He was hungry. He was afraid we would never make it without help. And he chose them. I mean, I guess I knew. I guess I always knew, somewhere in me, about Anthony. He was never brave. He was joyful and fun and so, so beautiful that I just wanted him to love me, and I couldn't be-lieve it when he did. So I brushed it off when he would avoid a confronta-tion, or side-step a hard question, or laugh at a gay joke if he was in a crowd who didn't know about us. I wanted him to be all the things he *should* be. The things a human being *can* be. But he was only the things that were easy. That's all he could do."

I stood, and went to the cupboard. I had a special bottle of red that I'd been hoarding—the last decent vintage left from before Hacker's Flu hit. I'd wanted to drink it many times since then, but I hadn't. I'd been afraid to—afraid it might weaken my tenuous resolve to keep breathing. Tonight seemed like a good time to share a drink with . . . a friend? I wasn't ready to go that far, but I poured us each a glass and brought them to the table. Rashad raised his in a toast.

"To having a fucking spine," he said.

I knew exactly what he meant.

⌐ ⌐

We drank the whole bottle that night. Rashad told me about his sum-mer in the mountains, after he left the cabin. He walked all night away from the cabin, stumbling in the dark, not knowing where he was go-ing or if the hunters would set out after him when they discovered he had gone. He was weak from hunger, and had left without anything but his jacket.

"I would be dead now if I hadn't run into some luck." Rashad held his glass out for more wine. "Kind of like you. Not that my little shack was anything like the garage—it was just a hunter's shanty, barely four walls and roof. But it was shelter, and it was so long-abandoned it had been almost hidden by the forest. Best part—I found a couple cases of canned beans and a six pack of beer. And my fancy survival-tool keychain com-plete with can-opener finally came in handy."

He survived the summer on beans and berries and fish. There was a lake up there, and he managed to rig up a fish trap that worked half the time. He hid his tracks and kept an eye out for the hunters, but he never saw them—he figured he'd gotten at least five miles from them before he found the shack.

"Did you see anyone at all?"

"I saw dead people." Rashad swirled his wine. "Nobody was left to clean up the bodies in the mountains. And plenty of people had the idea to wait out the crisis up there. Joel's cabin was remote, all the way up at the top of the mountain. But further down, there were park cabins, and I saw bodies in those. That was later in the summer, when I finally made my way down that far. Since I'm still alive, I figure the virus doesn't last very long, in terms of contagion—that was at least a month later." He gestured toward the French doors. "Out there—are there bodies in those marked houses?"

I shrugged. "I don't know. I don't go in those." I thought about the smell I'd noticed over the summer. "I'm pretty sure there *are* bodies in them."

"I did see one living person." Rashad frowned and took a drink. "I was almost down the mountain—headed this way to look for a winter shelter. He was on his way down, too, but he hadn't had the good fortune to find a case of beans. He was filthy, practically starving to death. We met on a deer trail, and I don't think either of us had the energy to be scared. He just held up his hands like I was the cops, and I did the same."

For a minute I was afraid. Was this man somewhere outside? Had Rashad tricked me—were they going to take my house from me and . . . I knew it made no sense. Like he'd said, if he wanted to kill me he could have when I was hurt. But what if he didn't want to kill me? What if—

"I can see your mind racing from here, Julie." Rashad was shaking his head at me and he was smiling but there was something irritated about the smile. He heaved a sigh. "He's dead. At least I think he is. He didn't want to keep living."

That made me feel bad. Bad about what he'd just said, and bad for doubting him, too. "Tell me."

Rashad nodded. His smile had disappeared. "His name was Pradip Patel. He and his family—a wife, their six-year-old boy—had headed for the mountains, hoping to avoid the flu. They had an RV, had some supplies. He said they drove as far up the mountain as they could and then turned off on a logging road. It was pretty muddy from the spring rains and they got stuck, but Pradip figured it would be fine. He said they were pretty far off the main road and someone would have had to really look to see the RV. Once things dried up a bit, he planned to get the RV back out on the main road and head back down to town. He thought the worst of the flu would be over by then and things would be back to normal.

"And it *was* fine, at least for the first couple of weeks. By then it had already been dry enough for a few days to get the RV out, but Pradip said the last radio broadcast they'd heard had been pretty bad. His wife was too scared to go back right then. And they had enough food to last a month he said—he was a mini-prepper from what he told me. Nothing fancy, just a lot of canned goods and water, but it got them through.

"He said a gang snuck up and surrounded the RV at night. He wasn't sure how many, maybe four, maybe five guys. They beat the shit out of him, knocked him out, and when he woke it was daylight and they were gone. So were his wife and son. He said he looked for weeks. He saw some signs of people, but he never saw *them*. By the time I met him he'd given up hope. He was walking down the mountain to his house, on the off chance he'd find his family there. He said if he didn't, he would end it.

"I didn't have any more beans by then, but I had some fish and I tried to feed him up that night. I thought maybe with a full stomach he might feel different in the morning. But in the morning, he was gone." Rashad's voice had gotten quiet. "I'm pretty sure he's dead."

We sat in silence for some time, nursing the last of our wine. I thought about how small the world was now—how few of us might be left. "Rashad."

He looked up from his glass. "What?"

"Do you think it was the same men? Do you think the hunters from your friend's cabin were the ones who took Pradip's family?"

Rashad nodded. "Yep." He stood up and took his glass to the sink— we still washed things there even though the faucet no longer worked. "I think it was them. There weren't that many people wandering around that mountain after the flu got done with them. What I wonder is if Anthony was a part of that."

The lamplight barely reached across the room to light the hollows of his face. He looked so sad just then—sad and a little lost.

"I'm going to bed. I'll see you in the morning." He started out of the kitchen, but then he stopped and looked over his shoulder at me. "Julie."

"Yes?"

"We're going to have to do some damn trust falls or something. Where you went in your mind when you thought I might have someone out there waiting to ambush you—that's not cool. You know that?" He sounded angry, but I thought he was hurt, more than anything.

I was shocked at how accurately he'd read my expression. All I could do was nod. "I'm working on it."

I had trouble falling asleep that night. The murmurations would not fade; I couldn't regulate them the way I'd been able to lately, just listening when I felt like it and relegating them to the back of my mind when I didn't. They were strong, and insistent. And, oddly, they sounded happy.

Winter

THE FIRST SNOW took us both by surprise. I didn't think it could be later than early October—I had no way to actually know, but Rashad agreed with my estimate. So even with the strange weather patterns of the last few years, it was early to wake to the muffled stillness snowfall creates. The house was frigid, but we didn't dare risk a fire during the day.

"Damn, I wish we'd hauled water from the garage yesterday, instead of having to do it today." Rashad was peering through the plywood peephole in the French doors.

"Why?" The question wasn't even out of my mouth before I realized. "Tracks."

"Yep. If we go traipsing over there now, we'll leave plenty of footprints for anyone to see." Rashad slid the peephole cover down and turned to face me. "How much do we have here, do you think?"

I opened the cupboard where we stored the water jugs. "Enough for a few days, if we don't bathe and don't boil potatoes." I grinned at that thought. "Hopefully it melts and we can stock up."

Rashad ignored my jab about the potatoes. "He'll still have to go out." He contemplated Tyrone, who was wagging his tail and gazing up at Rashad, waiting to be let out into the yard. "We'll just have to hope nobody takes a look over the fence."

"I'll get the bucket." I started for the bathroom to retrieve the latrine bucket. It had become habit to empty it in the hole we'd dug at the far corner of the yard while Tyrone had his first trip out each morning.

"Nah." Rashad was the one grinning now. "If you don't want potatoes how about you figure out breakfast? I'll take him out." He got the latrine bucket and checked through the peephole once more before he took down the bar across the doors. "I would love some French toast," he said, just before he closed the door. "With loads of butter and maple syrup, please."

We did that sometimes now. We could spend twenty minutes doing nothing but listing types of food we'd probably never enjoy again. For me it was sushi, waffles, crème brulee; for Rashad it was steak and ribs and hamburgers.

"A triple bacon cheese, with all the trimmings," he would say. "Nothing better than that and an ice-cold beer."

I told him we were indulging in predictable B-movie behavior when we did this. He retorted that it was in the movies because art imitated life. "Besides, sometimes I can almost taste that burger when I name it out loud."

The snow did melt, after two days. We immediately made several trips to Greg's, hauling over all the water we could store and a dozen bundles of pressed logs. We decided to make certain we always had at least three weeks of supplies in the house from then on. There was bound to be more snow.

I was surprised how easy it was to have Rashad in the house. He seemed to know I needed a lot of space and would disappear into the office—which now served as a storeroom/bedroom—for hours at a time, reading one of the books I'd scavenged. He was kind of a neat-freak, too, which was a bonus. Even without modern amenities like vacuum cleaners, the house stayed spotless. And he did most of the cooking, which meant I ate better—I had fallen into grazing the garden produce or simply opening a can of something during my summer alone. Rashad said we had to try, at least, to eat like civilized people. And as he pointed out, good nutrition was more important now than ever. We wouldn't be able to keep going if we got sick, and there were no doctors anymore. At least not in Billington.

Most of the time I had tried very hard not to think about things like that during the summer. I'd been too busy surviving to have much time to worry about it, but one thing I had obsessed about was my teeth. I brushed them four times a day, doling out a miserly bit of toothpaste, carefully cleaning every surface, flossing every night until I ran out of floss. Rashad had been thrilled at my Dollarama toothbrushes, but he rolled his eyes at my preoccupation with dental hygiene. I didn't care. I couldn't imagine having a cavity now. The idea of the unrelenting pain of a toothache, or worse, of having to figure out how to pull one of my own teeth, terrified me.

The two of us went on a few house-scavenging trips that winter between snowfalls, but we didn't push it. We had everything we really needed to survive and chancing an encounter with others seemed fool-hardy. During one of our excursions, Rashad spotted a chicken, pecking at the grass outside a house. Before I knew what he was doing he'd run over, caught the poor thing and snapped its neck. I stood watching in horror as he brought it back to me, beaming with pride.

"Fried chicken to*night*!" Rashad held the limp body out to me like a bouquet of flowers.

"You . . . you killed it." I shrunk away from him.

"I killed it quick." He looked crestfallen. "It didn't suffer. I mean . . ." He stood in front of me, the chicken carcass dangling from his hand. "Look." I know you don't eat meat, but I *do*. And that's okay, that's my choice, right? And this chicken helps extend the food supplies."

I considered the bird, who's eyes were already glazing over. It hadn't suffered, that was true, and Rashad had a point about the food supplies. But I hated the whole idea. I didn't really think it was okay—his choice to eat meat. "It's a living being, Rashad. Or it was."

Rashad just narrowed his eyes at me. "Julie. What do you think that dried salmon you eat out of those survival rations from your friend Greg was? A *living being*, Julie, that's what. That salmon had *relationships*, Julie. That salmon had a potential lifespan of twelve point five years if it had been left to live, free and wild." His voice kept getting louder and louder and he was starting to wave the chicken body around, punctuating his argument. "That fish wanted a life, too. But you *ate* it. So don't stand there judging me. Don't stand there and tell me that you're better than me just because I want some damned fried chicken." He glared at me, out of breath.

For some reason, when Rashad got loud it didn't scare me. I never thought he might go further, never worried that he might try to hurt me. I'd gotten to know him a bit and I could tell that he was . . . good. I almost laughed at his tirade. "Relationships? Really Rashad?"

"Well, okay, maybe not *relationships*, at least not the way we think about them. Maybe I was making that part up. But they *are* still living beings. And you may not kill them yourself, but you're supporting killing them if you eat them."

The thing was, he had a point. I hated it, but he did. "Okay." I turned and started heading home.

"Okay?" Rashad rushed to catch up to me and Tyrone. After a few steps he made a production of clearing his throat. Then he spoke again. "So, Julie."

I didn't look at him—I just kept walking. I didn't really want to see the chicken. "Yes?"

"The feathers have to come off before I can cook this bird."

"So?"

"Um." Rashad stopped walking.

Grudgingly, I stopped too. Rashad looked at the ground, kicking at a tuft of grass with the toe of his shoe like some teenager. "I have a . . . a thing, about that." He finally looked up at me, embarrassed. "My grandmother always did that part, back home."

I folded my arms in front to of me. "Do I look like your grandmother?"

~ ~

Rashad won that one, though. He scalded the carcass, which stunk up the entire house, but I plucked the damn thing. I understood about having *things* about things. I couldn't take baths, for example, no matter how nice the idea of soaking in a warm bubbly tub sounded. For me, that *thing* was fraught with memories—flashbacks, really, of my childhood. Of my father coming to "check" on me at bath time, and shutting the bathroom door, and picking a bar of soap to use in places it shouldn't be used on anyone, let alone a six-year-old. Not nice memories. So I'd always been a showers-only kind of person.

I didn't probe about why Rashad couldn't bring himself to pluck the chicken. It didn't matter. I could, and I would do it for him. And the look on his face when he took the first bite was priceless. He caught one more chicken that winter, but I forced him to scald it out in the back yard, in a pot we rigged up over a temporary fire. The smoke was a risk, but I couldn't stand the thought of that smell permeating the house for days.

We saw smoke columns that winter three times. All three were east, up in the foothills. There were some houses up there, hidden in the trees, and judging by the size of the size of the first smoke column, one of them burned to the ground. The other two sightings were small enough that they might have been from campfires, or from chimneys. We kept to our plan of heating at night, so the smoke from our chimney didn't draw attention. The glass doors on the fireplace kept the risk of burning the house down to a minimum, but when we closed them before we went to sleep it also cut most of the heat from the pressed logs off, so the house was cold all the time. Rashad and I stuffed the heat registers with paper and plastic bags, and sealed them with some heavy plastic and duct tape, to try to keep the cold air out. We dressed in layers and sometimes wore our coats inside. Between snow storms, we hauled supplies from Greg's, but other than those trips we stayed inside as much as we could. I began to understand what cabin fever meant. The days were long and cold and boring.

One evening after we'd had our dinner and cleaned up, Rashad carried several of the books I'd scavenged to the living room where I was poking at the dying fire to try to get the last flames out of it. Tyrone rolled over and presented his belly to Rashad, who obliged him with tummy rubs. After Tyrone seemed satisfied, Rashad gave him one last pat and sat on one end of the sofa. He spread the books on the cushion. "Let's have our own little book club. We can read to each other every night and have a discussion."

"Have a discussion?" I glanced at the books he had selected. "About home canning?"

Rashad grinned. "Nah—that one just looked like something I might read on my own. But we have a lovely selection here of—" he picked up a book and glanced at the cover. "Well, this one looks like a thrilling romance, about a young Irish girl at the mercy of—" he grimaced and put the book down, scanning the others. One, a slim blue book, caught his interest. "Thinking Through Death." Rashad looked at me, raising his eyebrows, and flipped the book open. After reading for a moment, he quoted from the book. "*A philosophical anthology on death.* Now that sounds interesting."

"I mean, I guess. If you want to be depressed." I'd already read the book twice. It *was* interesting. But I wasn't so sure about this book club idea. We already spent our days together hauling supplies, foraging, improving the house. We ate together. But in the evenings, we retreated to our separate bedrooms as soon as our allotted fire log died. All that togetherness took a lot out of me. It made the time alone—restoration time—precious to me.

Rashad would not take no for an answer. "It's perfect!" He read from the first section. "We've got your ancient Greeks and then your ancient Oriental—wait a minute. Do we say *Oriental* anymore? I don't think so." He continued reading from the book. "And then we wrap up with Stoics and Epicureans and stuff. And then in volume two . . ." he consulted the cover "Damn. Unless you have volume two we're missing out on all the modern guys."

"No volume two."

Rashad looked disappointed. "Oh, well. Still works. We can read a topic each night and then we'll discuss."

I was unaccustomed to having someone around to discuss ideas with; Roger had been sweet at the start of our marriage, but he was never a conversationalist. I'd only had real talks with Gina. The thought of her made me remember everything that was gone now. My only friend, ever, really. We'd talked about all sorts of things. I missed her. But talking about ideas with Rashad would mean either treading that exhausting, surface-level-only line, or actually revealing my thoughts and feelings, at least to some extent.

Rashad must have surmised by my expression that I was dubious. "Come on, Julie." He closed the book. "What do *you* think happens when we die?"

That was easy. "I think our bodies rot and that's that."

"No soul? No reincarnation or heaven or hell or whatever?"

"Nope."

Rashad waited a couple of beats. "And what do *you* think, Rashad? Do you have any opinion on what happens when we die?" He smiled at me, trying for beguiling, almost succeeding. "Come *on*, Julie. I'm about to go crazy from boredom. Let's do book club." He watched my face, hoping, I guess, for some sign of enthusiasm. Then he started chanting like a three-year-old asking for candy. "Let's do book club, let's do book club, let's do—"

"All right, all right, all *right*." I shook my head at him. "And what, Rashad, do you think happens when we die?"

Rashad tilted his head and pursed his lips. "Hmm. I don't . . . I don't know. But I think maybe what matters more is what happens while we're alive."

Friendship

RASHAD AND I talked a *lot*. We started with the death book. We took turns reading aloud to each other and after each section on death we talked about what we thought. We never did come up with a final decision on who was right and who was wrong on death, but we had some enjoyable arguments. Then we moved on to a dystopian novel, and as the winter passed, we began to talk more about ourselves. It wasn't as bad as I'd anticipated.

He was originally from Alabama, some little town where racism was still the order of the day in overt, every-day ways, not hidden in subtlety like it was in bigger cities.

"It was just a known factor that you stepped out of line for the white man, there. *You* moved out of the way on the sidewalk, not them." Rashad frowned, remembering.

Without thinking, I said "I know. I've heard it's really bad still in some place down south."

"Oh, you *know*, do you?" Rashad's southern accent flared, like it did whenever he was excited or agitated or mad. He leaned back against the sofa, something like a sneer twisting his lips. "You've *heard*. What do *you* know?"

I held my hands up next to my ears, signing acquiescence. "Nothing, I guess. All I meant was that—"

Rashad shook his head, almost laughing but not quite. He sighed. "Never mind. I know, I know. But I can't help but get pissed when I hear some white lady say she *knows* about the south. She *knows* about what it's like for me, even here—even here in Billington. It may not be the South, but it's still full of bullshit. It's just slyer here. Just more underground. But it's still right there, right in *my* face. If it's not my skin color, it's the fact that I'm gay. Or at least it was, before. Hell, even after. Think of those poachers. *We can't have none of that.*"

I shut my mouth. He was right. I *was* some white lady acting like I knew what he had had to live and breathe every day. I was a straight person, acting like I knew. I didn't know shit about that. I knew about other things, that Rashad didn't have a clue on, but not about that.

Rashad gave me a look—an I-*forgive-you, idiot* look, and continued his story. "My mother saved me. My father, too, I guess, since he kicked me out of my house and that town when I was seventeen. But Mom had a plan for that—she'd been saving part of her paycheck from the Food Mart since forever. She knew somehow, before I did, that I was gay, and that he would send me out when he realized. So she already had a place set up for me at my Aunt Tanesha's. I went to community college and I was good at it—got scholarships to three universities. And then I went on to get my Master's, and then my PhD." He stared at the fire burning in the fireplace, but he was seeing something else. "I imagine she must be dead now. Mom. And Aunt Tanesha, too, probably."

I nodded, thinking again of Gina. The silence stretched between Rashad and me, and we let it, watching the fire, each thinking of what we'd lost. Tyrone, who'd been sleeping on the floor, yawned and rolled onto his side. Idly, I scratched his stomach. When I looked up at Rashad he was watching me.

"What's yours?" He spoke quietly.

I shrugged my shoulders, giving him a quizzical look.

"Your story—your pain." Rashad poked at the fire log. "I mean, I know you have it—I can see it in your face."

I thought about it. I thought about telling him my history, about dredging up all the old shit, but I'd only ever shared it all with Gina. And I was exhausted at the idea of saying all the words, of hoping they conveyed the history of me—the why of the way I was now. I shook my head. "I don't think you'd understand mine, any more than I do yours."

"Hmm. Okay." Rashad picked up the book we had been reading earlier—a detective novel. He flipped the pages back and forth. "I get it. I guess maybe the best we can do is understand that we have it, right, not exactly what it is? You have yours, I have mine, and maybe . . ." he thought for a minute. "Maybe it's all the same, in a way." He looked up at me and smiled. "My pain, your pain. We can just try to understand we all have it, and treat each other accordingly."

⌒　⌒

I thought about what Rashad had said that night as I lay staring at the darkness in my bedroom. It seemed like such a simple thing, and yet it had been proven impossible so many times in the world. *Treat each other accordingly.* Was it beyond us mere humans, to see that our pain, our joy, our lives, were all the same?

I knew it was beyond *me*. I didn't really believe it—I thought of humanity as a disconnected, bumbling bunch of idiots who acted on their own selfish impulses without regard for anyone or anything else. Destroying each other, destroying the planet, tuned out of anything but their own desires. I knew I was one of them. But that didn't stop me from not wanting anything to do with most of them. I'd spent most of my life avoiding eyes on the street, avoiding intimacy, avoiding trust. But Rashad's eyes were there every day now, looking into mine, inviting me to trust. I didn't like it. I didn't want to trust him, or depend on him, or let him know me in any way deeper than our potato jokes went. That's what I told myself, that night. I told myself I'd be glad when spring arrived and Rashad could move on, on to where ever he was going. I'd been doing fine on my own, and I wanted my solitude back. It was safe.

Thinking about it made me tired. The murmurations were pushing forward in my mind, surging up with an insistence I was starting to get used to—it was happening more and more. I let them take center stage. Tonight, there were no sorrowful strains. Instead, allegro melodies soothed me, though as usual I couldn't understand what they meant. I fell asleep listening to them, wondering at the change, unable to fathom it but happy to have it.

— ~

In the morning, every morning, there was Rashad. Again. Taking Tyrone out, emptying the latrine bucket, stacking some pressed logs on the fireplace hearth, cooking his latest concoction for dinner. Arguing with me about the ending of a novel. Asking me whether we should read the dystopian or the mystery next. Helping me with the dishes. Asking me how I slept. Laughing at me, in gentle ways. Being a good roommate.

Being a friend. Asking me, without any words, to be a friend back.

And the maddening thing was, it worked. I didn't know if it was because the end of the world adjusted my attitude, or because reading all those novels let us share things about ourselves in a non-threatening way, or what. But Rashad and I became friends.

Actually, I *did* know a part of what it was. Rashad was, truly, a good man. He had saved my life. When he could have walked away, or taken my life, he saved it. That was hard to dismiss. That was more than any other human being had ever done for me. Rashad had, as he put it, a fucking spine.

I kept that in mind. It was worth *a lot*.

Not that Rashad was perfect. Oh, no, he was far from perfect. He could get moody, especially when he was thinking of Anthony. He was reminded, at those times, of his loss. He'd lost the person he had thought was the love of his life. Not just physically. Worse, Rashad had lost faith in the idea that Anthony was—or could be—the kind of person he'd believed he might be. To relive that moment in the cabin, that moment when Anthony turned on him and laughed, *laughed* with those poachers, in order to save his own skin—that would make anyone moody. Knowing that sort of thing about humanity had certainly turned me away from the whole of it. I tried to give him room when those moods struck.

We talked often about Hacker's Flu; about who released the virus, why, how much of the world had been decimated. We wondered if somebody somewhere still had a finger on a red button, just waiting to push it. Rashad figured North Korea was a candidate; they'd never really stabilized. I was betting there was more than one red button left.

"But what would be the point of pushing the button now?" I couldn't imagine more destruction and death.

"What was the point of Hacker's Flu?" Rashad shrugged. "Power. Mad, stupid fear."

Still, he was convinced that civilization existed somewhere, not just in Europe, or Asia, but in America. And he wanted to find it—to find, or build, a community. He pored over an old atlas he had liberated from one of the houses we raided, figuring out how far it was to the nearest big port, how many days it would take to walk there. He would go on and on about the possibilities, how the point in life was to be a part of something, to work together, how we could build new hope. It all made me uncomfortable. And one night, I had to shut him down, because he kept saying the wrong word. He kept saying *we*.

"We could make Seattle in a couple of weeks, if we were lucky." Rashad flipped back and forth between two pages in the atlas, checking distances.

"There is no *we*." The sentence was out of my mouth before I knew it. I felt bad, but I also felt like I had to put a stop to his dreaming. Or at the very least, to my playing some part. I'd actually been letting myself think about what it would be like if Rashad stayed, if we became a team of sorts. Waking up each morning *not alone* had been growing on me. And if there were two of us, we'd have a better chance at survival. But Rashad kept thinking there was more than just survival.

"I mean, our agreement was that you could stay for the winter. That was it. Spring is almost here and I have no intention of doing any traveling when it arrives. I'm going to plant another garden and keep my head down." I felt something close up inside of me when I said the words. Some amorphous, blooming tendril shriveled and died.

Rashad closed the atlas. He placed it on the sofa next to him and folded his hands on his lap. He kept his eyes on his hands as he spoke. "Well, maybe I didn't mean *you*. Maybe I meant Anthony. I plan to go back up the mountain this spring, to see if Anthony is still alive."

I was dumbfounded. "Why would you do that? He betrayed—"

"I know. I know what he did. But I also know I loved him for four years, and he loved me, too. At least, as much as he could. So I'm going to go see, and if I find him and it looks like he's in trouble, I'm going to try to get him out of there." Rashad moved his head toward me but he wouldn't look at me. "I won't bring him back here. I won't say a word about this place. So you don't have to worry about that." He put his hand on the atlas. "Either way, Anthony or no Anthony, I'm eventually heading for Seattle. That's the closest big port."

I could only shake my head. "There's no reason to think there's anything there. And as for Anthony, he *turned* on you Rashad. Who knows what else he would have done if you hadn't left?"

Rashad sighed, rubbing his eyes. "It's late." He rose from the sofa. "Time for me to go to sleep."

I couldn't let it go. "Would you have done that to *him*?"

Rashad didn't have to think about it. "No. No, I wouldn't have. But I also know what it's like to be afraid. I've seen plenty of people do things they would never do if they weren't afraid." He opened the door to the office, where his air mattress waited. Looking back, he waited until he was sure he had my attention before he continued. "I've also seen plenty of people *refuse* to do things because they're afraid, Julie. Refuse to hope. Or trust. Or love. Hard to say which is worse."

I stayed in the living room for a while that night, after Rashad closed the office door and went to sleep. Thinking about fear. Thinking about all the things fear had made me do—and not do—in my own life. There was no way to change it now—now that the old world was over, now that all the opportunities for change were gone. I stared at the front door, at the bars across it, at the plywood covering the window. I thought about the people who'd been, most recently, outside that door. In this new world, fear was a good thing. It wouldn't make me betray someone, but it might keep me alive.

It wasn't until I was almost asleep, listening to Tyrone snoring next to me, that I realized the irony of my situation. For most of my life, when mere survival was assumed, it had been optional to me, because of the pain it involved. I'd always considered suicide a viable alternative. Why was it that now, staying alive seemed paramount?

Staring in the dark, I knew why. It was because staying alive was all that was left.

Trust

IN THE MORNING I woke to the smell of frying potatoes. I groaned, tired, because though I'd fallen asleep listening to Tyrone snore, I'd been awakened through the night by murmurations. They'd been so strong, and so dark, they'd made sleep almost impossible. I'd never been disturbed from slumber before by the murmurations, but no matter how I'd tried to relegate them to the background, they had refused to go. And they were back to being gloomy. No joyous choruses for me now, just dirge-like refrains.

Rashad was in the kitchen, humming a tune while he finished making breakfast. When he saw me emerge from the bedroom he nodded toward the table, where two glasses of powdered orange drink waited, illuminated by the kerosene lamp.

"Tyrone's already had his outing." Rashad brought plates heaping with potatoes and onion. He pulled out his chair and sat.

That's when I saw it. Rashad's shotgun leaned against the door frame. Next to it was a duffle bag I recognized; Rashad had taken it from the same house he got the atlas. Instantly blood rushed to my face and I felt . . . shame? Sadness. Loss. I tried to fix it, words spilling out in an attempt to repair the damage.

"Rashad. It's at least two weeks too early. You don't have to go *now*. I didn't mean to be so harsh last night. I was just—"

Rashad, mouth full of food, waved his fork at me. He finished chewing and swallowed. "It's not about last night." He looked as sad as I felt. "It's just time. I need to go see about Anthony—"

"Who cares about Anthony?" I raised my voice more than I'd intended, but I couldn't believe what I was hearing.

Rashad's eyes got wide. He leaned back against his chair and stared at me for a minute. When he spoke, it was in a measured, tight tone. "I do. *I* care about Anthony, Julie, even if he shit all over me. And I *am* going to go see if he's still alive. And if he's still alive and in trouble, I'm going to try to help him." Rashad leaned forward. "Now, on the other hand, if he's still alive and happy as a clam to be in good standing with those assholes on the mountain, I'm going to sneak back down and head for Seattle. But for me, staying human means I have to go check, first."

"I understand, Rashad." I didn't understand at all. "But you could get killed up there. And Seattle? There's no reason to think things are different in Seattle than they are here. At least here, there's some food. There's some shelter, and the garden, too. I've been thinking and maybe we could catch some of the chickens—"

"I thought there was no *we*." Rashad watched my face.

"I didn't mean that." I had hurt him, so much, with my stupid remark. "I really didn't mean it, Rashad. I'm sorry I said it. I just . . . why can't you just stay here?"

Something in his face relaxed; his eyes smiled, even if his mouth didn't. "I didn't want to think you meant that." He took a deep breath, let out a huge sigh. "I can't stay here forever, Julie. It's been a wonderful respite, this winter with you. I have to admit I wasn't too sure about you at first," he laughed. "But you grew on me. And I know you're one of the good ones."

"Then why not stay?" As I spoke the words I knew he wouldn't stay, and I knew just as strongly that I wouldn't go with him to Seattle, Anthony or no Anthony. It was too much, too much. There was nothing in Seattle besides bodies, and worse, more survivors. Survivors like Ski Coat guy or the boy who wanted to eat Tyrone. I was tired. And I was afraid.

"Maybe I'll come back next winter." Rashad looked at me, his expression inquiring. "Who knows how long it might take on the mountain? If it's too long, I'll need to wait out the winter before I head for Seattle. What do you think?"

My expression must have revealed my thoughts.

"Not with Anthony. I won't come if Anthony's with me." Rashad pushed his plate away from him. "To be honest, I think he's dead, by now. Those men up there weren't playing, and Anthony would have been way out of his depth. I just need to know. Before I move on."

"If you need a place to crash for the winter you know you're welcome." I looked at his duffle bag. It wasn't packed full—probably just some clothes. "That thing looks like it could use some supplies."

"I didn't want to presume." Rashad pulled his plate of potatoes, now cold, closer, and started eating. "I did take a few cans of tuna."

"Rashad, stay one more night." I talked right over his attempted protest. "No, really. One night won't make any difference. We can finish that novel." We'd gotten almost to the end of our latest pick: a science fiction novel written by some guy I'd never heard of before. "We can choose some more supplies—maybe some of the dried meat, since you're the one who eats it. Lighter than the cans of tuna. And you can get to sleep early and head out after a huge breakfast. I'll even cook." I waited for his answer, surprised at how much it mattered to me.

"One more night can't hurt." Rashad grinned. "But I'll pass on the offer of you cooking."

— ~

We finished breakfast and chanced a long backyard play session with Tyrone, throwing a tennis ball for him, which he silently and happily retrieved. It was cold out, but the snow was gone. I still thought it was too early for Rashad to try to make the trip to the mountain, but he insisted it would be fine.

In Greg's garage, we sorted through the dried meats and selected as many as we thought could fit in the duffle bag. I opened the **TRADE** box and removed one of the bottles of whiskey. Rashad raised his eyebrows, but didn't comment.

"We'll have a bit after dinner. A little celebration." Immediately I felt stupid. What would we be celebrating? Rashad walking off to his likely disappointment, finding his lover dead or worse, possibly dying in the process?

When we got back in the house, we packed Rashad's duffle bag full with food and some water bottles and I slipped in some antibiotic ointment and an extra toothbrush. The day passed, filled with routine. Each second seemed, to me, to go by too quickly, each minute taking us closer to the next morning. After dinner, we sat together in the living room, the novel on the table waiting to be finished. But first, I poured us each a small drink and raised mine in a toast.

"To friendship." The smile Rashad rewarded me with made the risk I felt speaking those words worth it.

In the glow of the lamplight, we talked. And I decided to take another, bigger risk. Maybe there was really nothing to lose; Rashad was leaving in mere hours and I might never see him again. I'm not sure why I did it, but I think it was about being accepted. Accepted by someone, even after they knew the biggest secret I had. There weren't many *someones* left.

I told Rashad about the murmurations.

He listened quietly while I haltingly described them. I tried to look at him while I did it, but I found it easier to keep my eyes on Tyrone, who had flopped at my feet when we settled in the living room. When I was done I looked up at his face, trying to gauge his reaction, but his expression was inscrutable. I waited, wondering if I'd just lost my only friend, so soon after I'd finally admitted, even to myself, that I had found him.

Rashad took a sip of his drink, and leaned forward to set his glass on the table. When he settled back on the couch, he said "Are you serious?"

Are you serious. Exactly what Roger had said when I confided in him. I could feel my face flushing hot. I shouldn't have said anything. I *knew* it.

"I mean, that must be a trip. So that's what's going on when you're looking all other-worldly?" Rashad was watching me. I wondered what he was thinking. But at least he wasn't acting like I had suddenly grown horns.

I nodded, slowly. "Yeah. Well. Shall we finish that book?" I reached for the sci-fi novel.

"Ummm." Rashad's eyebrows leapt upward; his brow furrowed. "No?

I mean, you just lay that out there and now you want me to read some novel? I want to hear more about your thing."

"Why? So you can confirm I'm a freak?" I felt so stupid.

Rashad just stared. "I don't think you're a freak." He put his feet up on the table. "Any theories?"

I was one or two steps behind. "You don't?"

"What?"

"Think I'm a freak?"

"I mean, maybe, but not for the . . . murmurations? Is that what you called it? I mean, you can't cook, you smoke too much, you snore—"

"I do not snore!" I couldn't help smiling.

"You do." Rashad grinned back. "*Freakishly* loudly. Seriously though, any theories?"

I shrugged.

"Is it—is it *telling* you things? Or is it random? What is it coming from?" He waited, as though I had the answers.

I thought about it. I'd never talked to anyone about the murmurations before, in terms of trying to figure them out. "I don't think it's an . . . it." The words came out before I had a chance to edit them, but once they were out they made sense to me. "It doesn't feel like an individual intelligence."

"What do . . . *they* sound like?"

I had to stop and consider that question. The murmurations were such a private part of my world, I'd never really thought about describing them to someone else. "Hmm. Maybe . . . whale song? You know? Those moans, those sighs. Closest I can come to how they sound."

"Wow." Rashad nodded. "I've heard those, on YouTube and like that. They sound like something out of this world." He closed his eyes, like he was replaying whale songs in his head.

"What does it feel like? To hear them, I mean?" Rashad opened his eyes and looked at me. "Must feel a little crazy sometimes."

I searched his face, but I couldn't see any judgement, just sympathy. He was honestly trying to understand.

"It does feel crazy sometimes. I think of it as a *them*. I mean, I don't know why, but I do. And I know it must sound even crazier than it feels, but it's real."

Rashad nodded, as if to say *of course it's real.* "Maybe it's a gift. My grandmother had one—she called it *the information.* She would just get a feeling about something, whether the latest couple to get engaged would be happy, whether the job grandpa got would work out, and she would proclaim that she had *the information.* We used to laugh about it but she was usually right."

I shook my head. "It doesn't seem like it has anything to do with my own life, or the lives of anyone around me. It feels more like a mood ring."

Rashad frowned. "A mood ring?"

"Yeah. You know those rings they used to sell—they were novelty items. They had some sort of liquid inside a glass dome and they would change colors depending on temperature, but they were advertised as mood predictors. You know—if your ring was blue then you were happy, if it was orange you were angry." The more I thought about it the more the mood ring theory described the murmurations pretty well. "That's what it feels like—like the murmurations are a temperature check. Like the world, or something, is conveying its mood."

Rashad was silent for a minute. "Julie." He waited until I was looking into his eyes. "You aren't crazy. There is so *much* in this world. We can't understand all of it. But that doesn't mean it's not real." He chuckled. "I'm not saying I can understand what you experience, but I believe you when you tell me you experience it. And I have to think that it's a kind of gift, even if it may not feel like it to you. You're tapped into the great collective, somehow. Whatever that collective turns out to be. Can't be a bad thing to have an ear to the ground on that, even if you don't totally understand what you're hearing."

And just like that, I felt . . . okay. Just like that, just because another human being listened to me, and tried to understand what I was saying, and didn't roll his eyes or close up and walk away or dismiss me as crazy, I felt . . . accepted. I tried, but I couldn't stop the tears that sprang to my eyes.

"Hey, hey, hey there." Rashad put his arms around me and hugged me. "No need for tears."

We'd never hugged, and it felt both wonderful and awkward. After a second of not knowing what to do, I hugged him back. "They're not bad tears." I let him go, and wiped my face on my sleeve. "I've never . . . I've only ever told one other person about the murmurations."

"And how did that go?" Rashad's expression conveyed he knew exactly how it went. "Kinda like how it went for me back home trying to tell people I was gay, right?"

"Right."

"Well. That part I totally understand." He thought of something. "Did it—they—whatever—change any? When it all happened?"

At first I wasn't certain what he meant. But then I realized. "Since the flu?"

Rashad just nodded.

"No. I mean, now I hear them all the time, where before it was only now and then. I don't know why that is. Over the summer they were just sort of neutral-sounding, most of the time, but sometimes they sounded sad. And last night . . ." I stopped talking. I didn't really want to share what the murmurations had sounded like last night, though I wasn't sure why. "They didn't seem to change around the flu, though. I mean, there was no big change when it was all going down and everyone was dying."

"Do you think it's God?" Rashad narrowed his eyes.

"No." I didn't hesitate to answer. "I mean, I don't believe in God, so maybe that makes any guess I have about that biased. But no, I don't think it's God."

"Energy. Some sort of universal spirit. Our alien overlords." He listed ideas as fast as he thought of them. "The unknowable noumenon."

"Ah, Kant." Rashad looked surprised that I knew that one. I just shook my head. "I've stopped trying to know. It just is." I wasn't being totally truthful. The previous night had given me some food for thought.

"Yeah." He nodded. "So many things are." He drained the last of his whiskey and when he set the empty glass on the table, he took my hands in his. "Listen, I'm going to bed. And when I leave in the morning, I'm going to knock on your bedroom door, so that you can get up and lock the doors after me. But I don't want to say good bye in the morning. I want to just leave."

"Why?" I asked the question, but inside I thought I knew why. Even though he'd tried, Rashad couldn't understand my confession about the murmurations. He thought I was strange, now.

"It's not the murmurations." Rashad smiled and squeezed my hands. "Julie, seriously, I don't think any differently of you because you told me that. In fact, knowing how you are, I feel honored you told me. I know you don't trust easy." He let go of my hands and stood.

"But why, then?"

He leaned down to stroke Tyrone, who'd awoken when Rashad stood. Without looking at me, he answered. "Because I don't really want to go. And I'm afraid. But I know I have to, Julie. It's right, to go and see if Anthony needs help. It's the right thing for me to do. And if I get up tomorrow morning and you're up and we have a nice little breakfast and talk about the garden we could put in this spring I don't know if I would go. So, I need to just go."

I wanted to ask him, again, to stay. But I bit my tongue, silenced the words. He'd been a good friend to me, and I knew I should return the favor no matter how stupid I thought he was being.

"Then I'll say good bye, Rashad." I stood, and held out my hand for him to shake.

Rashad just laughed. "Give me one more hug. And who knows, maybe I'll stop by on my way to Seattle."

"If you do, you better have some smokes. I'm running low."

He was clearly relieved that I was going to keep it light. "I keep telling you to quit. Those things will kill you."

In the morning, he knocked on the bedroom door just like he said he would. Tyrone woke and tilted his head at me, as if to ask why I wasn't getting out of bed. But I stayed under the covers, listening as Rashad unbarred the French doors and opened them. I listened as he closed them, quietly. I listened to his footsteps as he walked across the deck. Once I knew he had had ample time to walk to the gate and leave, I got up and went to the kitchen. I locked the French doors, replaced the bars, and began my morning alone.

The murmurations were there, though, as bleak as I'd ever heard them.

Loss

I TOLD MYSELF it didn't matter. That I didn't miss Rashad, that I was better off alone, that I'd be just fine. I woke up every day and went through the motions of getting on with it. I didn't venture outside the house except to allow Tyrone his required toileting and to dump my bathroom bucket. I didn't change my clothes. I didn't even brush my precious teeth, most of the time. I had no appetite, but I drank two bottles of cheap, red wine from the **TRADE** box that Rashad had brought in from the garage. I spent long evenings perusing the death book by the light of the kerosene lamp, seeking passages that resonated.

I didn't find any I liked better than the first bit I read from the introduction, when I was taking the book from the house it had been in—the snippet about "how we understand death determines how we should live." I'd always thought when I died, that would be the big *end*; there would be no heaven or hell, no nirvana or reincarnation, just . . . the end of existing.

Earlier in my life the big end had often seemed like it offered respite, from pain, from difficulty, from the endless challenges that being around people presented for someone like me—someone so damaged by life that every interaction meant danger. I would sometimes even reassure myself, bolster myself through one more day, by thinking of the fact that when it all got to be too much, I could just kill myself. But since Hacker's Flu, I'd done everything I could to avoid dying. It wasn't the first time the thought had occurred to me, but discovering my will to live after the end of the world seemed sadder than ever, now. Now that I was alone again. I laughed out loud at the irony.

Tyrone, who had been following me from room to room, his head hanging lower and lower as the days passed and I turned into a sad, inanimate couch potato, raised his head, startled from his nap next to me on the floor.

"Sorry, buddy."

He looked up at me accusingly, then settled his chin on his paws and closed his eyes again, heaving the biggest sigh.

"I'm just a misery lately, aren't I?" I reached out from where I lay on the sofa and stroked his head. "Well. Rashad's gone." Tyrone looked around, eyebrows up, at the sound of Rashad's name. "But *we're* still here. And tomorrow we'll start getting the garden plot ready for spring."

My voice sounded fake even to me.

My self-imposed house arrest had lasted at least two weeks—maybe more. Too much time lost, when there was surviving to do. And that was all there was left to do, really. I trudged off to bed, a little tipsy from the wine, hoping I could fall asleep quickly. I was tired of feeling. I wound the alarm clock, which had fallen silent not long after Rashad's departure because I stopped winding it, to an approximate time, and then set the alarm for six A.M., determined to get out early the next morning and begin again.

But sleep refused to come. I realized that night, as I lay in the darkness of my bedroom, that I was mourning, and that what I was mourning was trust. I'd never felt it for any person but Gina, and even that had been a qualified trust. Finding it with Rashad had been a gift. It was *trust* that made life meaningful. Trust and acceptance. And those both required more than one person. I thought of all the shared laughter I'd had with Gina, and all the times I couldn't wait to get home to call her to tell her the latest *whatever*, or the times she called me to talk out some problem. And then, our relationship faded, until we were two people who remembered each other, instead of two people who *knew* each other. We kept up a fiction, but our conversations dwindled to mere pleasantries. Then, Gina was gone, and *everyone* was gone, and the only people left were people who would kill me so they could eat my tuna fish or my dog.

But then, there was Rashad. And despite my misgivings, I'd grown to trust him. And to feel accepted by him—something I'd never fully experienced. Rashad had known everything about me. And he'd still accepted me. And because of that, we'd begun to share . . . meaning. If there was such a thing.

Now, Rashad was gone, too. If he ever did come back, if he didn't die out there on the mountain, it would be only to leave again for Seattle, and I *wouldn't* be going with him. Rashad was a good person, but he was one in a million. All his talk about community was drivel; he was blind. Even the way Anthony had turned on him hadn't dimmed his belief that there were good people out there. Good people. *Right.*

My heart actually hurt, physically, that night. I thought of all the moments we had shared here, in this house; I laughed remembering his disgust at my smoking, his derision of my cooking. I cried remembering how he had listened to my confession about the murmurations and simply accepted it, accepted *me.* He hadn't made me feel like a freak. He hadn't ever hurt me, in any way. Until he left.

The murmurations accompanied my reflections, the tones alternated between lamenting and hopeful. I could have learned a lot that night, but of course, I wasn't paying attention.

― ―

In the morning, I rose to the alarm for the first time since Rashad left. My pounding head made me regret the wine of the night before. I had to get it together. I had to keep living. And that meant I had to keep growing food, which meant I had to go back to Jenna and Solly's. My head was pounding, and I felt like crawling back into bed, but I needed to begin, again, to survive. And so, without letting myself think, I did.

I took a cold bucket-bath, dressed, strapped on my homemade holster and slotted my gun into it. After leashing Tyrone, I headed for the garden. As I walked I felt oddly exposed, hyper-alert to any noise. It felt strange and frightening walking unaccompanied, after only a few months of walking with someone else. Something about that made me resentful. I hadn't realized how much I'd come to depend on Rashad, how much his presence had begun to mean in my every-day.

The lawns were scruffier than ever, just coming out of their winter stasis. Weeds were sprouting for a second season in all the ornamental beds, clearly destined to win the battle for space between them and the more refined plants so carefully cultivated by the people who had once lived in the neighborhood. I walked slowly, tired and stiff.

Rashad and I had checked on the garden and greenhouse during a break in the snow a few weeks before he left and they looked much the same as they had then. I shut the gate to the yard and let Tyrone off his leash. The ground in the raised bed was thawed now, ready to turn and plant. I stood next to the greenhouse for a few minutes, listening, to be certain Tyrone and I were alone, thinking of Solly and Jenna, the couple who had lived here, who had built the raised garden bed and the greenhouse. I thought of the Valentine note on the refrigerator in their house, and wondered again about their fate, wondered if they had somehow escaped the flu and were somewhere safe, or if they ended up dead somewhere on the road.

Sighing, I opened the greenhouse door and nearly fell when three rats exploded out of a fertilizer bag under the shelves. They ran frantically around the interior until one found the open door and the other two quickly followed. Tyrone lunged at them, but they disappeared into the bushes at the edge of the yard. Once my heart had resumed a normal tempo, I grabbed a shovel from the stack of garden tools by the door and poked at the rest of the bags and empty pots under the greenhouse shelves. No more rats appeared.

I was glad I had decided to store the seeds I had left in the house. The whole garden could have been lost in one winter of rodent damage. As it was, I knew I had to find more seeds soon if I wanted future gardens; I'd managed to save some from the heirloom tomatoes that I hoped would produce plants, but the rest of my supply was from store-bought packets at least two years old. I didn't know how long seeds remained viable. The supplies from Greg's garage were still plentiful, but they wouldn't last forever.

The dirt in the raised bed turned easily and I made good progress despite my headache. The morning passed quietly, the only sounds the soft thuds of earth falling from my shovel, the birds chirping their early spring songs, Tyrone grumbling at the bushes where the rats disappeared. After about an hour of digging, my muscles ached like I had been hauling rocks for days. The headache was worse, too. I dropped to the grass next to the garden bed and leaned back on my elbows, wishing I had brought along some water. Tyrone came to join me, hoping for a game of fetch, but I hadn't brought one of his tennis balls. When he brushed against my arm, my skin hurt.

Sore muscles, raging headache, sensitive skin. I lay there, taking stock. My ears felt hot, and when I held the back of my hand against my forehead, I could tell I had a fever. There was a tickle in my throat and it hurt my chest when I coughed. The moment I put all the signs together I felt an instant sense of panic. I didn't have a simple hangover. I was ill. Really and seriously ill.

"Crap." I hauled myself up off the ground and got Tyrone leashed up. I started to reach for the shovel to stow it in the greenhouse, but dizziness engulfed me, my vision cloaked with darkness at the height of the wave. As soon as it passed, I left the shovel where I'd dropped it and headed home.

By the time I got there, I felt shaky and my hands trembled as I locked up and set the bar across the French doors. I lit the kerosene lamp on the counter and grabbed the flashlight, flicking it on as I headed to the medicine cabinet in the bathroom. The beam of light from the flashlight illuminated the interior of the cabinet and I scanned the rows of pill bottles. I'd sorted them in order of drug type—antibiotics were front and center. I took one, and kept rummaging until I found some acetaminophen to bring down the fever.

Tyrone, who had followed me to the bathroom door, moved out of my way so I could get back to the kitchen, pill bottles in hand. I poured some water into a glass and drained it, then poured another. I couldn't tell if it was just the fear at work or if I was really feeling as much worse as I thought—all I knew was that I needed to get to the bed. I blew out the lamp and found my way through the darkness with the flashlight.

I didn't bother to take my clothes off. All I wanted was to crawl under the blankets and try to rest. Tyrone settled at the side of the bed, watching, but I was barely aware of him. My head hurt so much, the pain pulsing in my temples with each heartbeat. Chills ran through me and I hugged myself and tried to relax my body. Rest, I just needed some rest.

— —

I woke coughing. My throat was swollen and tender and I could tell I still had a fever. But I had to pee. Clambering out from under the blankets, I stumbled in the dark to the bathroom. When I was done I followed the walls to the kitchen, found the lighter and lit the kerosene lamp, which cast a yellow glow. Just that effort exhausted me and I slumped over the counter, eyes closed, trying to muster the strength to move. Another coughing fit overtook me, and when it was done I checked the palms of my hands, with which I had automatically covered my mouth, for blood. I remembered the news coverage of the doctor who was the first to die, how she coughed up those deadly, crimson drops in the hospital. Thankfully my skin was clean.

Tyrone grunted; he was at my side, as always, eyes glittering up at me in the lamplight. I realized I had no idea how long I'd been out. When was the last time he ate?

"Let me . . . let me get some medicine, Tyrone. Then I'll feed you." I found the bottle of acetaminophen and took three more pills. I managed to get a jug of water from the cupboard and set it next to the pill bottle. Then I opened the lower cabinet and dragged the half-full bag of kibble out, letting it fall open on the floor. I filled Tyrone's water dish, but after a moment of thought I set a large pot on the kitchen floor and filled that, too. I could smell dog urine, but I was too spent to care. It was all I could do to blow out the lamp and drag myself back to my bed. I collapsed onto the mattress and coughed myself to sleep.

I don't know how long I was ill. Days, days that passed in a strange, disjointed manner. I woke occasionally and guzzled water from a jug I didn't recall bringing to the bedroom. I took more acetaminophen from the pill bottle next to the jug when I remembered, until I knocked the bottle off the nightstand and couldn't find it. I coughed so hard I wet the bed. I remember thinking I needed to open the French door, open it and let Tyrone out, so he wouldn't die in the house with me. But I couldn't get myself up to do it.

And then one day I opened my eyes, lucid, covered in dried sweat, still shaky, but able to stand. I found the flashlight on the nightstand and holding it with one hand, leaning on Tyrone with the other, I made my way to the bathroom. Tyrone snuffled at me and licked my hands while I tried to balance on the bathroom bucket.

"Oh my, I *smell*, Tyrone." I reeked, in fact, of sweat and urine and staleness. After a little work with a washcloth and a change of clothes I felt fresher, but drained. I had to sit and rest for a while before tackling the mess I knew awaited me in the kitchen. I'd been out long enough for the pot of water I'd left Tyrone to be bone-dry, so the first thing I did was fill it. He lapped at it so enthusiastically I felt terrible. I felt even worse when I saw the piles of dog poop neatly lining the floor in front of the French doors, both because Tyrone had been forced to deposit them inside and because I was about to be forced to clean them up.

It took me most of the day to restore the house to some sort of order. I had to stop working often because I was so weak, and after I'd cleaned the worst of the kitchen and changed the bedsheets I decided that nothing else was really that important, at least not immediately. I fed Tyrone and stood at the open door holding the gun while he ran around the yard, whispering him back inside too soon for his liking. Food didn't sound enticing but I knew I had to eat, so I opened a can of tuna. Then I fell back in bed and slept.

Over the next few weeks I grew stronger and as I did, I realized just how sick I'd been. I tried not to think about what would have happened if I had died, about Tyrone, slowly starving inside the house, tried to remind myself how lucky I was to have recovered. But I didn't feel lucky. I felt bereft, though I was trying hard not to think about it. Bereft because Rashad was gone. I kept seeing his grin, flashing at me while he cooked his damned potatoes. I heard his laugh in my mind, saw his face crumple with grief when he talked about Anthony. I missed him. I missed my friend. I'd built a reason around him, without knowing it, a reason to live. And now that was gone.

Still, if I was honest with myself I'd built a very *customized* reason to live. I'd envisioned a life where Rashad came down from the mountains every winter and we spent long, comfortable evenings cooking and reading and talking, a life where Rashad eventually just came and lived with me year-round, or maybe he lived in the house next door. We could watch out for each other, and the world would seem less frightening, less empty, more like it used to be. We could be friends, until the end of our days. It would be safe. He would be safe. *I* would be safe.

I knew none of that was what Rashad wanted. He wanted to find others, find community, move forward, and if there was nothing left of the old world, to build something new. He still believed that it was possible. Because he still believed there was goodness in people. He still believed in humanity. I admired him for it, but I didn't share his feelings. Still, *Rashad* was a good human. I knew that in my bones. If he existed, couldn't there be more? I quickly shoved that thought to the back of my mind. It felt like too much to hope for.

I was still weak, and couldn't seem to shake the cough. It didn't help that I refused to stop smoking, even though each drag caused terrible coughing fits. My dwindling supply of cigarettes probably shouldn't have been uppermost in my mind, but some days it was. I wondered what all the heroin addicts were doing to get by. If there were any left. Heroin addiction had been on the rise for decades before Hacker's Flu, and nobody had seemed to know what to do about it. Every night on the news there'd been another story about how heroin was infiltrating the suburbs, or the high schools, or the Midwest in its entirety. Sometimes, watching the reports, I had wondered if there were just too many things wrong and the whole human race was simply imploding.

I decided the best thing to do was stick close to the house until I was back at full-strength. There was still time before the first seeds needed to be potted in the greenhouse. There were things to do around the house: a thorough cleaning inside, laundering the sheets I'd sullied during my illness, which was not an easy task post-washing machines. Maybe reorganizing some supplies. When I was stronger I'd get back to the garden. In the meantime, I could assess my fortifications, too. I'd noticed that the gutter on the front porch was clogged, and I knew I'd have to tackle that if I didn't want the place falling down around me. Maybe it was time for more bars across the doors, just in case. I'd always toyed with the idea of rigging up some sort of early-warning system for the yard, too, and now might be the time to figure that out. There was a lot I could do to be safer, more secure.

It's funny, in a way, that for all my careful planning and safety precautions, I ended up on the front porch, napping in the sun with my gun in my lap. Gina would have laughed, and said I wasn't too good at the whole apocalypse thing.

I had to wonder, later, if in fact, *nobody* could be that good at the whole apocalypse thing, all alone.

The Chicken

A DEAD CHICKEN, its once-creamy feathers flecked with mud, head lolling on a broken neck, hits the porch boards in front of me with a thud. Next to it, I see a man's boots, equally muddy, and as I look up, ragged jeans, a filthy canvas jacket, a wool ski cap so worn it looks felted. Then, a familiar face, covered in a couple of months' worth of fuzzy beard.

"Last of the suburban ones." Rashad sounds a bit mournful.

I lower the gun. I don't recall raising it. Even sleeping, some part of me was listening, like a prey animal. "You should give me more notice than that, Rashad. You could have got yourself shot." I try to decipher the emotions competing for dominance in my body—is that joy pushing up through the adrenaline? I'm so happy to see his face and that feels strange. It seems like it's been a long time, even though he's back much earlier than I had ever imagined he would be, if he returned at all. Too early. I wonder what's gone wrong.

Rashad finally notices the pistol. "Hell, I thought you heard me coming." He sounds a little rattled. "I went around back first, but you didn't answer. What are you doing out front?"

I don't tell him I was dozing—I hope he doesn't guess it. Not smart, dozing outside, especially out front. I'd been cleaning the gutter but I was so tired still, from the illness, and the warmth of the sun had felt so good. I'd climbed down off the old iron porch chair and taken a seat on it to rest my back for a minute and before I knew it, I'd nodded off.

"I was doing some deep thinking. Next time, be more careful." I assess the chicken. "Looks pretty scrawny. How do you know it's the last one?"

Rashad shrugs. "Well, I'm being dramatic. But last fall I saw more on the way here. Just that one this trip, and I didn't see any in the neighborhood. And scrawny or not, I'll still give you these for plucking it." Rashad slings a line of four tiny trout, leathery and crinkled from drying in the sun, off his shoulder and lets them drop next to the chicken. He must have made it as far up the mountain as the lake, at least. I wondered if he found what he was looking for.

"Or," he takes a step back, looked me up and down, "I'd split the bird with you." He pokes at the third porch step with his boot toe, where one of the boards is rotting through. "You're looking a bit scrawny. Doesn't seem like that vegetarian diet is doing you any favors."

"Not vegetarian. *Pescatarian.* I still eat fish, as you well know." I sound prissy and prim, even to my own ears.

Rashad just laughs; that roar of a laugh I've missed so much since he left. I was hoping I'd hear it again, but it was just a hope—one I kept hidden even from myself, most of the time.

"Well, I'm hoping you still pluck chickens, too."

"You have no qualms about killing the thing, but you can't disrobe it." I shake my head at him, rise to unlock the front door.

He smiles, but only for a moment. Then he gets serious. "You should have Tyrone with you when you're outside. He'd warn you if someone was coming."

"Maybe. But you and I both know he's no guard dog. I just wanted to get the gutter clean and get back inside." I want to get back inside *now*. The fact that I fell asleep on the porch—on the damn *front* porch—like some granny in her rocker in better times, has sunk in, and thoughts about what could have happened keep flashing in my mind.

Tyrone breaks from his usual station by the fireplace when he sees Rashad enter, and butt wiggles his way across the living room in the gloom. I light a lamp and head to the kitchen while the two of them reunite, to get some water on to boil so I can scald the chicken carcass. By the time I light the stove, Rashad, Tyrone still dancing at his heels, joins me. He drops the chicken and trout on the counter and walks to the French doors, peers out the peep hole in the plywood.

"You sick? You're really not looking good." Rashad keeps looking out at the back yard.

"Well, thank you, Rashad. Appreciate the kind words. You helping or what? There are some potatoes that need peeling." There's something off in his manner. I turn and take a good look at him. The back of his head doesn't reveal anything to me.

"Am I invited to stay?" Rashad still doesn't turn his head to look at me.

"I guess," I say, in answer to his question. "*If* you brought any smokes."

Rashad groans. "I thought I told you to quit." But he hunches over his pack, and soon enough he's pulling out a whole carton of cigarettes.

I don't know where he found them; some hunter's shack on the mountain, maybe. I've smoked almost all the ones I've scavenged and I'm out of places to look. Or at least the places I'm willing to look. But he found them, somehow. I can't stop the smile stretching my lips. A whole carton.

"Damn junkie." Rashad scowls, but he hands the cigarettes over.

"Your air mattress will be fully inflated in no time." I grin at him. "Even with these lungs."

"Let's turn this off for a minute." Rashad dials down the stove flame.

"I need that water boiling to—"

"I know." He turns to face me. Something is definitely up. "But for now, there's something I have to show you." He heads for the French doors, looks back at me.

I stay where I am. "Something outside?"

"Yeah." Rashad motions for me to get up. "It's kinda time-sensitive."

I stand and join him. "Tyrone staying or going?"

He considers Tyrone. "Staying, for now."

After I lock the French doors behind us, we descend the steps to the yard and Rashad heads for the back gate. Halfway there I tug on his jacket sleeve.

"Is it . . . Anthony?" He'd promised he wouldn't bring Anthony back here. If he has, I'm not sure how I'll handle it.

"Anthony's dead." Rashad pronounces the two words precisely, woodenly. He opens the back gate a crack and checks the alley.

"I'm . . . I'm sorry, Rashad."

He looks back at me. There's something hard in his eyes. "I think we both knew it was likely." He opens the gate wide. "I told you to stay out of sight."

I'm momentarily confused because I think he's speaking to me, but then I look past him, through the gate. Right outside there's a stump, the remains of a tree some previous owner had removed.

There is a boy perched there.

He's a praying mantis of a boy—all legs and arms and head, awkwardly splayed out around the stump, trying to sit, but with appendages too elongated from a growth spurt to do so with any grace. When we step through the gate he keeps his eyes on Rashad.

"I waited in the bushes like you said. You didn't come." The boy speaks softly, but there is a hint of defiance in his voice.

"I'm here now." Rashad turns to me. "Julie, this is Amit." He takes in my expression and sighs. "Amit, this is Julie."

The boy doesn't move from the stump, but he looks at me, his expression carefully guarded. There are deep shadows under his dark brown eyes, eyes that are the star feature in a delicately-boned face. He's waiting, but for what, I don't know. He's dressed in filthy jeans and a red sweatshirt that's three sizes too small. Is he Pakistani? Indian? I'm not sure, and I'm ignorant enough that his name gives me no clues. He looks as tired and hungry as any child I've ever seen, but he doesn't look away from me—he holds his ground. I switch my gaze to Rashad, glowering, and cross my arms.

"Well?" Rashad crosses his arms right back at me. We hold dueling glares for a minute and then I break and turn toward the open gate. I walk through it and back into the yard, heading for the deck. For a moment there is only silence behind me, but then I hear Rashad whisper.

"Let's go, kid."

"She's letting me stay?" Amit's voice just sounds scared, now that he's not facing me down.

"So far, so good."

I'm standing on the deck with Tyrone by the time they reach it. The boy hesitates when he sees the dog, but Tyrone's tail is wagging and that seems to reassure him. Rashad pats Tyrone on the head to show the boy he's friendly. Then he looks up at me, eyebrows raised, as if to say *Your move.*

"Amit." I ignore Rashad, for now. "You look like you could use a bath and a meal. Am I right?"

Amit looks up at me, measuring something. He nods.

"Then let's get Rashad here on hot water duty while I fix you some food."

Rashad makes a production of clearing his throat. "I think Amit might appreciate it if we switched those tasks." He winks down at Amit. "She's not the best cook."

Baggage

AS IT TURNS out we do switch tasks, sort of. I heat pots and pots of water on the camp stove, though Rashad insists he do the hauling and dumping in the tub, because I'm so worn out. He gets the air mattress blown up in the office and soaks some dried tomatoes and mushrooms with the dried trout, to go with the chicken he's going to fry. Amit sits, visibly uncomfortable, on a kitchen chair, watching Rashad go back and forth between rooms.

As soon as there are a few inches of lukewarm water in the tub, I call him into the bathroom, where I've lit one of the kerosene lamps. Tyrone, who's taken an interest in the boy, follows him.

"I've got some clean clothes here." I'd rummaged through some of the things I'd brought back from various houses and come up with a pair of jeans, a clean sweatshirt, some socks and some boxers. There was a pair of tennis shoes that were too small for me, too. Nothing was a perfect fit, but they were at least clean. "And there's the soap and shampoo. And a towel, and here's a toothbrush and some tooth paste." I look around the bathroom, as though something on the walls might tell me what to say next. Finally, I attempt a bright smile, which falters as soon as I really look at Amit.

He can't be more than seven years old. Whatever happened to him is inscribed on his face—he looks wary, drained, mouth set in a straight line, eyes avoiding mine. His head isn't bowed, but it's pretty close.

"Hey." I say the word softly, waiting until he looks me in the eyes to go on. "Do you need any help with your bath?"

He shakes his head, watching me intently. Actually, it's as though he's watching something just in front of me. His expression flickers into something less anxious and he seems to relax just a tiny bit.

"Okay." I point to the door. "It locks, if that would make you feel safer. When you're done, come on out and we'll get you some food."

I shut the bathroom door behind me and a millisecond later I hear the lock click into place. Rashad looks up from the pot of trout and vegetables he's tending. The chicken is scalded, set aside on a plate. I start plucking it.

"He all set?" Steam from the pot wafts up around him as he stirs it.

"What the—" I rip at feathers and lower my voice to a hiss. "What the hell? Who is that kid and why is he in my bathroom? And how could you have left him outside the gate by himself?" A cacophony of confusing murmurations swells up, negative and positive, happy and sad, but I mentally bat them away. I have no time for that now.

"His name is Amit, like I said, Amit Patel. And I told him to hide good out back until I came for him. Should I have just left him up on the mountain?" Rashad is playing it totally straight. "I mean, I know you don't want any encumbrances, so maybe I should have just stayed up there, too." He lifts the pot over to the sink and pours the contents into a colander. "Maybe you'll just let him have a meal and then we can be on our—I mean what the hell is *right*, Julie. What the *hell*, indeed."

He's getting loud, so I shush him.

"What do you care if he hears me?" Rashad whispers, though the whisper might as well be a shout given his expression. "You don't even want him in your house." He pours the vegetables and trout from the colander back into the pot. Then he takes a deep breath and exhales it slowly, shaking his shoulders out, trying to compose himself. "Where's the salt shaker?"

"Where it always is." I open the cupboard next to the sink and hand him the shaker. "It's not that I don't want him in my house. It's that suddenly you show up, months earlier than I would have expected you if I even thought you were coming back this way, and you have a child in tow and you . . ." Suddenly I'm crying, which makes me mad, but I can't help it.

Rashad starts toward me but I hold up my hand. "I'm fine."

He smiles. Then he chuckles. "Damn. We are *none* of us fine, Julie." Shaking his head, he salts the vegetables, then takes the chicken and starts cutting it up to fry.

I watch him. He looks almost as tired as the boy. "What happened up there? How do you know Anthony is . . ." For some reason, I can't finish the question.

Rashad doesn't answer. He gets plates from the cupboard and I automatically start getting silverware from the drawer. We set the kitchen table for three. I clean up the mess from the feathers, and then sit at the table while he fries the chicken, waiting, but he doesn't explain anything. Just as I'm about to ask again, the bathroom door lock clicks.

"After he's asleep. I'll tell you then." Rashad turns off the propane on the camp stove and grabs the plate of chicken, carries that and the pot of vegetables and trout to the table. We both stand by the table, watching the bathroom door.

Amit emerges, dressed in the clothes I gave him, hair wet, grime vanished. He's holding his old clothes, a neatly folded bundle. "I wasn't sure what to do with these." He offers up the bundle like it's something shameful.

"I'll just take those for now—we'll wash them later." I stash the bundle in my bedroom and return to the table. "Let's all eat, Amit. I bet you're hungry." I take a seat, and Rashad, after dishing us each servings of food, follows suit. Amit stands for a moment more before he pulls out his chair and sits down. He looks down at the plate of food in front of him, his expression still inscrutable. The three of us sit in the glow from the kerosene lamp. It feels odd, as though we're imitating a family.

"Dig in." Rashad grins. "*I* cooked it, so no worries."

Amit's first bite is tentative, but once he tastes the chicken he does dig in and I watch with awe as he consumes the entire serving without pausing. I get him another helping and he finishes that too, though his pace is more leisurely. When he's done, he carries his plate to the sink and carefully sets it down, then rejoins us at the table.

He looks at me—again it feels more like he's studying the space three inches in front of my face—his eye curiously unfocused for a few seconds.

Then, as if he's returned from some far place, he blinks and I can tell he's seeing *me*.

"Thank you, Ms. Julie." Amit pronounces the words precisely.

"You can just call me Julie."

Amit nods, but his eyelids are sliding down and he's swaying a bit in his seat. The food has hit his system and he's drunk with fatigue. Rashad and I exchange a look and without words we agree; it's bedtime for Amit.

"Let's get you settled in for the night, bud." Rashad stands and ushers Amit, who gravely says good night to me before he goes, to the office, where he's made up the air mattress for him. I clear the table and rinse off the dishes. By the time I've poured a glass of wine for Rashad and one for myself, he's back. He pulls up a chair and reaches for his glass, swirling the wine against the light from the lamp.

"So?" I light a cigarette, and Rashad grimaces. He looks half triumphant, half worried when my first drag causes a coughing fit.

"Don't worry. I'm over the worst of it." I stub the cigarette out. "It was just some regular type of sickness. Not Hacker's."

"Well, you'd be dead otherwise." Rashad takes a sip of his wine. "You're going to need some recovery time, build your strength back up. He will, too." He tilts his head toward the office. "Then, we have to go."

"Rashad, you know I'm not walking to Seatt—" I stop mid-sentence. Amit's appeared in the doorway. He's in an old tee-shirt and the boxers, his hair mussed, eyes droopy. Tyrone hauls himself up from where he's been laying by me and walks over to Amit, pushing his nose into the boy's hand.

"What's up, Amit?" Rashad sounds like he's used to kids—at least more than I am.

Amit put his hand on Tyrone's shoulders. "Can . . . can he sleep with me?" He poses the question hesitantly, as though he's afraid.

Rashad nods toward me. "That's Julie's call, Amit. Tyrone's her dog."

I'm not sure what to do at first. Tyrone seems fine with the boy. Maybe sleeping with the dog will help him rest. "Let's go in the office and see how Tyrone feels about that." I shoot Rashad a look over my shoulder to let him know we're not done and lead Amit and Tyrone back to the air mattress.

I wait while Amit crawls back under the covers and then I sit next to the mattress and call Tyrone over. He stretches out next to the bed like he's always slept there, heaves a sigh and closes his eyes. Amit lets an arm trail over the side of the mattress onto Tyrone's back.

"Well. Looks like it's okay with him." I start to rise, but Amit sits up.

"Can . . . can you stay until I fall asleep?" Again, he seems almost afraid to ask. When I think about what he's probably been through, it's not surprising.

"I . . . um, sure. I can stay." I'm not certain what else to say, so I just sit next to him. He lays back down and puts his hand on Tyrone again, still watching me. At first, I'm uncomfortable, but as the minutes pass, I feel myself begin to relax. I try to breath in a steady, even way, hoping he'll relax, too, and fall asleep. At some point the murmurations push forward in my mind, and I let them soothe me, listening to the rhythms, the high notes and the low notes. When I open my eyes, Amit is staring at me intently.

"Do you see it, too?" He looks so hopeful.

"See what?"

"The . . ." his voice drops to a whisper. "*Everything.*"

I stare back at him, thinking about how he'd looked at me today, looked at the spaces in *front* of me as though he was seeing something I didn't. How Rashad told me once that when I was listening to murmurations I looked like I was on another planet. That's how Amit had looked today, at least twice.

"No." I say, awareness clicking into place in my mind. "I *hear* it."

Amit purses his lips, thinking about it. Then he nods, as though it makes sense to him. And then, before I can ask him about what he sees, what he meant by *everything*, he falls asleep.

⌒ ⌒

I creep out of the office, leaving the door cracked in case Tyrone wants out later. When I return to the kitchen Rashad is dozing sitting up, hand still wrapped around his glass. He looks thinner than I remember, and older, with the beard. I sit down across from him, trying to be quiet, but he wakes.

"Hey." I don't smile. I'm not going to make it that easy on him.

"Hey," he says. "Amit okay?"

I nod. "I think Tyrone has a new best friend." I take a sip of my wine. "You seem pretty comfortable with kids."

Rashad laughs. "*You* don't. Looked like you were going to run when he asked if he could sleep with the dog. What took so long in there—did you actually try to sing him to sleep, or what?" He takes in my arched brows and backs off. "Lot of kids, back home, when I was growing up. Everybody helped." His eyes soften. "I always thought maybe someday . . ."

"Well." I don't know how to begin asking what he's been through since I saw him last, or what the hell he's thinking now, so I voice a thought that's just occurred to me. "Patel?"

Rashad frowns. "What about it?"

"That man you met coming down here the first time. The one with the RV. His name was Patel, right?"

Rashad thinks, then nods. "But there are . . . were . . . a lot of Patels around here."

"Patels who lost their wife and son? If I remember, that's what he told you. And his son, you said he was around six years old when it happened." I tilt my head in the direction of the office, where Amit is, hopefully, asleep. "He's got to be no more than seven. That's about the right age."

Rashad nods. "Could be. When I asked him about his father, he just said he was gone. Wouldn't say anymore. He's acting more normal today then he has—I think he's pretty shut down."

We sit in silence for a few minutes. Rashad's eyes are bloodshot and he rubs his face with his hand. "Listen, I'm sorry, Julie. I know it's a lot. But I just didn't know what else to do, where to take him. And I needed to warn you."

"Warn me?"

He leans on his elbows, supporting his chin with his hands. "I'm so tired right now, Julie, I just need to sleep. I'm going to crash on the sofa.

In the morning I'll tell you everything. And if you want to kick us both out, you can."

I want to defend myself; protest that I'm not that cold, but I realize I haven't acted very warm and fuzzy since he arrived with Amit, so I just nod.

"It's good to see your face." Rashad smiles, reaches out to touch my hand across the table.

"Yours, too." I grab his hand and squeeze. It *is* good to see him, alive and well and sitting in the kitchen. "Let me get the sofa made up for you."

"Nah, I can do it. I know where you keep the sheets." He stands, looks down at me. "One thing, Julie."

"What?"

"I think . . . I think the kid has your *thing*." Rashad frowns. "I mean, not the *same* exact thing, but—a thing. Like yours."

"I think you might be right."

He looks surprised. "How do you know?"

I just smile up at him. I'm feeling tired, too. "I'll tell you in the morning."

The Mountain

"I'D GOTTEN TO the third rest stop, the one at the foot of the trail that leads to the cabin."

Rashad keeps his voice low; Amit is still sleeping. We're in the kitchen, drinking coffee, both trying to wake up. He looks like he got more rest than I did. I spent my night tossing, trying to ignore the murmurations. Thinking about all the people in my house, and how I didn't hear Tyrone's calming breathing next to my bed, and what Rashad could have meant when he said he'd needed to warn me. Thinking about Amit, and his strange question—*do you see it, too?* And his answer, when I asked what he saw—*everything.*

"I camped there, and in the morning I was packing up, getting ready to head for the cabin. I wasn't sure I remembered the way. Amit was hiding in some brush—I only saw him because he was wearing that red sweat-shirt, just saw a patch of color in the bushes. He'd run from the cabin, said he'd been in the bushes for two days."

"*The* cabin? Your friend's cabin—where you went right after Hacker's hit?"

Rashad nods. "Amit says the men are still there. He described them— same crew that stormed the cabin that day. They abducted him and his mother. Held them all winter long." Rashad lowers his voice even more. "I think they killed her when they were done using her up. Amit just said one day one of them took her outside and she never came back."

I was almost afraid to ask, but I did. "Was Anthony there?"

"He was." Rashad stares at the table top. "He was there. Amit de-scribed him perfectly. Although he called him Tony."

I wait. Rashad had said Anthony was dead. I try to work out what it meant—Anthony alive at the cabin, then dead.

"Amit said that after his mother, well, as he puts it, after she *didn't come back*, one of the men started in on him. Anthony didn't like it. Kept telling the guy Amit was just a kid. He tried to stop it, put himself between Amit and the guy who was coming for him." Rashad didn't look up from the table. "I guess there was a struggle and then one of the other guys shot Anthony. Amit was able to run out the cabin door during the commotion and he just kept running. He said he saw Anthony fall—that his whole chest was blown open."

I just sit, stunned, unsure what to do or say. Rashad's fist hits the table, making the coffee cups clatter and jump. I jump, too, startled by the display.

"Damn him." Rashad's face is twisted, and tears streak his cheeks. "He let those men rape Amit's mother for months and did nothing. *Nothing.*"

I grab his hand and hold it tight, wanting to cry, wanting to make the world different than it is right now. Maybe different than it's always been. And then it dawns on me. "Rashad."

He looks up at me, his face so full of pain. "What?"

"Anthony grew a fucking spine." I squeeze his hand and I'm smiling, even though I'm crying just like him. "He didn't save the woman, but finally, finally he grew a spine. He *saved* Amit."

The expression that slowly transforms Rashad's face is something to see. It's the release of all that Anthony had done to him, all he had not done for him, the realization and the relief at knowing he'd finally done *something* for *someone*. It's perfect. It's . . . *meaning*. He smiles, and then, through his tears, he laughs. "Damn it, you're right."

"Morning." Amit's awake and standing in the kitchen doorway. His hair is sticking up all over his head from sleeping on it wet. He looks as tired and worn as any child I've ever seen.

Rashad swipes at his cheeks furiously. "Morning, kiddo."

Amit's not buying the façade. "You okay?" He walks over to Rashad and touches his sleeve. Tyrone is right behind him.

"I bet this dog needs to go poddy." I stand and Tyrone ambles over to the door, waiting expectantly.

Rashad gives me a weird look; I've never used the term "poddy" in my life and it sounds odd coming out of my mouth. I shrug at him; how am I supposed to know what to say in front of a kid? "We'll be right back."

When Tyrone and I return from the yard, Rashad is cooking pancakes on the camp stove and Amit is seated at the table, drinking a glass of the awful, powdered orange mix from Greg's stores. There are tear streaks on his cheeks and he won't look at me. He watches Tyrone closely, and when the dog sidles up to him and puts his head in the boy's lap, I think I see a hint of relief, a subtle relaxing of his shoulders.

"Bet you haven't had a decent breakfast since I left, right?" Rashad puts the first stack of pancakes on a plate in the middle of the table. He's already set three places.

"You know I'm not that much of a breakfast fan." I sit down and Tyrone has the decency, finally, to come over and snuffle my hand. I forgive him silently for his infidelity. He doesn't seem too concerned.

"Want a pancake, Amit?" I fork one onto his plate. "There's no butter but we do have a bottle of maple syrup."

Amit looks at me, just me, I think, no invisible things in front of me. He studies my face for a long moment before he speaks, his voice low and tremulous. "Tyrone will come with us to Seattle, won't he?"

"Um." I look toward Rashad but he's suddenly very busy at the camp stove. "I think for now we should just focus on getting you rested up."

Amit's insistent. "But when we do go, we have to take Tyrone. The men will kill him if he's here when they come."

I drop my fork, mid-bite.

Rashad shuts off the propane on the camp stove and brings the last stack of pancakes to the table. "I haven't explained everything to Julie, yet." He's speaking to Amit but his eyes are on me.

"They're coming here?" I look at the fork, fallen beside my plate. I pick it up, lift the triangle of pancake halfway to my mouth. Amit can only mean the men from the cabin. Coming here. I stare at my plate, my plate on *my* table, in *my* kitchen, in *my* house. My *haven*. I don't realize I'm shaking until Rashad takes the fork from my hand and sets it down.

"We need to talk." He keeps his voice even, but the look he gives me is intense. He continues in a lighter tone that rings false. "For right now, though, let's eat these pancakes."

We all sit silently, not eating. Amit looks from Rashad to me and back again. He shakes his head slightly, and fresh tears begin to fall on his cheeks. "You promised," he whispers to Rashad, his voice toneless, hopeless. "You promised we wouldn't let them get us."

Rashad is instantly at Amit's side, arm around him, wiping away the tears. "And I'm going to keep that promise, Amit. They won't come near us." He glares at me over Amit's head. "I just haven't had a chance to explain things to Julie, yet, like I said. We're going to have a grown-up talk, just between us adults, and then she'll understand."

"I can take my pancakes in the living room if you need adult-time." Amit's lower lip trembles, but he fights back his tears.

I glare back at Rashad. I feel horrible watching Amit cry, but I didn't ask for this. "Do we need *adult-time*?"

Rashad stands and picks up Amit's plate. "Let's get you set up on the sofa, Amit. Grab your juice."

Amit follows Rashad out to the living room, giving me a long look over his shoulder. Tyrone starts to follow, too, but he must sense how upset I am because he backs up after two steps and settles at my side.

I can hear them setting up Amit's place on the sofa; the clink of his plate on the table, Rashad lighting the candle out there and joking about flipping on the television. I push my own plate away and take one of my cigarettes out of the pack in my pocket. Removing the glass chimney from the kerosene lamp on the kitchen table, I light up and take a long drag. By the time I replace the chimney Rashad is back.

"So." He sits across from me. "Not going to finish that?" Rashad nods toward my uneaten pancakes.

"Feel free." I shove the plate his way. "But you better talk before you eat." I take another drag off my cigarette.

"Yeah, well, what with all the second-hand smoke in here my appetite is gone." Rashad squints at the layer of haze hanging just above our heads, illuminated by the glow of the lamp. "Long and short of it is, we *do* have to leave, Julie. They're coming before winter. I figure we've got until early fall to get ready and get gone."

"What do you mean, they're coming?" I stub the cigarette out half-smoked; a terrible waste, but I can feel my lungs preparing to revolt.

"Amit heard them planning. While he was being held in the cabin. Winter up there on the mountain is rough, so they're looking to hole up down here. They plan to head down in time to set up somewhere before the snow hits, just like I did last year."

The thought of those men trekking down the mountain toward my house gives me chills. They sound like even more evil versions of Ski Coat and Denim Jacket. "What makes you think they'll come here, though? There are plenty of neighborhoods to choose from."

Rashad shakes his head. "Why do you think *I* came here?" He ticks the reasons off on his fingers as he lists them. "Billington's not that big, and your neighborhood is one of the first you come to off the mountain. Most of the other neighborhoods have quarantine marks on *every* house and from what Amit said, these guys are scared to death of contagion—I mean, I was, too. I think Hacker's Flu is probably over, that the virus is dead, but I skirted those **Qs** pretty religiously myself last year."

"*My* house has **Qs** on it."

"Yes." Rashad's using his patient voice. "I would have avoided it, too, if I hadn't caught sight of you and that man and his son, alive and well and uninfected. But Julie, even if they don't pick *your* house for one of their places, they'll be close, and if we stay, we'll be discovered. We *have* to go outside sometimes. Either a trip next door for supplies, or a bathroom out-ing for Tyrone, or the smell of smoke from one of our fires will tip them off. And then we'll all be dead. Or worse, at least until they get tired of us. We have to *go*."

I suddenly feel so tired. Down to my bones, an aching fatigue that makes it seem impossible to move. "Go where, Rashad? To Seattle? Like we'd make that trip alive—over 200 miles on foot, with a kid and a dog?"

"Yes, to Seattle." Rashad reaches across the table for my hand, but I refuse to give it to him.

He withdraws his hand. "But not on foot. I have a plan now, a better one. I thought about it all the way down the mountain with Amit." He pauses dramatically. "We take a boat."

"A boat?" Before I can say more Rashad is off and running.

"We're four miles from the marina. We find a manual transmission car, so we can push-start it, load it with all the supplies we can fit from the garage, pile in, push-start it, drive down to the marina and unload everything into a boat. Then we sail to Seattle."

All I can do is stare at him. "Do you know how to sail?"

Rashad shrugs. "Can't be that hard. I've been out a few times with friends and it seemed pretty straightforward."

"Don't sailboats need motors to get out of the marina onto open sea? We can't push-start a boat motor, and the batteries will all be long-dead." I'm reaching; I know nothing at all about boats.

"No?" Rashad sounds less than positive. "Look, I don't think they do—I think outboard motors are like lawnmowers—you just pull a cord to get them started. And after that, you use the wind. This will *work*, Julie. And I will put money on the fact that there are people in Seattle."

I have to laugh. "Oh, I bet there *are* people, Rashad. People like those men on the mountain."

Rashad makes fists and raises them at the ceiling, shaking with tension. Then he sighs and lowers his hands. "Julie. There's more to life than this. There's more than existing in your safe little house, alone, waiting to die. If we could find like-minded people, a community . . ." His voice trails into silence. We've had this discussion before.

The thing is, I *like* my safe little house. I even like existing away from all the complications people bring into the picture. The world is what it is, now, and it seems to me, most days, that surviving in it requires *avoiding* people, not seeking them out. I don't know if I can believe, like Rashad, that there might be other people like him. I don't know if I can take the risk. The murmurations crescendo in my mind, their tone indecipherable.

"What about *him*?" Rashad's whispering. "What about Amit? He's a child, yet. He deserves the chance for more. And if he does have the thing—*your* thing—he's going to need you, to help him. He's going to need someone who—"

"I'm not his mother." I cover my ears, though only half of the noise I'm hearing enters through them. Between Rashad and the murmurations I feel like I'm under attack.

Rashad stares at me. "No, you're not his mother. But who *is* now, Julie? The kid's got nobody."

I stand, shoving my chair back so fast it almost hits Tyrone. "I'm going to go see if he's finished with his pancakes."

"We're not done talking about this."

"We're done for now." I walk into the living room without a backward glance for Rashad, trying hard not to think about anything at all.

Amit

AMIT IS SITTING on the sofa, his empty breakfast plate on the table next to the candle Rashad lit for him. He's doing that thing, staring into space, but not exactly . . . space. He looks like someone who's watching a film, but there is no film. I say his name softly. "Amit?"

He blinks, blinks again, as if clearing his vision. He turns his head and focusses on me for a moment, then quickly lowers his eyes, refusing to look at me. "Did you have adult-time?"

"Um. We sort of did." I watch as Tyrone, who's followed me from the kitchen, lopes over to Amit and nudges his knee. "I think he likes you."

Amit smiles— a tiny smile, but the first I've seen on his face. It lights him up, competes with his eyes for center stage. "I like him, too." He scratches Tyrone's head. "That's why he has to come with us." He still won't look at me.

I ignore his comment and sit down next to him on the sofa. "Amit. Last night, when you asked me if I saw . . . everything. Were you seeing it just now?"

Amit nods. He turns his head, finally looks directly at me, narrowing his eyes. "You *hear* it, you said."

"I hear *something.* I don't know if it's the same thing you see." I watch him ruffle Tyrone's fur, this young boy who might—might—have the same thing, gift or curse, that I have. "Does it just happen? When you see . . . it? Or do things have to be just right for it to appear?"

Amit shrugs. "I just have to look."

"What does it look like?"

"Depends." He frowns, thinking. I can tell he doesn't fully trust me. I can't really blame him, given what he must have gone through. He shifts the question onto me. "What does it sound like when you hear it? Is it like music?"

"Kind of. Kind of . . . music that talks. But it talks in a language I don't know." I'm about to try to explain more fully, but Rashad pokes his head around the corner.

"You two doing okay?"

We both crane our heads back at him from the sofa and shrug in unison.

"Well. Um, okay." Rashad can tell he's interrupted something. "I'm going to run next door to get some water. Looks like we only have three gallons in the cupboard."

"Key's in the—"

"I know." Rashad's head disappears.

Amit and I sit in silence, listening to the sounds of Rashad leaving the house. The bar being removed, the key in the French door lock, the door closing. I don't know what he's thinking, but I'm trying to work out how I feel about meeting another person who seems to be tuned in to the same strange frequency I've been tuned into since I was a child. Someone like me.

I'm drawn from my thoughts when Amit taps my hand. When I turn to look at him, he quickly averts his eyes.

"They're really bad men." His voice is barely audible, and I can tell he's trying very hard to not to cry. Tyrone, sensing Amit's distress, pushes closer to him on the sofa, nuzzling his hands. "They did . . . bad things." He's begun a little rocking motion, his upper body moving forward and back, forward and back, ever so slightly. He buries his fingers in Tyrone's fur, as if to anchor himself. "They hurt Papa. They . . ." he gasps, a sob wracking his small frame.

I rub his back, tiny circles, feeling him shake and heave, feeling him fight against his pain. He keeps his hands and his eyes on Tyrone, who stares back at him calmly. The murmurations rise in my mind, louder and louder. For some reason, while this helpless child is sobbing on my sofa, they sound hopeful.

After a while Amit draws a long, shuddering breath, and continues. "They hurt Mama." His voice is stronger, but still ragged with emotion. When he looks up at me his eyes are haunted, like so many of the children at the safe house I volunteered at; like my own, in the mirror sometimes, even now.

"I know." I 'm not sure what to do but keep rubbing his back. I try to think of what words to say, what might make it better, but nothing could ever make that better. "We won't let them hurt you, Amit."

"But they will. If we stay here. They'll come and they *will* hurt all of us." He sounds desperate. "They'll hurt Tyrone." He dissolves into tears again.

"Look." I stand, holding out my hand. "What you need right now is some more sleep. You must be exhausted after . . . after that long trip down the mountain. Let's get you tucked in for an after-breakfast nap." I wait, hoping he'll take my hand, at a loss as to what to do if he doesn't. It feels like forever before he lets go of Tyrone and reaches out. I help him up from the sofa, wondering where the hell Rashad is when he's needed, trying to ignore the murmurations, which are practically deafening, and making no sense whatsoever.

Amit follows my lead into the office and I get him settled on the air mattress. I pull the blanket up to his chin and make some room for Tyrone, who insists on climbing right up next to him. Within a minute, he's sound asleep, tear stains on his cheeks, dark circles under his eyes. He looks so gaunt, and I realize how frail he really is right now. It seems like he could just . . . disappear.

I back out of the office quietly, leaving the door cracked so Tyrone can get out if he wants. When Rashad returns with more water jugs, I'm sitting at the kitchen table, smoking.

"He okay?" Rashad stows the water jugs in the cupboard.

"He's absolutely exhausted." I stub out the cigarette, take a sip of my cold coffee. "I put him back to bed."

"There you go, see? You *do* know how to handle kids." Rashad joins me at the table, and the grin he's trying out dies a quick death when he sees my expression. He holds up a hand. "Look, Julie—"

"Don't *look Julie* me." Emotions are warring inside me; I'm so glad to see Rashad, alive, here in my kitchen again, and so angry that he's brought a child here—a child who's in such pain and so frail from the terrors he's endured. A child he expects *us* to be able to protect. And though I know in my rational mind that it's not his fault, I blame Rashad for the specter of those men, men who even now could be making their way down the mountain toward us. I wouldn't even know about them if it wasn't for Rashad, and ignorance seems like a bliss, right now.

"He's really frail, Rashad." I won't look at him. "He's not just starved and tired, he's . . . he's destroyed. What he must have witnessed—"

"He needs some time, yes." Rashad places his hands flat on the table top, carefully, as though their placement matters crucially at this moment. "He's been through a lot. But he'll be able to gather his strength here, while we get ready—"

"Ready for what?" Even while I'm snapping at him, I notice again how worn out Rashad looks, and how, even now, exhausted, he's being kind and gentle. I want to get him some more pancakes, heat some more coffee for him, and I want to scream at him and tell him to get out.

Rashad looks up at me, his eyes seeking mine, waiting until I meet his gaze. "Julie. I know this is hard for you. I know you don't want to leave here. Hell, I don't blame you. This is . . . was . . . almost a perfect set-up for you. You had food, you had—"

"We could have made it work!" I don't want to hear him. "We could still have made it work, if you hadn't gone up there—" I stop myself. "I know that's not true. I know that you going to see about Anthony has nothing to do with this." I think about Amit, up there on the mountain alone hiding in some bushes, and where he'd be right now if Rashad hadn't gone up there. He'd be dead. Or worse. "I just . . . I just don't know."

Rashad nods, and reaches out me. This time, I take his hands in mine. He's alive. He's safe, and so is Amit. For now, that's what I'll think about.

"There's something out there for us." Rashad squeezes my hands. "Something better. I *know* it."

I don't know it, though. I shake my head at him, exasperated. "There may be something out there for you. And for him." I tilt my head toward the office. "But I'm not so sure it's for me. For now, I think you need to follow his lead and sleep. You're both going to need a lot of rest if you're going." I try to stand, but Rashad won't release my hands.

"Julie, come on. We can *do* this, if we—"

"Seriously, let's let it go for now." I keep my voice light, and extricate myself from his grip. "I'm going to get the dishes, and I suggest you go crash. You look like hell." I try to make it into a joke, but it falls flat. From the look on his face, Rashad isn't amused, either.

"I *am* tired." Rashad stands, pushing himself up like an old man. "And I will go sleep for a while, but Julie, we *are* going to talk more. I'm taking Amit to Seattle and I can't just let you—I can't just leave you here." He starts toward the door to the living room, heading for the couch, but he doubles back, stopping in front of me. He puts his hands on my shoulders, looking down at me with a solemn expression. "You're my *friend*, friend."

For just a moment, I want to believe him, believe that we'll all troop off together and find some beautiful future. But I just smile back up at him. "Take my bed. You need some quiet."

They both sleep most of the day. I spend it sorting through my clothing stores to find more outfits for Amit, and trying to think about what else they might need for the trip to Seattle. A couple of times during the day I break down, tears splashing on the supplies I'm organizing into piles, while I imagine Rashad gone forever.

But I snap out of it soon enough. I just remind myself that I've been through this before—I've already lost him; I've already mourned him. The fact that he's back, even briefly, is just a gift, and I tell myself to look at it that way. What comes after he and Amit leave will come. And I'll get through it. Or I won't. I don't care much, anymore.

The murmurations have fallen silent.

Respite

RASHAD SLEEPS MOST of the day, or at least, the bedroom door remains closed. I wash up the breakfast dishes and putter, tidying the living room and finally settling on the couch with a book of poetry. It doesn't hold my attention for long, and soon enough, I extinguish the lamp and stretch out, staring at the ceiling in the dark. Tyrone noses his way out of the office and joins me, laying next to the couch.

I imagine I can hear all the breathing in the house—Rashad from the bedroom, Amit from the office, Tyrone from the floor. And my own breath, in and out, in and out. All four of us existing here, in my little house, in this moment of stillness. All four of us separate, and yet together. I hear the wind outside, buffeting the trees, an early spring storm gathering strength. I feel nothing. Nothing but regret, and sadness.

A moan from the office brings Tyrone to his feet in an instant, and I light the lamp, follow him to the door. Amit is stirring, troubled by dreams. I enter, kneel beside the air mattress, afraid to touch him. I can't even guess what nightmares he must have, what terrors haunt him from his time in the cabin on the mountain, and the time before that. His father, beaten by those brutes, left for dead; he and his mother abducted, dragged to the cabin where he must have witnessed such horrors, where they killed his mother, where they would have killed him, too, if not for Anthony.

"I'm so sorry, little boy." I whisper the words. "I'm so sorry no one protected you." I feel a tear slip down my cheek and wipe it away with my hand.

"Papa protected me." Amit whispers, too. His eyes gleam in the lamp light. "Mama protected me." His voice catches, and he chokes down a sob. Then he continues, stronger. "Even Tony did. And Rashad brought me down the mountain." He rubs his eyes, props himself up on his elbows. "That's why I'm here." He stares at me. "Why are you here?"

"You were having a dream. Maybe a bad dream? I came to check on you."

"No—I mean why are *you* here?" Amit keeps staring. "Who protected you?"

"Nobody." The word is out of my mouth before I think. "I mean . . ." I stare back at Amit. He lets his head fall back on the pillow, the picture of exhaustion. After a moment he turns on his side, curls his hands under his cheek.

"I'll protect you, Miss Julie." He mumbles the words, and I wonder if he's actually awake, or sleeping. After a moment, his breathing tells me it's the latter.

Once I'm sure he's going to remain asleep, I creep out of the office, closing the door almost all the way, and return to the couch. Tyrone huffs and settles, and we lay quietly together. I think about my own childhood, sifting through the people in it, trying to identify a protector. I come up with some kindness, some concern, but not a single act of what could be called protection.

The things that happened to me as a child were *allowed* to happen. No one stopped them. Certainly not my mother—I always thought of the saying *The meek shall inherit the earth* when I thought of her—yes, the meek. Because all they do is go along to get along, keep their heads down, and let others get hurt because it's safer. So yes, they probably will inherit the earth, but what kind of place will that be?

Nobody came to my rescue. The first time I felt protected was when I protected myself, from Roger, by leaving him. And I've protected myself ever since, by staying away from people. It seems like a working solution to me. At least, it had been working, before Rashad. But he'll be gone, too, soon enough.

— ⁓

I awake to the smell of food. Sounds in the kitchen; quiet talking, dishes clinking. It's dark in the living room, but light spills from the kitchen doorway. Tyrone, still on the floor by my side, nudges my hand.

"They're up, huh?"

Tyrone stands, stretches, and takes a step toward the kitchen. He looks back at me, cocking his head as though to ask what's taking so long.

"Oh, okay." I haul myself up from the couch. "I'm coming."

The scene in the kitchen is like some heart-warming greeting card illustration. Rashad stands behind Amit, who is stirring something in a pot on the camp stove. He holds the wooden spoon awkwardly, moving it in careful circles.

"Like this?" He's intent on his task.

"Just like that. Now we just need some salt." Rashad turns to get the shaker from the counter and sees me. "Hey, there. You're up."

I nod, and enter the kitchen, Tyrone preceding me. "Yeah. Something smells good."

Amit holds the spoon aloft for me to see. "I'm making almost-jambalaya. Rashad says it's *almost* because we're missing some of the ingredients."

"Yeah, like everything but the rice," Rashad grins, "but we're improvising." He points to Tyrone. "I was just about to give this guy an outside-break. I bet he's got to go by now." He unbars the French doors and makes a smooching sound at Tyrone, who is at his side in a flash. "Can you supervise the stirring while I run him out?"

The daylight streaming in from outside surprises me—it must still be late afternoon by the looks of it. "Sure." Rashad lets Tyrone out and follows him onto the deck.

I walk to the camp stove and stand near Amit. "So . . . where are we at with this jambalaya?"

Amit corrects me. "*Almost*-jambalaya. It's different. Rashad said regular jambalaya has sausage, and celery." He looks up at me, still stirring. "We don't have that. But we have the rice, and we have dried onion and dried meat and stuff. So it should be okay."

"Did you get some sleep, Amit?" I lean against the counter, trying to look casual. I don't feel very casual. I've never been in total charge of a seven-year-old, even for a minute. Amit seems better than he did earlier—there are still signs of fatigue on his face, but he sounds fairly chipper.

He tends to the pot. "I did sleep. You slept, too, and Rashad. I guess we were all tired."

"I guess so." I have no idea what I'm supposed to do next. As I'm wondering how to make small talk with a child, Rashad and Tyrone return. Rashad sees my face before I can wipe the relief off of it, and chuckles.

"We all ready for supper?" He drops the bar across the doors and walks over to Amit to inspect the almost-jambalaya. "Looks perfect, Amit." Rashad turns to me. "Shall we eat?"

Throughout the meal Rashad and Amit keep up a steady patter of conversation, and I try to contribute, but I feel as though I'm seeing them, them and the whole scene, through the wrong end of a telescope. Here they sit in my house, acting as though we're all part of a unit, passing the salt and refilling the water glasses, and they don't seem to notice that we're really flying apart, hurtling away from each other, that we always have been and we always will be separate.

"Do I remember maps, Julie?" Rashad starts to clear the table, and Amit hops off his chair to help. "Didn't you have some somewhere? A city map, I think, and some others?"

I nod. "From one of the houses. I thought . . ." I'd thought they might come in handy, long ago—it seems like years, now—when I'd stumbled across them in one of my house raids. No Internet anymore, no way to download the fastest route. I can see the house in my mind, the desk they were in—just a couple of city maps and an old, Rand McNally Road Atlas. I'd brought them home and stashed them in the bookshelf in the living room. "They're in the bookshelf."

"After we get these dishes done let's take a look at them, see if we can chart the best course to the marina." Rashad ruffles Amit's hair, and Amit nods enthusiastically.

They spend the rest of the evening engrossed in a Billington map, crinkled folds spread out on the coffee table in the lamp light, index fingers tracing various roads. Amit asks question after question, and Rashad patiently responds. Finally, after I take Tyrone out for one last bathroom trip, I interrupt them from the doorway.

"I'm going to turn in."

They both look up. Rashad smiles, stands. "Yeah, maybe we all should. I'm still beat even after sleeping almost all day."

Amit carefully folds the map, gets up and walks over to me. He pats Tyrone on the head, and then, hesitant, steps closer. "Good night, Miss Julie." He holds out his arms, waiting, I realize belatedly, for a hug.

"Um." I stoop, and wrap one arm halfway around him, pat him on the back. "Just Julie's fine, really." Straightening, I ignore Rashad's expression—a combination of hilarity and mock seriousness that I don't find funny. "I'll see you both in the morning."

— ~

The next week seems interminable. The three of us fall into a routine—breakfast, lunch, a nap, since all of us are still tired—me from being so sick, and the two of them from their journey down the mountain. Then, lots of planning, at least from Rashad, with Amit chiming in excitedly about what Seattle might be like, how we'll get there, what we'll need to take. We make trips to the garage for what we need, we do what has to be done to get through each day. Then we eat dinner and not long after we all go to bed.

Rashad takes every opportunity to press his case. He goes on about how we have to try for more, how we have to make sure Amit is safe, how we can't stay here. At first, I argue back, but soon enough I just listen, and let him talk. I can see his frustration grow when I don't engage, but I don't know what else to do. I want the time before they leave to be good, I want it to be as easy as I can make it, for him and for me.

The murmurations remain silent.

The Garden

ONE MORNING AFTER breakfast, we're all in the living room, Rashad poring over maps while Amit plays a game of indoor fetch with Tyrone. I sit on one end of the couch, cleaning the gun. I've no idea how often one is supposed to clean a gun, and am not exactly certain I'm doing it correctly, but I'm doing my best to oil it up. Rashad holds up one of the maps and points out the port to Amit.

"Only a few miles to the water." He runs a finder along the roads leading from the house we sit in to the bay. "Then it's hop a boat and off sailing we go." He folds the map in order to study a section more closely.

Amit's especially excited about Rashad's boat idea, and very proud that before Hacker's hit he learned to swim.

"Mama took me to lessons at the Y." Amit makes swimming motions with his arms. "I was not even four yet, and I was scared, but Mama said I could learn to swim just like I learned to walk." He looks up at me from the floor where he's been rolling a ball toward Tyrone, and Tyrone's been rolling it back with his nose. "We all had to *learn* to walk—did you know that, Julie?"

"Yep." I like seeing Amit play with Tyrone. It's how a kid should act— it gives me hope for him. And Tyrone is already in full-on love with him.

"We all have to learn a lot of things, Amit." Rashad doesn't look up from the map. "Some of them we have to learn even when we're older than three." He raises one eyebrow, and even though he's not looking at me, I get the message.

"I'm going to make a trip to the garden." I announce it the same moment the thought enters my head. I just want to get out, away from all the planning and the stifling sense of loss that pervades every conversation they have about the future.

"The garden?" Rashad and Amit both say the words at the same time, but with two totally different inflections.

"You have a garden?" Amit looks curious.

"What for?" Rashad looks concerned. "I mean, we've got everything we need for the trip next door."

I ignore the assumption that we're all going on *the trip*. I'd planned to go check the soil, get back to the tilling I'd begun when I fell ill. Soon enough it would be time to plant, and it was already time to start seedlings in the greenhouse. But I don't want to argue, so I make something up.

"Seeds. You'll need—it would be good to take seeds to Seattle, in case there are none. I stored all the extra seeds in the greenhouse." I wipe the last of the excess oil off the gun and begin to reassemble it. I stored all the seeds right here in the house, to protect them from rodents, but Rashad didn't know that.

Rashad grunts—his *I'm thinking* grunt. "Well, maybe. But it's risky— we'd all have to go, and I wonder if it's worth it for a few seeds. There's bound to be some in Seattle."

"You don't know that. It's better to take what's available here and be prepared." I stand, and Tyrone jumps up from his ball, sensing he might have an outing in store. "We don't all have to go. I'll be fine to make a quick run while you two stay here."

"I want to see the garden." Amit sits up, looking almost as eager as Tyrone. I imagine he's just as sick of the inside of the house as I am, for different reasons.

"We go together." Rashad's tone doesn't leave room for discussion. "When?" He watches me, waiting for my response.

"Um, well, I was thinking now? Ish?" What I'm really thinking is that my whole plan is ruined. I won't be able to get any work done in the garden bed without starting another argument about me going along to Seattle. No need to prep for planting a garden nobody will be around to harvest. And Rashad will jump right on that and start wheedling about how I have to go with them. I won't even be able to get away from them for a bit, just to have some silence, some space.

"Fine." Rashad stands, too. "Let's get ready."

We're out the door in less than half an hour. I manage to grab a few of the seed packets I have stashed in the kitchen and shove them into my coat pocket before we leave. I'll plant them later, at the greenhouse, so Rashad will never know about my subterfuge, I hope. I feel bad lying to him, and even worse dragging him and Amit on a trip for nothing, but I also feel trapped. And I need to get out.

It's brisk out, but we've all got warm coats on. I lead the way, with Tyrone at my side on leash, just to be safe. Amit follows close behind me and Rashad brings up the rear. It feels good to be outside, even though it will be sort of a wasted trip. I remember the last time I made this walk, unaware that I was ill, how I felt alone without Rashad by my side. I feel all alone now, even though I'm not. *They will be leaving soon.* I keep repeating the words in my mind. I need to protect myself.

Everything is silent. We move along carefully, stopping often to scan the yards and houses ahead, listening for any sound. Amit is watchful and quiet, and I realize he's had practice at this, coming down the mountain with Rashad. I see bright green tips on the shrubs, ready to burst into new growth. Another spring will be here in no time.

We arrive at the garden yard and examine the ground in front of the gate.

"Looks pretty untouched." Rashad scuffs a clump of grass with his foot. "Seem good to you?"

I nod, and unlatch the gate. Inside the yard, nothing looks disturbed. Holstering the gun, which I've kept at hand on the walk, I move to the greenhouse. Amit is right behind me, and when I stop to open the door he runs into me.

"Sorry." His eyes widen when he sees inside the greenhouse. "Whoa." He scoots around me to the shelves of pots. A couple of seedlings are sprouting, pale and thin, stretching toward the light. They give me a bit of hope, hope for this coming spring, and the summer after it, when I'll be alone again. I can do this. I can *do* this. I have to do this.

"Mama had a garden." Amit speaks softly, reaches out to touch one of the tiny plants. "She had lots of plants."

I can't see his face, but it sounds like he might be near tears. All of the pain this child carries, all of the loss. "I bet her garden was much better than this one. I'm just learning."

"Oh, no." He turns to me, worried that he's offended me. "I bet it was great. I bet you did a good job."

"She did." Rashad enters the greenhouse. "All those potatoes are because of Julie." He looks around, checks out the neat stacks of pots, the shelving along the sides of the structure. "I tied Tyrone's leash to the deck rail for now. Where do we find these seeds?"

I haven't had a moment to stash the seeds in my pocket somewhere in the greenhouse. "Um," I stammer. "I think I left them in the house, maybe. Yes, it seemed more secure than here." I hope I sound convincing.

"The house it is, then." Rashad steps to the side and gestures for me to lead the way out of the greenhouse.

I start toward the door, but freeze in my tracks at the creaking sound I hear outside.

Turning my body without moving my feet, I whisper to Rashad. "Did you latch the gate?"

He looks confused, then his eyes widen. The creak sounds again, long, and low. Someone is opening the gate to the yard.

The three of us stand, motionless, bathed in the cold, early spring light, aware that any movement will be seen through the glass by whoever's outside. I've brought us here, to this risk, for no reason at all, except my own selfishness. I hear Amit behind me, breathing hard, and imagine the fear he's feeling now, because of me, after all the fear he's already endured.

I unholster the gun without thinking, raise it and rush toward the door. Whoever's out there, I can't let them hurt Rashad or Amit. I won't.

"No!" I hear Amit scream the word and in the same moment somehow he's in front of me, we're both out of the greenhouse, exposed, and I wave the gun and scream myself at the gate—it's halfway open and moving. I feel Rashad grab me from behind, and I lose my balance. Amit throws himself on top of me like a shield, knocking the wind out of me.

From the grass, I see a deer peering in at us, halfway through the gate, looking as surprised as we are. I'm laying half on, half off of Rashad, covered by Amit, still holding my gun out at the deer. The creature takes in the scene, lowers her head to sample the grass, raises it again and stares. We stare back.

"You're not going to shoot the deer, are you?" Amit whispers.

"Lotta steaks there, though." Rashad struggles to get out from under me.

The deer bolts, and we can hear it running down the alley.

Rashad and Amit stand, brushing grass and debris from their clothes. Rashad starts to chuckle, and soon enough Amit joins in, laughing.

"Did you see that look it gave us?" Rashad straightens Amit's jacket collar. "I think we offended it."

"What the hell is so damned funny?" I lay on my back, still breathing fast, thinking about what could have just happened. "Amit what the hell were you thinking? Running out in front of me?" I am furious, and finally the two of them hear it in my voice.

"Whoa, whoa." Rashad extends a hand, helps me to my feet. "Easy. He was just—"

"I was protecting you, Miss Julie." Amit's head is bowed, his voice tremulous. "I *told* you I would protect you. Don't you remember?"

And I do remember. This little boy, waking from a nightmare, promising to protect me. I let my head fall back into the grass. This little boy, not knowing what he might be facing, put his body in front of mine in order to protect me. "Oh, Amit." I don't know why but I burst into tears.

"I'm sorry, Miss Julie." Amit drops down next to me, distraught. "I didn't mean to make you mad. Or . . . sad."

I push myself up into a sitting position, and drop the gun so I can wipe my face with my hands. "I'm not mad, Amit." When I hold out my arms he comes to me, and I hug him. "I'm not mad. You were very brave." I ruffle his hair. "And it's just *Julie*. Okay?"

"Um." Rashad's untied Tyrone from the deck, and he joins the hug, licking Amit's face and mine in turn. "I was protecting you some there myself, you know. *Miss* Julie. I mean, not as good as Amit here, but still."

All I can do is laugh.

But we're all three shaken. When Rashad says "Let's get out of here" we do. On the walk back to the house, all I can think about is how that deer could have been something much more dangerous; how we could be dead. And over and over, I hear Amit screaming *No*, see him running out in front of me, protecting me from danger. I can feel Rashad grabbing me from behind, trying to get me down, out of the line of fire. They could have both been killed if that deer was some guy with a gun. And I have no doubt there are a lot of guys with guns in Seattle.

After a light supper, we turn in early, adrenaline-weary. I lay in my bed, seeing a bloodied Amit, a battered Rashad, hundreds of different ways they could perish, and tell myself I'm relieved I won't have to witness any of them.

— —

The next morning at breakfast, Amit pushes a piece of potato around on his plate, and sighs.

"Do you think there will be hamburgers in Seattle?"

Rashad laughs out loud. "Getting a little sick of the rations, huh, Amit?" He grins across the table at me. "I bet there will be. But what I really hope for is onion rings—deep-fried, salty onion rings with dipping sauce."

Amit smiles. "Maybe there will be ice cream." His eyes get big.

"Or waffles and bacon!" Rashad points at Amit. "Your turn."

"Um . . . cotton candy!" Amit points back at Rashad.

"Lasagna!" Rashad points to me.

"I wouldn't know. I'm not going to Seattle." I say the words without thinking, so focused on protecting myself, but as soon as I say them I want to slap myself. The first sign of fun from Amit, the first tiny hope of a hope, and I have to open my big mouth and ruin it. Rashad's expression goes flat. Amit immediately lowers his head, and in an instant he's weeping, trying hard to hide it. I reach out toward him.

"Oh, Amit—I'm sorry. I didn't mean—"

"Amit." Rashad's voice is gentle, but his eyes are stormy and he's staring at me while he talks. "Why don't you go into the living room and see if Tyrone would like to go with you? I bet he'd like some of that potato. Just take that big piece and see if he likes it."

Amit scoots his chair back and forks the potato off of his plate. "Tyrone," he whispers, head still down, "look." He holds out the fork and Tyrone, happy to oblige, follows him from the room.

Rashad is sitting very still, shaking his head in disbelief.

"I'm sorry—" I don't get a chance to finish my sentence.

"For fuck's sake." Rashad whispers fiercely. "Get it together." He stands and takes his plate to the sink. He keeps his back to me for a moment, holding the edge of the counter, breathing in, breathing out. I can see his shoulders rise with each breath. The he turns to face me. "I'm going to the garage for water, for Amit's bath. When I come back, and that bath is ready, I hope you will have done whatever you need to do make him feel better."

"I didn't mean to upset him. But, I mean, it's true. I'm not going, and he may as well know that." I shrug my shoulders, feeling sick inside.

"Oh, he *knows* it Julie. He knows it. He asks me about it every time you're not in the room. He's scared for you, and damn it, Julie, so am I. *So am I.*" Rashad is shaking mad. He strides to the door, lifts the bar, opens it. Then he turns back. "Think about what you're doing to that poor kid. Think about that. And maybe, think about what you're doing to me. How do you think I feel, wondering if you're ever going to wake up and realize you have a responsibility? To me. To him," he jabs a finger toward the living room. "To yourself, for fuck's sake." And then he leaves, without a backward glance.

I watch him hop off the deck and disappear through the back gate. I clear the table, stacking all the dishes in the sink, trembling. I take my own deep breaths, and then I go out into the living room.

Doing

"JULIE." AMIT'S BEEN waiting for me.

I look at him. This boy, just a child, sitting on my couch, petting Tyrone. Is he my responsibility now? "Yes, Amit?"

"Do you want to sit down?" He pats the sofa next to him.

I sit, carefully, keeping a few inches between us.

"Rashad says you won't come with us because you hate people." His expression is very serious.

"I don't hate them. I . . . it's just, lots of people are . . ."

"Bad." Amit makes the word sound terrifying. "There are a lot of bad people. I'm afraid of them." He takes hold of my hand. "You're afraid of the bad people, too."

I start to deny this, but then I realize it's true. I *am* afraid. "It just doesn't seem like a good idea."

"But if you stay here, even if the mountain men don't kill you, you'll die. And in the meantime, you'll be alone. And then, when you do die, you'll die alone." Amit recites these facts with something that sounds close to sadness. "So you won't have much chance to do." He pauses, working something out in his mind. "I mean, you *can* do, but not really, not if you're alone. Because then, what does your doing matter?"

I'm stymied. "What do you mean, *do*? Is it something about what you see when you . . . see?"

Amit shakes his head. "Doing is for *people*. We're the only ones who can do." He taps his temple with an index finger. "Because we can pick. We have . . . choice. Doing is the only thing that matters. Mama *said*." He repeats a rhyme, in a sing-song voice. "It's not who you are, it's not what you own, it's not who you love, it's not *you* alone. It's *what* you *do*, and *how*, to *who*." He smiles, but almost instantly his lip trembles and he's in tears, and I remember his mother is dead.

Tyrone and I both move at the same moment; Tyrone puts his front feet up on the sofa next to Amit and nuzzles him, while I lean in and gather him in a hug. It's not a natural movement for me and I hope Amit can't tell. "I'm so sorry," I whisper, over and over. We rock like that in the dim light in the living room, until Amit has hold of himself again. He wipes his tears away and sniffles.

"She said all we have is our effect." Amit pronounces *effect* carefully. "That means what your *actions* do. And she said you can only do actions that matter on *others*." He looks at Tyrone, who is still nuzzling his hand. "She would have counted Tyrone as others. So I guess you *can* do to Tyrone, because you won't really be alone, but if you decide to stay here, you would be doing *wrong* to him."

"Because the mountain men might kill him?" I'm starting, crazily enough, to follow his logic.

"You say you love him, but they *would* kill him. All because you're afraid to go. Mama would say you aren't doing it right." Amit's still sniffling a bit.

"Did you tell her about seeing things?" I wondered; was his life before Hacker's Flu like mine had been, a lonely child with a unique ability, unable to share his experience, even with his parents? I hoped not.

"Visions. She called them visions." He looks sleepy; worn out from crying.

"So, you have visions, I have murmurations. I guess we both have the same thing, in a way." I smooth his hair back from his forehead. "Did your mom tell you what the visions mean?"

"She said maybe someday I would figure it out." Amit sighed. "She said it wasn't most important to know what they are. More important is *doing*. More important is my *effect*."

"Ah." I wonder aloud. "Do you think *doing* and the visions—and my murmurations—do you think those are connected?"

He looks confused.

"I mean, do you think what you see and what I hear—our *things*—are they about us? About *people*? Whether we're all doing okay or not?"

Amit shakes his head. "The visions aren't just about people. They're about *everything*. Like I told you." He frowns at me as though I'm being dull-witted. "We—people—are only a *little* thing. We're in there—we're a *part* of everything, but we're only a tiny part." He yawns. "I think that's why Mama said the doing is most important. Because for us, for people, that's all we have. Our effect on others. We can *never* understand the great everything, even if we see some of it." He looks at me. "Or hear some of it."

I reach out for Amit's hand and give it a squeeze. I think I understand what he's saying, but the translation of the world's mysteries by a seven-year-old makes it a bit murky. "Your mama was very wise."

Rashad pokes his head in the doorway. "Bath water's heating up, my man. Two pots done, three to go." He ignores me. "I could use some help. Want to watch a pot while I dump some in the bath tub?"

Amit hops up, looks at me. "Are you okay, Julie?"

I nod. "I'm okay. Go get your bath." I watch him go, and when I think about all that's happened to him, I don't quite understand how he's still functioning at all. When I look at him, I still see echoes of the faces of the children at the safehouse, but there are no caseworkers here to provide whatever counseling or therapy they might to help him. There is only me; me and Rashad.

I settle back on the sofa for a while, thinking. Thinking about *doing*.

I see Tyrone shivering in his death row kennel, and think of how I stopped at the intersection that day, how I could have kept going when that light turned green. But I didn't. I pulled into the shelter parking lot instead. I picture Rashad standing over me as I bled from a knife wound in the kitchen, see him help me to my bed, nurse me back to health. I see Anthony, walking right up to Rashad in that wine shop for the first time, and I imagine the invisible thread connecting Anthony to Rashad to the men in that cabin on the mountain, and then to Amit, to saving Amit's life. And Rashad, meeting Amit's father on his way down the mountain before he saved me, and meeting Amit on his way back up. I think about Gina, borrowing that cigarette during the break from poetry class, how she'd become such an important part of my life. She understood me when I needed it so badly, she taught me to begin to trust. My mind fills with connections. What of the man and his son who would have killed me for Tyrone's meat? What about Ski Coat and Denim Jacket, or Mark the gun-toting neighbor?

Were we all moving together, forming a pattern on our own version of the sky, just like the birds in a murmuration? Each of us in a certain place at a certain time, free to go left or right but part of a larger pattern? And were we all a part of that whole, as Amit had said, *a part of everything*, even if we were only a tiny part? All of us choosing, all of us *doing*, as Amit's mother had said? Choosing and doing, for better or worse.

The Plan

I'M SITTING AT the kitchen table, smoking another cigarette, when Rashad shuts the bathroom door behind him, having gotten Amit settled for his bath. He goes to the French doors and unbars them, fetching three more gallons of water from the deck, brings them in and leaves them on the floor while he locks and bars the door. I don't offer to get up and stow them in the cabinet. After he hauls them to the counter and gets them put away, he sits down across from me at the table.

"Even if *they* don't come, others will." Rashad makes the statement with no preamble. "The reality is that—"

"You think they'll come late fall, right?" I take a drag of my cigarette.

Rashad raises his eyebrows and I can see him trying to figure out what I'm thinking. "Right."

"So, that means we need to be out of here in a month or so." In a month it will still be late spring, early summer, but I don't want to cut it close. "We'll need to assess the stores, see what we should bring on the . . . boat." This still seems like a major weak spot to me. "Seriously, Rashad, a boat?"

He nods. "Yep. A boat. I had a chance to really study the atlas last night and if we just hug the coastline we should be fine." He rubs his stubbly chin dramatically, as though he's combing his beard to a point. "You didn't happen to find any *Sailing for Dummies* books in your raids, did you?"

I can't help but grin. "This is not a joke, Rashad."

"Oh, don't I know it." Rashad stops goofing and gets serious. "Why the change of heart?"

I stub my cigarette out. "You know the death book? All the time we spent last winter reading that thing? Talking about what happens when we die, what death might mean?"

Rashad just nods.

"Well. I finally figured out that the most important part of that book is in the introduction. That one line, where it says *how we understand death determines how we should live*. For me, the way I understand death is—"

"I know. You think we rot and that's it, right?"

"Right." I shake my head, thinking of all the years I've tried to keep safe. "But I don't *know* if we rot, for certain. I don't *know* anything about death. So how I understand death is . . . I don't. All I can ever really understand, or try to understand, is life." I watch Rashad's face, wondering if he comprehends half of what I'm trying to say. "Amit and I had a conversation about his thing, and my thing—the mumurations and the visions—about the meaning of life. And I guess I finally understand there is no meaning, without doing, without *effecting,* as Amit says. And you can't have an effect on *nobody*. You need *people*. So I better start doing something besides hiding from people and trying to keep myself safe. I better start being a part of it all, at least the tiny part I can be, of the *everything*."

Rashad looks scandalized. "I *told* you that. *I* told you that last winter. Um, except whatever that *effecting* shit is about. And you *finally* get it from a seven-year-old?"

I laugh at his expression. "The way *he* said it made sense."

— ～

We spend the next week taking stock of which supplies we'll need to pack and feeding Amit as much as possible. He is painfully skinny, and the dark circles under his eyes linger despite hours of sleep. Tyrone sticks close to him, though he does check in with me often. Watching the two of them sometimes, Tyrone leaning against the boy's leg, Amit with his hand on Tyrone's head, I'm even more happy I adopted the dog. He brings Amit a comfort neither Rashad or I can, just by being quietly *there*.

Greg's garage still holds a surprising amount of supplies; we could never take it all. Rashad makes list after list of priority items, changing his mind so many times it drives me crazy. Finally, after the fourth discussion about whether the rice or the beans are more important to take, I suggest we figure out how we're hauling it all, first.

"I told you." Rashad looks irritated. "We're finding a stick-shift."

"Well. Let's find it, and get it here."

Rashad shakes his head at me as though I'm a disappointing student. "We have to push-start the thing."

"So?"

"So, we can go locate our vehicle, but that vehicle better be on a hill, and close enough to haul our supplies to, and it will stay on said hill until we're ready to go."

He's right. I hadn't thought about it but my street is level ground; letting gravity provide the momentum to push-start us made sense. Thankfully, just a couple blocks from us the streets turn hilly as the suburban sprawl rises to the foothills. Still, it seems risky.

"We'll have a lot of work hauling the supplies."

Rashad nods.

"And what if we get the thing totally loaded and ready to go and it doesn't start."

Rashad nods again, as he moves a sack of beans to the *take* pile.

"Most of the cars I see now, the tires are flat. And what about the gas? How long does gas stay good?"

Rashad sits down next to me on the bin I've been using as a seat. "We can drive on rims if we have to, if we go slow. It's not that far to the marina. As for the gas, all we can do is hope. Worst case scenario, we're going to be hoofing it with very few supplies." He nudges me with his shoulder. "It's not like we can go look it all up on the Internet. It is what it is."

"I hate that saying."

"Doesn't make it any less true." Rashad eyes the dead laptop on the workbench. "Damn, I miss the Internet."

⌐ ¬

The three of us set out the next morning to find our chariot. Amit wants to bring Tyrone but I tell him we can't; I want to locate a vehicle and get back home with no distractions. I feel a little guilty when we leave, Tyrone's tail wagging hopefully right up until I shut the door on him, but I tell myself I'll make it up to him with some ball when we get back.

Amit is feeling stronger and he seems to enjoy the light and fresh air. I imagine the dark, stuffy interior of my house is getting old. He troops along behind Rashad, who leads the way. I follow last, gun in holster, checking behind us often. The streets are quiet, but I'm worried about eyes we can't see. Amit is silent, careful, any trace of childhood removed from his being by his experiences. I think about that smile he gifted Tyrone with, still one of only a few I've seen from him, and wonder if he'll ever recover from what's happened to him already in his short life.

I'm afraid we'll have to trek to the hills a half-mile away before we find a vehicle situated appropriately, but not even three blocks from home Rashad holds his hand up, signally us to stop. He's looking toward a cul-de-sac, the houses laid out in some suburban planner's dream configuration, all elevated above a perfect circle of street-slash-playground awaiting neighborhood children who will never again burst through front doors to play. There's a dusty basketball hoop in front of one house. A faded skateboard lays on its side on the pavement. Each house features a huge, front-facing garage, all perched above sloping driveways spilling down into the street. Most of the garage doors have home-made quarantine **Q**s on them.

"Bet one of those has our car in it." Rashad scans the houses. "Right at the top of its own little hill. We can start from there." He points at the house closest to us. We walk up the driveway to the garage door and Rashad leans down to lift it. No luck.

"Side door." I try it and it's open. But inside the garage there's only grease-stained cement and an empty bike rack on the wall. "Next." I lead the way, skirting the garage for the next house.

We hit gold on the third house. The roll-up door is locked like the two before it, and so is the side door, but it has a window which Rashad breaks. Inside, there's a red pickup truck. It looks like it must be from the 1950's and it was clearly someone's baby, lovingly restored, spotless, except for the layer of dust coating the surface. Even the tires are still inflated. Rashad tries the door and it's open.

"Stick shift." He leans in, flashlight probing, checking the truck's instrument panel. "If the gauge is right it's got half a tank of gas." He fumbles around in the cab. "And holy . . ." Rashad backs and turns to face Amit and me, eyes wide.

"What?" I brace for bad news.

"Keys." He holds up a key with a chain dangling. "Right under the seat!" Rashad laughs and grabs Amit's hands, coaxing him into an impromptu dance.

I climb into the cab myself and check out the minimalist dashboard. There's a round, bubble-glass fuel tank gauge, an identical speedometer and a push-button radio. The steering wheel is attached to a metal stalk coming right out of the floor. There's a stick shift labeled with three gears plus reverse. "What good do the keys do if we have to push start it?"

"The ignition has to be in . . . start mode." Rashad mumbles the last words. "Maybe. I think."

I climb out of the truck and give Rashad a skeptical look. Did you say *start* mode?"

He attempts a dignified tone. "I believe that's the technical term." Then he turns his back on me and high-fives Amit. "Doesn't matter. We have the keys, we have the hill, we have some gas, all systems go!"

Rashad and Amit both seem thrilled, but I'm feeling a strange numbness. I touch the fender of the truck, feeling the grit of the dust and then the smooth, cool surface of the metal underneath. The idea that we will be loading that empty truck bed with everything we can fit, and then climbing in the cab and hoping to hell that the thing starts, and then driving away from all I've known since the flu hit and setting out to sea? Based on the dicey proposition that there are people somewhere up the coast who won't kill us on sight for our supplies? That all seems insane. And imminent.

I watch Amit, who is almost playful with Rashad. I think about what kind of life he would have here, what future would unfold for him. If Rashad's right, it would be a short life, ending brutally when the men come down the mountain. We won't be able to out-fight them. We have to go.

The garage is tidy, a tool chest against the back wall, a storage cabinet next to the work bench. Rashad bags some of the tools while I peek in the cabinet. Inside, most of the shelves are stacked with car-wash supplies; wax and road goop remover and chamois cloths. Oddly enough, the bottom shelf has a stack of board games. I wonder if the people who lived here were empty-nesters, storing the last of the kid-relics away under the new, adult-hobby accoutrements. I read the sides of the boxes: Scrabble, and Monopoly and Pictionary. On the top of the stack is a travel version of checkers, small enough to fit in my backpack. I take it.

"We can keep the main garage door closed until we leave, and truck our supplies through the side door with the wheelbarrow." Rashad slings the bag of tools he's gathered over his shoulder. "Let's see if there's a back route here from home that's less exposed than the streets." He heads for the side door. "Ready?"

After a couple of false starts, we do find a better way to the cul-de-sac house. From its back yard, we can cut through a small, sparsely wooded area and connect with an alley, jog south on that for a half a block and then cross to the alley behind my house. The route is less exposed than the streets we took to get there, and it's quicker, too. By the time we get back home we're all feeling pretty good about the plan. I've decided that focusing on the practical details is the only way to stay sane; it keeps me from fretting about the huge unknown.

We make two trips to the truck with supplies before calling it a day, taking mostly clothing and bedding, because those can be replaced if someone raids the truck. The rest of the day is spent estimating what we can fit in the truck bed, and how long it might take us to get it all there. Amit pushes himself to help, but he still looks tired and weak to me. I say as much to Rashad once we're back in the house and he's taking a pre-dinner nap.

"I think he'll need at least a couple of weeks to rest up before we try this."

Rashad, rummaging through the cabinets to come up with dinner, nods in agreement. "I was thinking the same thing about you. That cough is still hanging on."

He's right. I haven't been able to shake the damn cough and I still feel more exhausted at the end of a day than I should. I haven't mentioned it to Rashad because I don't want any lectures on smoking. I'll run out of cigarettes soon enough. "I'm okay. Just taking some time to get over it."

"Yeah, well, *you* may need to be taking naps along with Amit." Rashad looks over my shoulder. "Speaking of whom . . ."

Amit's awake. He enters the kitchen slowly, still groggy from his nap. Tyrone is on his heels, nose up, sniffing at the odors Rashad's cooking is producing. I pull some plates from the cabinet and start to set the table, while Amit gets the silverware. Tyrone settles on the floor near us, ever hopeful that he'll get some people-food. Before too long, a pasta dish is ready to be served and Amit and I hold our plates up so Rashad can ladle out our shares. Then he joins us at the table and as I look around at the scene illuminated by the kerosene lamp I'm struck—we look like some sort of family, again. And this time, it doesn't feel so odd.

Healing

IN THE DAYS that follow, time takes on a strange mutability, sometimes whizzing by, sometimes dreamily unhurried. We settle on a trip per day to the truck, loading in everything we can think of that might be necessary; it seems less likely we'll be observed with only one trip, and it's a good way to limit Amit's physical exertion. He's getting stronger, but Rashad and I both want him to have time to rest, both physically and emotionally, and we can't bring ourselves to leave him home alone while we make the supply runs. Fear of returning to some horror, fear of us not returning at all, prevents us.

The murmurations have returned. They sound . . . pleased.

Amit looks better with each accumulated night of sleep, each meal, each confirmation that we aren't going to hurt him. He's a brave boy, I can tell. He trusts Rashad the most; their time coming down the mountain together helped with that. He seems to love Tyrone. I'm the unknown factor to him, and I can't blame him, considering the uneven welcome I gave him his first day here. I catch him watching me sometimes, measuring the way I talk to Rashad, the way I treat Tyrone. I watch him, too. I watch how he always helps set the table without being asked, how he tucks in the sheets and blankets on the air mattress each morning, how he tries to hide his sadness.

I try to imagine myself at his age, and I remember how it felt then, always knowing I had to take up the least amount of space possible, keep my head down, try my hardest not to be any *trouble* for anyone, because if I was, there would be a price. I remember how aware I was that I didn't matter at all. *The child who is not embraced by the village will burn it down to feel its warmth.* I thought of that proverb a lot, growing up. I don't remember ever wanting to burn anything down, but I certainly never wanted to help build anything up, either. The endless damage humans can do, one to another, on and on down the line. Could it ever be stopped? I wonder, watching him, if it's too late to stop it for Amit.

One day, while Rashad is taking a bucket bath, I get the miniature checkers game out of my backpack and bring it out to the living room, where Amit is sitting quietly on the couch, petting Tyrone. I kneel and open it up on the coffee table.

"Want to play?" I try to sound casual. I can see Amit trying to process the question, wondering what the right answer might be.

"It's okay. I just wondered if you might be bored." I start to get up, but he leans forward on the couch.

"Checkers. My father taught me how." Amit smiles, a small, sad smile.

"Red or black?" I settle back down on the floor, start setting up the board.

Amit shrugs. "Which do you want?"

"I'm really happy with either." I wait until he hesitantly points at the red pieces, and swivel them toward him. "I guess I go first, then. Is that how your dad taught you? Black first?"

He nods.

"You sure you don't want black? First move? I'm pretty good at checkers." I smile so he'll know I'm kidding.

Amit smiles back, a smile with no sadness in it. "I'm pretty good at checkers, too."

I study the board, with no idea what a good first checkers move might be. Finally, I just pick a piece and slide it diagonally.

Amit groans. "Going to be a short game." He quickly checks my expression to see . . . what? If I'm mad?

"Come at me, bro." I waggle my head at him, laughing. "You have no idea what my secret strategy is in this game." I'm rewarded by a grin, and the game is on.

He beats me in three minutes. We reset the board, and he goes first, this time.

"Amit," say, after I make my own, sure to be ill-fated move. "I realized today that we've never asked you what you think of us all going to Seattle. I mean, I know I haven't, and I doubt Rashad has, either."

He stops mid-move, his checker frozen above the board. Keeping his eyes on the board, he speaks.

"What do you mean, ask me about it?"

"I mean, how you feel about it. Do you want to go?"

Amit sets his checker down beside the board. He doesn't look up at me. "Do *you* want me to go?" He waits, silent and tense.

"Of course I want you to go, Amit." I get up and sit next to him, but he still won't look at me. "I want us all to be together. I just thought you might have some feelings about it, too. And I wanted you to know that your feelings matter." I wait, hoping I haven't made things worse.

"I'm scared." It's no more than a whisper. "But I do want to go." He turns to face me, uncertainty in his eyes.

I meet his gaze. "Want to know a secret?"

Amit nods.

"I'm scared, too." I realize just how true this is; I am petrified at the prospect of leaving this house for good. "It's a scary thing, going off to someplace we don't know, but we'll be together. And so far, we—you, me, Rashad, Tyrone—we seem to be a pretty good team."

Amit nods again. "I see that it's right, so even if I'm scared, I want to go."

I'm about to suggest, now that I know he's okay, that he move his checker, but that phrase stops me. "You see? You mean, you . . . *see* that it's right?"

"Don't you *hear* it? That it's right?" He frowns. "Aren't your murmurations telling you?"

"I thought you said your visions, my murmurations, that they aren't about people." It's my turn to frown. Just when I think I have it all figured out, I don't.

"No, I said that they are about *everything*. But people are a part of that." He watches me. "I remember you said they talk in a language you can't understand. Your murmurations."

"Like your visions, I imagine. They're both things we can't really understand."

Amit shakes his head. "I can't understand all I see, but I can understand some of it, when I really look. My visions say that going to Seattle with you and Rashad and Tyrone is the right thing. I can just . . . tell, when I look." He studies the checker board. "I wonder," he says, softly, "if you're just not listening."

Rashad chooses that moment to appear in the living room doorway, still rubbing a towel over his hair. "I thought someone might be making dinner while I was getting less grubby, but I can see it's all fun and games for the two of you." He makes a dramatic turn, flicks the towel our way and stalks, faux-upset, into the kitchen. Amit and I look after him, both of us shaking our heads.

"We should go help." Amit starts to rise.

"We will." I pat the couch next to me. "But first, one more game. I need fair shot at evening up this score."

⎯ ⎯

That night, I'm awake, thinking, for too long. Amit's words—*I wonder if you're just not listening*—rattle around in my brain, pinging off of old memories. I remember knowing, somehow, that my mother didn't hear murmurations, because she was too damaged to look for magical things. Because she would never have actually *listened* to them.

It appears that I have become my mother.

All those years, all those years of hearing pain, and joy, and sorrow and hope, my murmurations were telling me, plain as day, what might be right or wrong with my own actions—my own *doing*. It's easy to piece together now—the hope they sang to me when I became friends—real friends— with Gina. The sadness in the tones I heard when Roger hit me and I stayed. Even the soothing sounds the day I adopted Tyrone. How the murmurations became just a constant, almost neutral whisper in the back of my mind when I was truly all alone, except for Tyrone. The anguish they conveyed when Rashad was leaving, and I refused to go with him. The happiness when he returned and I let him back into my life, when I comforted Amit through his nightmares, and when I finally decided to go to Seattle. How much time had I wasted pushing them out, covering my ears, ignoring the magic? They were telling me about *me*, and not just about me, but about my part in things, my part in *everything*. My ability to *effect*.

I didn't understand it all. And I knew I never would. But somehow, I knew that Amit's visions and my murmurations were a part of the same thing, the same glimpse into the . . . the everything. I fell asleep that night to the sounds of my murmurations, contented sounds, certain for the first time in my life that I was doing the right thing.

The evenings are the best times. After dinner, the four of us sit around in the living room. Rashad studies his atlas and a local map for our trip. Amit and I play checkers. Tyrone stretches out on the floor, occasionally lifting an eyelid to peer at us. It feels almost as though nothing bad has happened in the world outside my little house, even though all of us know it has. I savor our leisurely evenings, because I know they will end as soon as we have the truck completely loaded.

And they do end.

We choose a day to leave, deciding that we'll depart as soon after dawn as we can manage. One last dinner together, one last game of checkers, and suddenly it's morning and time to go. As we make our way out the door, I turn, ready to lock it as I have all the days before. But I stop myself. I'm not coming back here, to this house I turned into a little fortress. I'm going forward, to a new life, with two people I have decided to make a part of it, come what may. There's no reason to lock away the life I had here in this little house.

And so I leave the door open. I lay the key on the deck, and I walk away without looking back.

Blue Skies

EVERYTHING APPEARS TO be as we left it at the cul-de-sac. When we get inside the garage, it looks like all our supplies are still in the truck. I get Tyrone and Amit settled in the cab and help Rashad do a last check on the bungee cords holding down the tarp we've spread over our supplies. He's tense, fussing with the hooks, smoothing the tarp. I'm tense, too.

"Looks like this is it." I meet his eyes across the truck bed.

"It does." Rashad walks to the front of the garage. He looks back at me. "Ready?"

I open the passenger door and position myself to push the truck. "Yep."

Rashad lifts the garage door as quietly as possible. Once it's up, he goes to the driver's side of the truck and leans in, puts the truck in neutral, inserts the key in the ignition and turns it. "Okay." He grins at me. "*Start mode*, check."

I shake my head but I have to grin back. "Hang on." I lean in to the cab and pop the glovebox open. Removing the gun from my holster, I put it inside. I'd hate to lose it. "And, commence pushing?"

Rashad's grin disappears. "Amit, you hold onto Tyrone, got it? And Julie." He ducks so he can see my face through the interior of the cab. "You make damn sure you're in the truck as soon as we hit the slope."

"Got it. You, too, Rashad."

We both lean against the cab, pushing to get the truck to the lip of the garage and started down the driveway. At first, it doesn't move at all, but then we get it rolling and things speed up. The front wheels hit the slope and Rashad jumps in the driver's seat and grabs the steering wheel. He shoves the clutch down and puts the truck in second gear. "Get in!"

I pull myself into the cab and slam the door shut, as the truck gains speed, rolling down the driveway. Rashad waits until we're at the bottom, steering the truck into the cul-de-sac, and then he lets the clutch out and we're all holding our breath. The truck lurches, and lurches again but then the engine catches and it's so loud, so impossibly loud. Rashad puts it back in neutral and gives it some gas, and we sit for a moment in the middle of the cul-de-sac, all of us stunned.

"Holy crap." I grab Amit and then Tyrone and I reach out toward Rashad. "Holy crap, it worked!"

Rashad's gripping the steering wheel so hard his knuckles are pale and he looks like he thinks the truck is filled with dynamite, like one wrong move and we'll all be blown to bits. "Damn." He stares at the gauges, beads of sweat appearing on his forehead. "Damn." Carefully, he eases the clutch in and shifts to first gear. "Okay. Here we go. We should be to the marina in twenty minutes or less."

We take the main road into town. Rashad has looked at all the side routes on the map and we both agreed that the most direct route makes the most sense as long as the way is clear, and the main road is, remarkably, fairly passable. There are vehicles here and there, some clearly abandoned in haste, parked crazily halfway in the street. Others are wrecked, driven onto sidewalks and, in one case, through the plate glass of a boutique. We go slowly, but even at fifteen miles an hour it seems to me as though we are traveling at an incredible speed. I've been walking everywhere for so long, I've forgotten how it feels to be in a vehicle.

All of us are silent, riveted by the scenes racing past. As we get closer to the heart of town, there are more cars clogging the streets, and evidence of unchecked fires; charred buildings gutted, spilling piles of unrecognizable debris. A ritzy condominium has **Q**s scrawled across the double glass doors of the lobby—inside I glimpse what look like desiccated bodies sprawled on the marble floor.

The truck engine coughs and misses, choking on old gasoline, but it doesn't stall. Amit hugs Tyrone tighter every time it belches, and I realize how frightened he must be. I hope he didn't see the bodies. I find his hand and wrap it in mine. "Almost there."

We pass through downtown and into the more industrial section above the marina. The train station is here, and there are warehouses that used to be cold storage or small manufacturing businesses. There are fewer cars, less damage to the buildings here, too.

"Shit." Rashad's looking at the road, about 200 yards ahead. A barricade blocks it, a barricade built from two burned out cars pushed together nose-to-nose, bolstered by piles of wood and unidentifiable metal. "Somebody built that for a reason."

"It looks like we can get around on the right." I am instantly saturated with dread, but I try to keep my voice calm for Amit's sake. "What do you think?"

Rashad slows the truck to a crawl, thinking. "Maybe it's old. Maybe nobody is actually still around."

"Somebody's still around." Amit points. "A lot of somebodies."

Rashad and I both look where he's pointing. From behind the vehicle carcasses, heads pop up, three, four, seven. People, watching us approach. They all have weapons of some sort—one holds an axe, another a long, sharpened stick, a third has a hammer. I don't see any guns.

"They'll expect me to go right, try to get around them that way." Rashad whispers, though there's no way they can hear us from where they crouch. "I'm thinking left, full speed, last minute." He turns to me and Amit. "You two get as low as you can, hold on tight."

I get the gun out of the glove box. "Amit, get down, and keep Tyrone down, too." Amit scrambles to fit himself and the dog into the space in front of the seat. I reach down and give Tyrone a head scratch to reassure him, though he seems much calmer than me. Then I straighten up and click the safety off the gun.

Rashad gives the truck a little gas and we crawl forward. "Ready?"

I take a deep breath. "Ready." I'm not ready.

We gain speed, and as we approach the barricade the people stand up, waving their weapons. It looks like they're all men and I can hear some of them screaming—no words, just savage sounds, meant to scare us. It works on me. Rashad heads straight for the middle of the barricade at first, then about thirty feet out he veers toward the right side, where there's clear passage. All the men surge toward the opening, gauging our speed and distance, ready to attack.

"Hold on!" Rashad floors the gas pedal and twists the steering wheel violently and it feels like we go on two wheels as we hurtle left. There's a pile of debris—wood, some old tires, a few plastic crates—blocking our way, but Rashad barrels through, and we bounce crazily as the truck hits things. In moments we're past the blockade, leaving the men behind. Through the rear window I can see them running after us, angrily brandishing their axes and sticks. One of them throws his hammer at us but we're far enough away that it falls to the street, bouncing once before it comes to a stop. Most of them are jumping up and down and yelling, but one man stands very still, and I see him extend both arms straight out toward us.

"Gun!" I scream, and aim toward the man with my own gun. At the same moment the truck jolts wildly, throwing Tyrone and Amit against each other on the floor and ruining any chance I have of a shot.

"Fuck!" Rashad struggles to keep control of the steering wheel. "They got a tire." He doesn't slow a bit and the truck lurches forward on the three remaining tires. I watch the men get smaller and smaller in the rear window, until they look like harmless, jumping dots.

When we're sure we've put enough distance between us and them, Rashad slows a bit and scans the road ahead. "The marina should be the next left. Bay Road. Can you read that—"

"Bay Road!" I shout as I make out the words on the street sign. "That's it."

Rashad swings the truck onto Bay and hits the gas again. The lurching worsens and I grab the back of the seat to try to steady myself with my free hand.

Rashad grips the steering wheel hard, trying to keep the truck on the road. "They'll be coming. We have to make time." He eyes the rearview mirror. "Amit, come on back up. Everything's good."

Amit struggles to help Tyrone up onto the seat and then pushes himself up, too. He looks at me, eyes wide, speechless, then peers behind us. "Are they gone?"

I wish I could tell him they were. "They're gone for now. We're fine, Amit." I take his hand and smile, hoping he's reassured.

"There it is." Rashad sounds relieved. "The marina."

He turns into the entrance and slows the truck. We all stare. There's a boat ramp to our right, and the main office is to our left. The marina is in front of us, row upon row of floating docks, all branching off from the main dock. Almost every slip is empty. There are perhaps seven boats in the whole place. The boats I can see are half submerged, some with obvious damage to their hulls, others so wrecked they're hardly recognizable.

For a moment, we're all silent. Then Rashad slams his fists on the steering wheel. "No. Man, no, can't be." His voice is ragged and harsh.

I want to cry. I can feel the men from the barricade behind us as if they are a physical presence, and panic constricts my chest. "They're all ruined."

"They'll be coming." Rashad sounds defeated. "We'd better find a place to hide."

"Look." Amit is practically standing in the truck cab, craning to see. "What about that?"

He's pointing to the last dock, about two hundred feet from us. I follow his finger, and I see what he sees. At the very end, there's a smaller sailboat with no cabin, not ideal for our needs. But the mast is intact, and the boat itself is floating. From a distance, it looks like it might be seaworthy. "Let's go."

Rashad drives to the dock and backs the truck up to the boat ramp there, easing it down the ramp as close to the water as he can. He puts the truck in neutral and pushes down the foot brake. "I'm going to check it out. If it's good, I'll get it to the ramp so we can load our stuff. You two stay here until we know." He hops out of the truck.

"Take the gun." I hold it out to Rashad. "There might be somebody in that boat."

"Julie, you get behind the wheel. Don't turn the truck off. If anything . . . if you need to, get the hell out of here." He takes the gun and runs down the dock.

Shaking, I open my door and run around the truck to the driver's side. Once I'm in the cab, I turn to Amit. "Listen." He looks up at me, his dark eyes serious and scared. "Rashad's going to be fine. We're all going to be fine." I wish I sounded more convincing.

Amit watches me for moment, and then he puts a hand on my shoulder. He doesn't say a word, just sits next to me, one hand on my shoulder and the other on Tyrone's neck.

I strain to see Rashad at the end of the dock, but my view of him is blocked by a larger, half capsized boat between us and him. Half-turning in the seat, I look toward the marina entrance, hoping not to see anyone coming. So far, there's no sign of the men but I know they can't be far behind. They saw the truck bed full of *something*, and they'll want it.

The sound of an engine cuts through the air. I'm confused at first, but then I see the mast of the boat moving and then the whole boat comes into view and there's Rashad, crouched next to an outboard motor. He's steering the boat toward us, angling carefully to back it in as close to the ramp as possible.

"Stay here, Amit! I'll be back for you." I scramble out of the truck and run to back, unhooking the bungee cords as fast as I can.

"Julie!" Rashad shouts over the noise of the outboard. "Here!" He throws a rope toward me.

I miss, and I have to clamber down the ramp into the water to get it. Once I've tied it to a post, I run back up to the truck and start unloading things. Rashad cuts the motor, jumps to the ramp and begins to load supplies onto the boat.

"Any sign?" He's gasping for breath, moving as fast as he can back and forth between the boat and the truck.

"Nothing yet." I keep working; I don't think we have long.

"We can't fit it all in—start picking what you think we need most. Water, for sure." Rashad grabs a bin filled with food and runs for the boat.

I leave the tools, at least most of them, and focus on food, water, ammunition and medical supplies. Once I've got those out, I throw the bedding and clothes out and grab the tarp. I run to help Rashad get the last of it aboard the boat.

And then Amit screams.

Both of us turn toward the truck. He's staring out the back window at us, pointing toward the entrance to the marina. Tyrone is jumping from one side of the cab to the other. I can't hear Amit clearly, but I can read his lips. They form two words—*they're coming.*

"Get him!" Rashad turns to the outboard motor. "Get him in the boat."

I jump off the boat and run toward the truck. As I climb the ramp, I see what Amit has seen. At the entrance to the marina there are men, and they're running toward us. Not seven, not ten, more like a dozen men, all shouting and all armed, though I can't tell if the man with the gun is among them. I grab the door handle and open it. Amit is frozen, so scared he's not sure what to do. Tyrone is frantic, trying to lick Amit's face and trying to get to me at the same time. I push past him and grab Amit by the wrist. "We have to go *fast* Amit, *fast.* Come on." I half-drag him from the truck. Once his feet hit the ground, he seems to come back to himself, and we run together to the boat.

Rashad's crouched at the outboard motor, pulling on the cord, but nothing is happening. I help Amit onto the boat and scramble in myself, watching the men run toward us. Their screams sound like some huge beast, a nightmare roar. I can see individual faces as they get closer. They all look brutal. I can imagine what they'll do to us when they reach us.

The outboard motor sputters again and I can hear Rashad cursing under his breath. I feel hope sliding away from me; it feels like an actual thing leaving my body, like blood, or breath. I wrap my arms around Amit, holding him. I want to whisper to him that it will all be fine, but I can't.

And then the outboard starts. Amit and I almost tumble over as the boat jolts away from the boat ramp. I see the men put on speed, running flat out as we put distance between us and them. I'm holding Amit so tight he pushes against me and I loosen my grip, tell him it's okay, but he's shouting, he's shouting with tears streaking down his face and he shoves away from me and screams. *Tyrone.* He screams for Tyrone and I realize he's not on the boat.

"He's on the dock!" Rashad is shouting at me and I look and see

Tyrone, sure enough, on the dock, running back and forth at the top of the boat ramp, leaping and running, watching us abandon him. The men are coming fast, they're not more than twenty, thirty feet away.

I run to where Amit is leaning over the boat. "Get back, Amit. You get back *now.*" And I stand as tall as I can and I scream his name. "Tyrone! Come here. Come! Tyrone!"

And he *does.* Tyrone launches himself into the waves. I scream some more, and I'm crying as hard as Amit and we're all yelling for him to *come* to us. And Tyrone is swimming hard now, but I see a man running down the boat ramp, the man with the gun. He levels it at Tyrone, and fires into the water.

He misses. Tyrone is still swimming, paddling hard to reach us. I see the man aim again, but nothing happens. He's out of bullets. But there's no time for relief—the man runs into the water, after Tyrone, and then he's swimming too, closing the distance.

"Julie!" Rashad can't leave the outboard but he's holding something out toward me—the gun. I make my way to him, holding the edge of the boat, and I grab it.

"Shoot at him!"

I turn and fire into the air, then point the gun at the man. I will shoot him, I will *kill* him to save Tyrone. When the man sees me, I think I witness the moment *he* realizes I will kill him for my dog, because he stops swimming and treads water. Tyrone keeps paddling toward us and Rashad slows the boat enough to let him catch us. I watch the man in the water for a moment more before I put the gun on the floor of the boat and grab Tyrone's collar.

It takes both Amit and me to haul him into the boat. Sea water streams off him onto the floor boards and he coughs up more, his legs shaking from the swim. But he's aboard, and safe, and all I can do is cry and hug him. I whisper into his ear. "I'm so sorry, boy. I'm so sorry."

Rashad points to the gun and I retrieve it to keep it from getting wet. The docks are receding, but we can still see the group of men standing in a ragged line, shouting, waving their weapons at us. The one who came after Tyrone walks out of the water up the boat ramp to join the others, but he doesn't shout, or wave anything. He just stands, staring at us. We watch until the men are so small we can't really tell they are men, anymore.

——— ⌐

It's just after dawn. Rashad is hoisting the sail; he actually looks almost like he knows what he's doing. Tyrone and I are sitting in the middle part of the boat—I have no idea what correct term might be. Amit is still asleep under the tarp we fastened across half the boat for shelter. To our left, the coastline is still visible but far enough away that I can pretend it doesn't hold any threats—that it's just a beautiful, harmless vista. To our right is a small island, one of many we've passed so far—there's a chain of them along this coast.

"Tempted?"

I shield my eyes from the sun so I can see his face better. "By what?"

Rashad nods toward the island. "I figured you might suggest we just find one of those, set up camp and stay, far away from any other people. After that bunch yesterday I'm almost tempted myself." He looks back toward where we've been, remembering, I guess, the horde of men who tried to catch us. The men who would, I'm certain, have killed us.

I *am* tempted, but I don't tell Rashad. I've decided to believe in his version of hope. I've decided to believe that Amit's mother was right; that we can only *effect* by doing unto others. I want to effect; I want to discover what community means. What living means. Before I die.

Tyrone moves toward the tarp at the same moment Amit emerges from under it, rubbing his eyes. He accepts Tyrone's eager, sloppy greeting and comes to sit next to me. He's still not quite awake. I offer him some water to drink, and scrounge around in a bin for some dried plums.

"Look." Amit points up.

At first, I see only a nebulous adumbration darkening the perfect, blue sky, but then a shape forms more clearly, and then another, and then I can see it's birds. It's a huge flock of birds—starlings—a bigger flock than any I've seen before, all swooping and soaring and twisting as one.

A murmuration.

We all three stare, amazed, as the phenomenon gets closer, until the birds are right over our little boat. Judging from his awed expression, Amit has clearly not seen a murmuration before.

"That!" He points to the sky. "Julie, that's what I see, only with colors, all the colors, and no birds."

I have to laugh. "That's what I *hear*, too, Amit. Only with sounds, all the sounds, and no birds."

We watch in reverent silence until the murmuration fades from view, until all that's left is that blue morning sky as far as we can see. When I look at Amit, he's smiling a *real* smile, one that lights his face and makes him look like a happy child. Like he *should* look. And then I smile, because I realize that *I* can be a part of keeping it that way.

Rashad adjusts the sail and it billows out, filled with wind. The boat leaps forward like metal to a magnet. He looks back at me. I understand, somehow, what he is silently asking. *Do we keep going?*

I nod at him. Yes. Yes, we do. We keep going. Because though the murmuration in the sky is gone now, I can hear my own murmurations, a jubilant serenade in my mind, that sounds just like the blue sky above, full of hope, full of promise. This time, I am truly listening.

And together, each a single dot in some pattern of meaning we will probably never fully understand, the four of us sail on.

Author Bio

Teri Hall's work includes the YA trilogy *The Line*, *Away*, and *The Island*. This particular book, *Murmurations*, was written well prior to the Covid-19 Pandemic, which makes the author wary of possible prophetic powers and cautious about her choice of new projects. Teri has always been drawn to themes of courage, integrity and what love really looks like. She lives in a small community in the Pacific Northwest with some rescue pets, one of whom—Tyrone, so sorely missed—was the inspiration for the Tyrone in this book.